The Lady
Who Cried Murder

A Mac Faraday Mystery

By

LAUREN CARR

The Lady Who Cried Murder

Published by Acorn Book Services

For information call: 304-995-1295
or Email: writerlaurencarr@gmail.com

Designed by Acorn Book Services

Publication Managed by Acorn Book Services
www.acornbookservices.com
acornbookservices@gmail.com
304-995-1295

Cover designed by Todd Aune
Spokane, Washington
www.projetoonline.com

ISBN-10: 0-9891804-8-4
ISBN-13: 978-0-9891804-8-1

Published in the United States of America

To the arrogant, envious, rude, self-centered, demented, and twisted souls amongst us. For without you, murder mystery writers would be without inspiration.

The Lady
Who Cried Murder

A Mac Faraday Mystery

THE LADY WHO CRIED MURDER

Cast of Characters
(in order of appearance)

Mac Faraday: Retired homicide detective. His wife had left him and took everything. On the day his divorce became final, he inherited $270 million and an estate on Deep Creek Lake from his birth mother, Robin Spencer.

David O'Callaghan: Spencer police chief. Son of the late police chief, Patrick O'Callaghan. Mac Faraday's best friend and half-brother.

Deputy Chief Arthur Bogart (Bogie): Spencer's Deputy Police Chief. David's godfather. Don't let his gray hair and weathered face fool you.

Robin Spencer: Mac Faraday's late birth mother and world famous mystery author. As an unwed and pregnant teenager, she gave him up for adoption. After becoming America's queen of mystery, she found her son and made him her heir. Her ancestors founded Spencer, Maryland, located on the shore of Deep Creek Lake, a resort area in Western Maryland.

Police Chief Patrick O'Callaghan: David's late father. Spencer's legendary police chief. The love of Robin Spencer's life and Mac Faraday's birth father.

Florence Everest: Mother of Khloe Everest. Her sudden death sets the wheels in motion for murder.

Archie Monday: Editor and research assistant to world-famous mystery author Robin Spencer. She is now Mac Faraday's lady love.

Lily Carter: Ex-best friend of Khloe Everest.

Bevis Palazzi: Senator Harry Palazzi's son and heir apparent to his father's political legacy, and don't you forget it.

Gnarly: Mac Faraday's German shepherd. Another part of his inheritance from Robin Spencer. Gnarly used to belong to the United States Army, who refuses to talk about him.

Khloe Everest: The lady who cried murder.

Meghan Bishop: The producer of E-Entertainment Live. She and her crew came to Spencer for a story about Khloe Everest and got more than they bargained for.

Audrey Connelly: Television show hostess.

Dr. Dora Washington: Garrett County Medical Examiner.

Chelsea Adams: Paralegal for Ben Fleming, Garrett County's Prosecuting Attorney. House guest at Spencer Manor. David O'Callaghan's first and current love, he hopes.

Molly: Chelsea's service dog, trained to sense and warn of seizures.

Ben Fleming: Garrett County prosecuting attorney. He's one of the good guys.

Edward Willingham: Mac Faraday's lawyer. Senior partner at Willingham and Associates. He chased Mac Faraday for three city blocks to tell him that he had inherited a fortune beyond his dreams. First lawyer Mac ever met who he actually liked—maybe because he works for him.

Jeff Ingles: Manager of the Spencer Inn, the five-star resort owned by Mac Faraday. His therapist is on speed dial.

Amber Houston: Murder victim. The media attention her murder garnished inspired Khloe to cry murder.

Tiffany Blanchard: Murder victim. Was a model in Hollywood before she ran into our killer.

Dee Blakeley: Murder victim from Mac Faraday's past.

Catherine Davenport Fleming: Ben Fleming's lovely socialite wife.

Senator Harry Palazzi: Former sheriff, now United States Senator.

Samuel Brooks: Senator Harry Palazzi's lawyer.

Hector Langford: Spencer Inn's chief of security.

Cameron Gates: Pennsylvania State Police Homicide Detective. Amber Houston's murder is her case.

Irving: Cameron's twenty-five pound Maine Coon Cat. You'd have issues, too, if you looked liked a giant skunk.

Joshua Thornton: Cameron's husband. Hancock County Prosecuting Attorney in West Virginia. Together with Cameron Gates, they are the Lovers in Crime.

Otto Grant: Burglar who spends the evening playing with Gnarly at Spencer Manor.

Kevin Cooper: Private Investigator, former police officer.

Nick Fields: Khloe Everest's gay best friend—at least, that is what he claimed on her reality show.

Sandy Patton: Nick Field's unfortunate next door neighbor.

Sheila McGrath: Nick's wife ... or sister ... or sugar momma, or maybe she's a killer.

Russ Burton: Nick Field's defense attorney.

Iman: Spencer Inn's head chef.

Officers Brewster, Zigler, and Fletcher: Spencer police officers.

The truest characters of ignorance are vanity and pride and arrogance.

Samuel Butler

PROLOGUE

Spencer Mountain on Deep Creek Lake, Western Maryland—Three Years Ago

"Are you ready for this?" Mac Faraday asked David O'Callaghan, Spencer's chief of police.

The two men peered through the window at the fleet of vans and SUVs blocking the mountain road. A mob of journalists and their camera operators filled the small front yard of the log A-Frame home built into the side of Spencer Mountain. The rear of the luxurious mountain house provided a bird's view of the valley floor and Deep Creek Lake.

"There sure are a lot of them," David said in a low voice.

Mac looked over at the handsome young man. A gold police shield was pinned to his chest. Shining, it stood out against his uniform's white shirt. Somehow, it seemed unfair that the police chief, only in his early thirties, should be introduced to the media with such a horrible case. Baptism by fire.

"You'll do fine," Mac said. "Use your officer's training from the Marines. When you go out there, take command. They're going to try to take control from you—don't let them."

"You make it sound like I'm going into battle."

"You are." Unable to look at the journalists, desperate for something to report—anything, no matter who it hurt; Mac turned away.

David followed him into the front sitting room. "When you were a homicide detective in DC, did you ever have to give a statement to the media?"

"Are you kidding?" Mac replied. "I'm the last person my superiors wanted speaking to one of those vultures." Grasping David's arm, he softened his tone. "You're going to do fine. We've practiced your statement. Remember, no questions because—"

"It's an open police investigation," David finished.

"It's okay to be firm with that," Mac said. "You're in charge of this investigation. A young woman is missing. Your first objective is bringing her home to her mother—not playing up to the cameras."

"I almost wish I wasn't chief of police," David muttered. "I remember how much Dad despised having to do things like this. They always seemed to take one thing he would say and twist it—"

"I know." A smile came to Mac's lips when he thought about the feelings he and his birth father shared, even though they had never met. There was something to genetics.

He caught a look in David's eyes, which were identical to his own. They had both inherited their deep blue eyes from their father, as well as his tall, slender build. The only noticeable difference was in David's blond hair, inherited from his mother. Mac had inherited his birth mother's dark hair, touched with gray at the temples that had crept in after he had hit forty.

As a teenager, Robin Spencer had given birth to Mac out of wedlock. Her parents had immediately whisked him away to be adopted. While Mac's mother went on to become a world famous murder mystery author, his birth father, Patrick O'Callaghan, had become Spencer's police chief. Eventually, he married and had a son.

It was only upon Robin Spencer's death forty-seven years later that Mac Faraday, a homicide detective in Washington, DC, had discovered the truth. She had left her entire estate, which included a mansion on Deep Creek Lake, to him. She had also left her journal to Mac. From that, the multi-millionaire had learned about his parents unending love for each other and his half-brother, who lived in the same town.

"I'm glad you're here to help me, Mac," David said.

Mac shrugged his shoulders. "It's better than losing another tennis match to Fleming."

Arthur Bogart, Spencer's deputy chief of police, came in from outside. "The natives are getting restless out there, Chief."

"I'm ready." David picked up a clipboard with his notes from the coffee table to go over his statement one more time.

"I'll give these to our officers to pass out to them." Bogie picked up a stack of papers that contained a drawing of their suspect and handed some to Mac.

"Chief O'Callaghan?"

They looked up the stairs leading to the upper levels of the home. Florence Everest was making her way down. Archie Monday, assistant to the late Robin Spencer, was behind her.

Focusing on the case of Florence's missing daughter, Mac pushed away the thought of how lovely Archie was. For the last four days, the petite blonde had been acting as friend and confidante to the distraught mother.

When Robin Spencer had left her estate worth two hundred and seventy million dollars to Mac, she had further increased his good fortune by stipulating that her assistant, Archie Monday, was permitted to live in the guesthouse for as long as she wanted. Mac had no desire for the emerald-eyed blonde who loved to go barefoot to leave. It isn't every man who inherits a house with a live-in beauty.

Under normal circumstances, it would be difficult to gauge Florence Everest's age. She was a tall, slender woman with the look of a movie star from the days of the silver screen or a runway model. Her presence was flawless. An interior decorator, she knew all about style, and she had used her talents to become successful in business as well as in high society, which was how she had risen up from a single working mother to the cream of Deep Creek Lake society.

For those on the A-list, Florence Everest was the only interior decorator in town.

Casting a fearful glance out the window at the crowd that seemed to be closing in while David's officers pushed them back, she asked, "Do I need to go out there?" Her eyes were puffy from a recent flow of tears.

"No," David said. "If you're out there, they'll be focused on you. I want them to listen to me and look at our pictures from the sketch artist."

A ruckus outside caused them to return to the window. The journalists looked like they were about to mow down the dozens of Spencer and Garrett County officers trying to hold them back when the front door opened.

A young woman and man rushed inside and slammed the door behind them.

While the woman rushed to hug Florence, her chubby companion hung back to glare at David and Mac. His penetrating gaze bore through his small dark eyes under his dark eyebrows and flabby cheeks.

"Ms. Everest, have you heard anything yet?" the woman asked. "I saw on the Internet that the police chief was going to make an announcement. Does that mean they found Khloe?"

"No, Lily," Florence said. "We've heard nothing yet."

"I wish I had insisted on Khloe going home with me." With a sob, Lily glanced over at the row of pictures that lined the fireplace mantel. "I saw that she had had too much to drink. None of this would have—"

"It's not your fault." Florence draped her arm around Lily's shoulders.

Everyone's eyes turned to the mantel, which contained an array of pictures of the dark-haired beauty. Like her mother, her hair fell in a thick wave past her shoulders. Her dark eyes stood out against her alabaster skin. Many of the photographs were professional shots that displayed her striking features that had won her leading roles in the local community theater circuit.

"We're passing out pictures of the man that you saw Khloe talking to down at the lake on Friday night," David explained. "If we can get it out across the media, maybe someone will recognize him."

"That's all?" Lily's friend exploded. "You're passing out drawings of this guy? Why aren't you out there looking? Why aren't you bringing in suspects to question? She's been missing for the last four days and all you bunch of boobs have been doing is hanging around looking at the view and contemplating your navels."

"Now look here, Bevis," Bogie said, "We've been doing everything possible. You don't know—" The silver-haired deputy chief who possessed the solid build of a wrestler was more than impressive enough to cause Bevis to back up a step to avoid contact with him.

"I know all about abduction cases." Bevis tried to avoid the imposing form of the deputy chief. "Back when I was a kid, my mother and her friend were kidnapped, and my father caught their killer. He was a sheriff in Frederick County in the 1970s, and he knew his job. He worked hundreds of abduction and murder cases, and it's because he was so good at what he did that they elected him senator. I know all about how this works. I also know that your handling of this case is totally unacceptable!" Threatening to strike the police chief in the chest, he poked a finger in David's direction. "If you morons would have listened to me four days ago, Khloe would be home now, and her kidnapper would be in prison."

There was something about the smug expression on Bevis' face that made Mac want to slap it. Sometimes, Mac wondered if it was who Bevis' father was that rubbed him the wrong way. Senator Harry Palazzi, a former sheriff, had earned every bit of the reputation of a sleazy politician. He could see by David's clenched jaw that he had the same effect on him.

"Everyone is on edge right now, Bevis," David said in a steady tone. "So I'm going to excuse your comments as simply that."

"Spoken like a man with no balls," Bevis replied. "How did you get appointed police chief anyway?" He cast a glance in Mac's direction before scoffing. "I'm sure rubbing elbows with the owner of the Spencer Inn had nothing to do with it."

"That's enough, Bevis." Florence stepped in to cut Bogie off before he was about to grab the young man by the front of his shirt to take him outside for a little talk about respect.

Seeing Bogie coming, Bevis backed up. His legs buckled and he fell backwards to land on his rump on the floor.

Without missing a step, Gnarly, another part of Mac's inheritance, scurried around from where he had moved in to trip Bevis and sit down next to his master. A huge German shepherd with a mind of his own, Gnarly and Mac had a love-hate relationship. When he listened to Mac, or took it upon himself to act in Mac or Archie's defense, it was love. When he was committing petty larceny, it was hate.

At this moment, it was love. "Watch yourself," Mac told Bevis, "that first step is a doozy."

Bevis pointed at the dog whose tongue was hanging out the side of his mouth in what appeared to be a laugh. "He tripped me on purpose."

Lily offered her hand to help him up. "Really, Bevis, he's a dog. They aren't capable of doing things on purpose. What is it with you two? You've been paranoid about him ever since you met him."

"I don't like the way he looks at me." Shoving his cell phone into his pocket, he smoothed his hair with both of his hands. "I know he stole my phone the other day. That's why I had to go out yesterday to buy a new one."

"Why would a dog steal your cell phone?" Lily asked.

When Mac cast a glance in Gnarly's direction, the dog scurried over to hide behind Archie.

"The sooner we get this started, the sooner we get it over with." David moved to the door with Bogie directly behind him. Mac, Bevis, and Lily fell in behind them. Archie grasped Gnarly's collar to hold him inside with her and Florence to watch through the window.

As soon as the media saw David step out of the house, a hush fell over the journalists. Cameras were poised to frame him in their shot when the police chief stepped up to the bank of microphones that they had set up on a makeshift podium in the driveway.

Bevis leaned against the porch railing with his arms folded across his chest. His tubby stomach rolled over his belt. Mac wondered if that smirk ever left his face. It seemed to be permanently etched there. Behind him, Lily chewed on her pinky finger.

Bogie, Mac, and two of David's officers positioned themselves behind him in a show of support when the police chief began his statement:

"Four nights ago, on Wednesday night, twenty-one year old Khloe Everest, accompanied by two friends, went out for an evening of clubbing. During the course of the evening, she became separated from her friends. Khloe Everest did not make it home. Witnesses have told our investigators that they saw Khloe parked at a boat launch on Deep Creek Lake. She was seen speaking to a young man. On Thursday morning, her mother, Florence Everett, who was out of town on a business trip, received a phone call from her daughter's cell phone, in which she was screaming and crying for help during what seemed to be an attack. They were abruptly cut off. Ms. Everest immediately contacted our police department. Since that time, we have been searching for Khloe Everest. All of you have received pictures of Ms. Everest. We are still searching for the young man with whom she was last seen. At this time, I would like to distribute composite pictures that have been made of him based on witness descriptions."

"Is he a suspect?" a journalist yelled out.

"Right now, we only want to talk to him," David said. "He is wanted for questioning."

"Do you think Khloe's disappearance is in any way connected to the Amber Houston disappearance and murder in Pittsburgh, Pennsylvania?" another journalist shouted out. "They are about the same age and disappeared in the same way. Could it be the same killer?"

Another journalist agreed. "Have you checked the dumpsters belonging to motels in the area... like the one in McHenry?"

"We are examining all possibilities," David said. "Until we get evidence suggesting otherwise, we're operating on the assumption that Khloe is alive."

Over the heads of the journalists, Mac saw a car pull up as far as it could go on the blocked road and turn off to get out of traffic. Squinting, he could see a young, dark-haired woman behind the wheel. She fluffed her hair with her hands and checked her lipstick in the rearview mirror before opening the door and sliding out of the driver's seat. With a broad grin on her face, she sashayed up the driveway in her high heels and fire engine red short skirt.

Mac was still trying to find the words to express his surprise when Lily abruptly screamed, "Khloe!"

It took a full moment for the journalists to react. Cameras followed the line of Lily's pointing finger to the young woman in the driveway striking a pose for the cameras.

"What's going on?" she asked with a giggle in her voice. "Has someone been killed?"

While the journalists mobbed the subject of the search, David turned to gaze at Mac in stunned disbelief.

Not only was Khloe Everest alive, but, judging by the glee on her face while posing for the cameras, she was doing extremely well.

Mac was the first to get over his shock and fight his way through the mob to grab Khloe by the wrist. "We need to talk," he hissed through gritted teeth before dragging her out of the throng of reporters to take her inside where her mother hugged her—until she discovered that Khloe had never been in danger.

Even Gnarly was cocking his head at her with an expression of disbelief in his eyes.

"We thought you were dead!" Florence screamed at her. "None of us have eaten or slept in four days. All of these officers all over the county and much of the state have been searching for you, and where were you? Shacked up in a motel with a boy?"

"You should have called your mother." While chastising Khloe, Archie stroked Florence's arm in comfort—or was it to calm her down and hold her back from throttling the girl?

"What motel were you at?" David asked her.

"It was some dive outside Morgantown," Khloe said with a shrug of her shoulders.

"Didn't you see the news about a tri-state-wide search for you?" Lily asked.

"We weren't watching television." Khloe's grin was wickedly naughty.

"What about the phone call you made to me?" Florence demanded to know.

"What phone call?" While her words communicated bafflement, her grin said she knew exactly what her mother was talking about.

"You really need to work on playing innocent," Mac said in a low voice in reference to the smile kicking at the corner of her lips.

"You called me on your cell phone," Florence said in a high-pitched voice. "You were screaming and crying and—"

"Oh!" Khloe wailed in laughter. "So that was you I called. It was a butt dial."

Blinking, Florence turned to David for help.

"That's when you have your phone in your back pocket," David explained, "and you sit down and accidentally call someone without realizing it."

"Once, a SWAT team got called out to a school because a teacher accidentally butt dialed his wife," Bogie said. "She heard voices, but her husband didn't respond when she tried talking to him. So she thought that the school had been taken hostage. The school was locked down and SWAT converged on it before the police realized it was a mistake."

"Why didn't you answer your phone during the last four days? Why have you had it turned off so that we couldn't locate you via GPS?" David asked her. "Why haven't you called anyone to tell them that you were all right?"

"I was busy," Khloe said with a toss of her head that sent her long hair back over her shoulder. She checked out the window to see if the media had left yet.

"Since when have you been too busy to text?" The anger in Lily's tone matched that of Khloe's mother.

"What's the name of this boy you were with?" David asked her.

"Brad…something or other," Khloe said with a shrug of her shoulders.

"You were in bed with a boy for four days, never checking the news, not calling any of your friends or family, and you didn't get his last name?" Bogie asked.

"She set us up." Lily glared at Khloe. "You set me up."

"Why?" David asked.

"Excuse me," Khloe said, "but my fifteen minutes of fame is slipping by fast and there are some people outside who want to talk to me." She turned to find David blocking her path. When she moved to one side, Mac blocked that escape. "Hey, I did nothing wrong."

"Actually, you did," David said. "It's called obstruction of justice. During the last four days, police from most of the state have been looking for you when we could have been focusing on people who were in real trouble."

"Hey, I didn't call the police!" Khloe pointed at her mother. "She did."

"After you set up that butt dial to make it look like you've been kidnapped," Florence said. "Think of all the young women who have really been kidnapped. Who have really been raped and humiliated, who really do need help, and you made a mockery of all of these officers to play this little game of yours—for what?" She pointed out the window. "Fame!"

Mac glared into Khloe's eyes, which were filled with satisfaction. "I know you're too young and cocky to understand this right now—but I've worked a lot of murder investigations that involved some very famous people—both as victims and suspects—and all of them had one thing in common."

"What's that?" Khloe said with a sigh to show him that she was humoring him.

"They paid a price," Mac said. "They all paid with their privacy. Some paid an additional price of their dignity. You," he chuckled, "you traded in your integrity. Too bad you're so young that you have yet to realize what a valuable thing that is."

"I'll think about that when I'm in front of the cameras on my way across the red carpet." She pushed her way through to make her way to the door.

"It's obstruction of justice," David said forcibly. "Five years in prison if convicted."

Khloe whirled around and shot him a glare. "First, you have to prove that I engineered all of this to make you look like a bunch of fools, instead of you doing it to yourselves."

"Considering that your own mother and best friend believe you're capable of it," David said, "we will prove it. No one makes an ass out of my people and gets away with it."

"Knock yourself out." With a flip of her hair, she stepped outside to strike another pose for the cameras.

Florence sighed. "It's all my fault…letting her grow up without a father."

Lily wrapped her arm around her waist. "Do you really think she'd be less self-absorbed if she knew her father?"

Mac saw that instead of David, it was now Khloe to whom Bevis was directing his beady-eyed glare while stroking his plump lips. Outside, the latest infamous newsmaker was being swarmed by the media.

"What do you think?" David drew Mac's attention for the unpleasant man's display. "Is there really any way to prove she did engineer this whole fiasco?"

"Even if there isn't," Mac said, "she'll get hers. What goes around comes around."

CHAPTER ONE

Present Day

David groaned when he turned his cruiser into the driveway at the Everest home and found it occupied by a van and limousine. A video camera operator rushed to the cruiser and focused his recorder on David in the driver's seat. Meanwhile, a young woman in jeans and a form-fitting winter parka ran to the door. David spotted the wire for the portable mic hanging out from under her coat and clipped to the top of her coat. She was wearing a mic and an earbud.

"Chief O'Callaghan, I'm Meghan Bishop, the producer of E-Entertainment Live. I'm the one who called you."

David slipped out of the driver's seat of his cruiser. "Then you're the one to arrest if this turns into a publicity stunt." After zipping up his coat and pulling the collar in tight around his throat, he gestured at the camera operator. "Turn off that camera."

The camera operator ignored his order.

Oblivious to the police chief's displeasure, Meghan continued, "Khloe Everest invited our crew to her house this morning for an interview. She was going to make an announcement—"

Turning around sharply, David was in the camera operator's face so fast that he didn't have time to react before the police chief grabbed the camera and yanked it down from his face. "If you don't turn off that camera, I am going to take it and stuff it down your pants," he said in a low tone.

In spite of the freezing winter temperature, beads of sweat popped up on the camera operator's forehead. The young man turned to Meghan, who waved her fingers across her throat in a gesture for him to cease recording. He backed away a few feet and bounced on the balls of his feet to keep warm.

David saw a familiar looking redhead freshening up her makeup in the warmth of the back of the limousine.

"Yes, that's Audrey Connelly," Meghan told him. "She's conducting the interview with Khloe Everest. She needs to be in New York by five o'clock." She planted her hands on her hips. "Khloe isn't answering the door."

"Maybe she got a better offer," David said.

"I doubt it," Meghan replied. "Khloe has been shopping around for a show that would be willing to give her camera time for this announcement, which she promises to be huge. None of the producers saw her as being much of a ratings draw. But when we found out that she lived in Spencer, we convinced the station that this mysterious announcement would be worthwhile and got them to foot the bill on a boondoggle at the Spencer Inn." She jerked her head in the direction of the porch and door. "Now that we're ready to go to work, Khloe's not answering the door."

"What do you want me to do about it?"

"Khloe Everest is a fame junkie," the producer said. "If she could answer that door, she would. She knows that when we go, we're not coming back, and no one else will. She'll be through."

Sucking in his breath, David tried to check his growing impatience. "If you called me for—"

"Are you going to press charges against Khloe for obstruction of justice for faking her abduction?" Audrey called to him out the window. Her breath came out to form a white cloud of steam.

"We're still investigating," David said. "She may be broke, but not too broke to have a lawyer putting up road blocks." He looked up at the front door. "Well, I'm here. It's about time for her to answer the door and lift the curtain on her show."

"We told you," Meghan said, "She's not answering the door."

Audrey added, "I haven't gotten any texts from Khloe for the last four days. Last night, I asked her to confirm the interview and got nothing. I check all of her social media sites and she hasn't posted anything there, either."

"That's big," Meghan said.

"Real big," Audrey said. "Khloe doesn't make a move without reporting it to her friends and followers. A week ago, when we scheduled this interview, she started a countdown to her big announcement. It ended four days ago. I think someone got to her to put a stop to it."

His hands on his hips, David fingered the grip of his gun.

So this is how it plays. I go in to check it out and find Khloe in the bubble bath naked with the camera crew behind me to film it all. Or, better yet, I walk in to find her unconscious from an attempted suicide. Why else would she have arranged to have a full film crew here? She's planning something to make her way back onto the media radar, and I refuse to be a part of it.

The two women were eying him.

"I'll go inside to check on her," David said. "I want all of you to stay here." He turned to the camera operator and pointed a finger into his face. "That means you."

His eyes big and his mouth open, the camera operator looked too scared to respond.

While crossing the snow-covered yard to go up to the front door, David pressed the button on his radio to report into the station that he was checking out the Everest residence due to no response from Khloe Everest. "According to this producer and show host, no one has heard from her in four days."

"Have you checked with the local motels to see if she's hooked up with a new lover?" Spencer police's desk sergeant Tonya replied.

"If that's the case this time, I'm cuffing her and dragging her in to spend four days in our holding cell." His irritation about being dragged into yet another publicity stunt came out when he pounded the door with his fist. "Khloe Everest! This is Police Chief David O'Callaghan. Answer the door! Now!"

The response was silence. The crew in the driveway craned their ears for a sound from inside the house.

He went around the corner of the house. Before turning the corner, he ducked back to see the camera operator attempting to creep across the yard to follow him. "Do I have to lock you up in my cruiser?"

Caught, the operator backed up to the driveway.

The Everest home was built into the side of the mountain. When David turned the corner, he only went a couple of feet before stepping up onto a deck that went around to the back. The patio from the lower level was under the deck off the main floor. In the back of the house, the second and third floors provided a view of the lake from their glass windows. The deck had multiple doors.

The second door David tried was unlocked. "Khloe, Chief O'Callaghan," he called when he stepped into the kitchen. The foul odor of decaying food hit him in the face. "I'm coming in."

The counter was a mess with dirty plates and empty take-out food cartons. There was also a half-eaten cocktail shrimp platter with ants crawling over the leftovers, an empty bottle of champagne, and two empty glasses.

The rest of the house wasn't much cleaner. Papers, mail, dishes and clothes were scattered all over. The doors to the entertainment center rested wide open. Disks were fanned out across the room. In the study, he found that all of the drawers of what had been Florence Everest's well-organized desk were yanked open with everything pulled out.

Has this place been robbed, or was Khloe looking for something?

David resumed his search. "Khloe, are you here? It's the police."

Still, the response was only silence.

David tapped the button on his radio to report. "Tonya, I'm not getting any response inside the Everest home. The place appears to have been ransacked. I'm going up to the bedroom level of the home to search for any sign of her. Stand by."

"Copy that, Chief."

Yelling came from the upper level—two women arguing in high-pitched voices—that sounded like a major cat fight. With his hand on his gun, David went up the stairs at a gallop. At the landing, he spotted blood drops in the carpet. *Oh, man! This is not looking good.*

A series of loud bleeps were followed by the crash of furniture overturning.

Bleeps? David followed the blood drops down the hallway to the door to the master bedroom.

"You're a slut! A bleep-bleep-bleep-bleep and the only reason Vince puts up with you is because you bleep-bleep-bleep!"

That psychopathic idiot is sitting here watching television!

Ready to teach Khloe Everest a lesson she would never forget for dragging him into her media circus, David turned the knob and shoved open the door. Like the rest of the house, the room was cluttered with clothes, especially lady's underwear, and wreaked of alcohol, liberally mixed with another odor that David recognized.

The top of the dresser was cleared off to make room for a big screen television. Khloe Everest's image filled the screen with another young woman. Dressed in cocktail dresses and high heels, the two women were in the throes of a cat fight.

A giant-sized garbage bag rested on the floor in front of the television. The walls, furniture, and clothes were splattered with blood sprays.

Crime scene! Thinking back to Khloe's past bids for publicity, David regrouped. On the off chance that it was a real crime scene, he slipped on a pair of evidence gloves. There was a lump under the covers on the bed. Half-expecting to find Khloe's bloody corpse, David pulled back the covers to discover the lumps were pillows. The sheets were stained red with blood that covered the width and length of the bed.

This is where it happened…if it happened. Where's the body?

Expecting to find Khloe's body in the bathroom, he opened the door and stepped inside. The sink and counter were splattered with blood across the mirror, counter, floor, and sink. The bathtub had a red bath ring around the edges.

Where is she?

Cursing under his breath, David came back into the bedroom.

The garbage bag.

He had dismissed it because it was not the shape of a body. Standing in the middle of the room studying it, he realized it was big enough to hold a body—if it was chopped up into pieces. The top of the bag was knotted to seal it tight.

"One day, bitch, you're going to meet someone who isn't going to put up with your bleep!" the other woman on the television was saying to Khloe.

"Oh, bleep off, Rain Drop!" Khloe said with a laugh in her voice.

Squatting in front of the plastic bag, David braced himself before pulling out his jackknife and slicing a small hole in the side, only small enough for him to see inside. As soon as he punctured the bag, the rancid smell of decomposition burst forth.

Holding his breath, David peered in through the hole and saw a tuff of long dark hair. "Damn!" he cursed while widening the hole only enough to see clearly inside. Assaulted by the smell of Khloe's decayed body, he grabbed his nose.

"Did you—?" Audrey got out upon making her entrance into the bedroom with the camera operator behind her.

Catching sight of Khloe's bloody head, the television show host began screaming hysterically. In an effort to escape, she whirled around to collide into the operator. Stuck within the confines of the doorway, they did what appeared to be a polka that ended with the two of them falling to the floor in the upstairs corridor. Audrey landed on top of the camera operator. When she pushed up to climb off, she threw up on his camera.

Chapter Two

Mac Faraday fought the yawn working its way from his lungs and up his throat while pulling his red Dodge Viper off the road behind the string of emergency vehicles. Once the car was in place, he suppressed the yawn with one hand while turning off the car with the other.

Wake up, Mac. You need to clear your head. Back to work. He laid his head back against the headrest. *Just one minute and then I'll...*

He woke up to the sensation of steam and the smell of coffee hitting his nostrils. Startled, he jerked straight up in his seat.

With a chuckle, David retracted the paper cup before Mac knocked it out of his hand with his chin. "First day back from vacation can be a killer."

"Tell me about it." Mac opened the door and slid out of the driver's seat. "Man, it's cold here." Shivering, he reached into the pockets of his leather jacket for gloves.

"Mac, you didn't have to come when I called you." David handed the coffee to him. "You're not an employee. You're a contractor. You're free to choose what cases you take. You can even come in later after resting up from your cruise."

Mac took as big of a gulp of the hot coffee as he could without burning his tongue and throat. "I like to see the crime scene while it's as fresh as possible."

"Well, this isn't too fresh." David led him up the driveway to the porch. "Based on the state of decomp, Doc Washington believes she was killed around four days ago. The crew that came to interview her said that was the last time she posted to her social media accounts, and supposedly she was always doing that."

Mac noted the van, limousine, and crowd pushed back behind the yellow crime scene tape. The camera operator was filming all the action. "We need to have our IT forensics team get a list of her sites and download those posts going back several weeks. Based on what I know about Khloe, she wasn't too private of a person. She may be able to point a virtual finger at her killer." At the front door, he bent over to examine the lock.

"No sign of a break in." David led him inside. "I think she let her killer in and knew him or her." He jerked his thumb up in the direction of the bedroom upstairs. "She was killed up in the bedroom."

"Any sign of rape?" Mac asked while slipping on his evidence gloves and plastic booties over his shoes to protect possible evidence on the floor.

David frowned. "Right now, that's hard to say." He caught Mac's eye. "Her body was completely mutilated. I was in Iraq and Afghanistan and saw a lot over there. Still, this ranks right up there as one of the worst I've ever seen."

"That bad?"

"That bad." David led him up the stairs. "How was the cruise to Australia?"

"Great," Mac said while observing the blood drops on the stairs.

"Was Archie right?" A smile worked its way to David's lips.

"About what?"

"That once you got on that cruise ship that you'd like it and not be as bored as you swore you'd be?"

"No, I was not bored," Mac said. "It was great spending a whole month with Archie and my kids." He shot David a grin. "It was like being with a family again. I would have enjoyed that even if we weren't cruising down under. Jessica and Tristan gave their blessings to Archie and my getting married."

"All right." David gave Mac a high five at the top of the stairs.

"Next cruise, you're going to come," Mac said. "You can bring Chelsea. By the way, how did Gnarly do while we were gone? He was quite mellow when we got in this morning."

"He was fine."

The high pitch in David's voice did not escape Mac's attention. "What did he do?"

"I took care of it." Avoiding the suspicious expression in Mac's eyes, David stepped around him and pointed to the blood on the floor. "This blood leads to the kitchen. We found a butcher knife in the dishwasher—cleaned and sterilized. If that's the murder weapon, we have no hope for fingerprints or DNA."

"He's a smart killer."

"Yep." David moved over to the wall to pass the two crime scene officers marking and photographing the blood spots.

"I hate smart killers." Gazing over the bannister to the floor down below, Mac noted the messy condition of the home. "This house was clean enough to eat off the floors three years ago. What happened? What was Khloe doing here, anyway? I thought Florence disowned her after that stunt she pulled."

"That's right," David said. "You had already left for your trip when Florence Everest died."

"Mur—"

"Accident," David said. "A drunk driver plowed into her company van when she was on her way out to Georgetown to remodel a brownstone. That was three weeks ago. As soon as she got word, Khloe came swooping in, expecting to collect it all. After all, she had no siblings or relatives."

"Florence had made it very clear that Khloe was disowned," Mac said. "She made a public announcement about it during the height of the publicity following—"

David was nodding his head. "Florence ordered in her will that her estate was to be liquidated and her attorney—"

"Ed Willingham, who happens to be my lawyer."

"—was to set up a foundation to provide legal and medical aid to female victims of violent crimes."

"Ain't it ironic?" Mac said, "Khloe lost it all to help victims of violent crimes because she pretended to be one. That doesn't explain how she ended up in this house and murdered."

"Unfortunately, no one changed the locks on the door before Khloe swooped in. She refused to leave. She's been squatting here illegally, and Willingham has been working through the courts to have her evicted so that he could put the place up for sale."

"Meanwhile, she trashed her mother's house," Mac said.

With a frown, David shrugged his shoulders. "I'm not sure this is all Khloe."

"Was someone shacking up here with her?"

"Khloe, or someone, was looking for something, I think," David said. "There are papers all over the place in the study. The safe door is hanging open and someone has gone through all of Florence's legal papers."

"Like maybe Khloe was searching for another will?"

"My thought exactly," David said. "But she's been here for three weeks. Why leave it like this?"

"Because Khloe was a slug in a bra," Mac said. "She was too lazy to clean it up."

David took him into the bedroom. The television had finally been turned off.

The medical examiner, Dr. Dora Washington, was poking around at the body inside the garbage bag while Deputy Chief Arthur Bogart peered over her shoulder. The expressions on their faces revealed that this was not your average murder.

As always, Mac was struck by Dr. Washington's flawless figure and blue-black hair that she always wore in a silky ponytail that spilled down to the middle of her back. In her black slacks and form- fitting white shirt, she looked more like she belonged on the cover of a fashion magazine than cutting up dead people in the morgue.

When he had first met the medical examiner, Mac was struck by how brilliantly smart she was—but only after he had gotten over her physical beauty. Dr. Washington had nailed Mac and David's sibling relationship by their second meeting based purely on their eye color, cheekbones, and jaw-line. During a consultation in her office, she had bluntly asked David for confirmation of her assessment. She had the class to keep that information to herself. While David and Mac's familial relationship was not a state secret, they preferred to keep it under wraps for the sake of their late father's reputation.

"This is one sick animal," Dr. Washington told Mac when she saw him.

"He spent a lot of time here." Bogie led Mac to the bed. "He killed her here in the bed."

"It's too early to know if she had sex with him, either willingly or not," Mac said.

"I'll have to find that out at the morgue," the medical examiner said. "She was stabbed several times. I see stab wounds on her chest. It almost looks like he skinned her, but I won't be able to tell anything for certain until I get her back to the morgue and lay her body parts out on the table. It'll be like putting together a mannequin."

"We believe that after killing her," Bogie said, "he took her body into the bathtub where he dismembered her. Forensics already found blood, hair, and body tissue in the drain. He didn't go to much trouble trying to clean up after himself."

Mac went to look in the bathroom. Squatting, he examined the floor. In the room, brightly lit with high-powered lights, he could see the drag path from the bathroom and across the hardwood floor to where the bag rested in front of the television. "After dismembering her, he put her in the bag and dragged it all the way across the room to leave it there."

"That's how it looked to me, too," David said.

"Why there?" Mac rose to his feet. "If he was going to move it, why not take it out to the garbage? If he wasn't going to get rid of it, why not leave it in the bathroom? Why move it from here," he gestured to the bathroom, "to there?" He pointed to where the body in the bag then rested. Struck with a thought, he asked them, "Was the television on when the body was found?"

"Yes," David said. "As a matter of fact, it was Khloe's show that was on."

"Wasn't that cancelled?"

"After one season," Bogie chuckled.

"It was a Blu-ray disc with all of the episodes," David explained. "It was playing one particular episode. The player was set to continually repeat it."

"What episode was it?" Mac asked.

Mac followed Bogie's and Dr. Washington's eyes to David.

"To tell you the truth, I was too preoccupied to watch it," David said. "When I came in, two women, one of them Khloe, were in the midst of a cat fight over what sounded like a man."

Mac looked down at the drag marks on the floor.

"You're thinking the killer set up the player to play that episode," David said. "How do we know Khloe didn't set it up herself before getting killed?"

"And she also dragged her dead body in the bag out of the bathroom and across this room so that she could sit there and watch herself over and over again until her body was discovered?" Mac asked.

"Well, when you put it like that..." David sighed with disgust. "I guess we're going to be watching Khloe's show."

"That will make a full viewing audience of two," Bogie said with a smile.

CHAPTER THREE

Spencer Manor on Deep Creek Lake

There's no rest for dog owners—even if you're a multi-millionaire. Mac Faraday's German shepherd was a die-hard morning dog. Gnarly got up at six o'clock in the morning, rain or shine.

For some unexplained reason, Archie Monday, who had moved into the main house and Mac's bed from the guest cottage, was not suitable to take Gnarly outside. The dog would ignore her when she got out of bed and called him to go outside with her. Instead, he would sit next to Mac's side of the bed and paw at him until his master woke up.

If Mac took too long to get up, Gnarly would jump up onto the bed and stomp on his chest until his master would curse and tend to him.

After securing the perimeter of all threats—most of them squirrels, ducks, geese, and low-flying birds and occasional aircrafts—Gnarly would return to scratch at the door and demand breakfast. He would finish about the time Mac poured his first cup of coffee. Then, Gnarly would have to go outside again.

Mac had come to assume Gnarly, a kleptomaniac, would use that time to case Spencer Point for potential items to steal. Every couple of weeks, Mac would search Spencer Manor for the stolen goods and return them to their owners.

By the time Gnarly had finished breakfast and returned outside, Mac would be fully awake. If Mac was lucky, he could catch a nap after Gnarly returned from his second outing at nine o'clock.

This morning, Mac decided to catch his nap on the sofa in front of a roaring fire. Between the hot flames and the toasty afghan he curled up under, he was able to drift back to sleep until he heard one of the bedroom doors upstairs open and close. The click-clack of high heels on the granite floor told him that it wasn't Archie. She went barefoot except for when she absolutely had to put on shoes.

A freelance editor, Archie had jumped right back into work upon their return from the cruise. She had stayed up until well after midnight editing a novel for a mystery writer whose publisher had a tight deadline.

"Good morning, Chelsea," Mac greeted their houseguest without opening his eyes. "I guess you're going to work."

"Some people do have to work for a living," she said with a smile in her voice.

Trying to hang onto a thread of sleep, Mac squinted up at her. In the bright morning sunlight bouncing off the lake to spill in through the windows, Chelsea Adams resembled an angel with her platinum blonde hair framing her face in wispy waves. Chelsea's light blue eyes and ivory skin gave her an almost albino appearance. Her turquoise suit brought out the blue in her eyes.

Her hair was almost as white as her service dog, Molly, a German shepherd, who was also dressed for work in her gray vest with "Service Dog" stenciled in red block letters on the sides. Suffering from epilepsy since a serious car accident years before, Chelsea had enlisted the aid of Molly, who was trained to pick up early signs of seizures, which allowed her mistress time to take the medication to stop it.

Since Chelsea's arrival in Deep Creek Lake, Molly and Gnarly had become fast friends. When she and her mistress came downstairs, Molly galloped over to sniff Gnarly, who had curled up on the rug to warm himself in front of the fire.

"I'm very aware of that," Mac said. "Do you need a ride? I heard David come in around three o'clock this morning. He may not be up yet." He fought a smile when he saw a flicker of disappointment come to her eyes.

"You know," Chelsea said with a cock of her head, "I discovered something very interesting yesterday at the county prosecutor's office."

"What's that?"

"You and Ben Fleming go to the athletic club together twice a week."

"You didn't know that?" Mac asked with mock surprise. He folded his arms across his chest.

Chelsea sat down in the chair across from him. "How is it that the county prosecutor called out of the blue to offer me a position as paralegal in his office when I was looking for a job here in Deep Creek Lake? Not only a good job with a good salary, but they'll pay for my law school as well."

"How is that?"

"And the rent for the lakeside condo that I'm moving into, which has a view to die for, is a fraction of the other condos in the area and is managed by Spencer Properties, which you own." Her voice rose in octave.

"I knew that."

"My mother used to say that if it is too good to be true," Chelsea said, "it usually is. What gives, Mac? You're calling in favors and losing money on rent to make it almost impossible for me to not move back here to Spencer? Why? What's in it for you? You certainly aren't looking to date me, because I see how you look at Archie." She glanced in the direction of the guest cottage where Mac's half-brother lived. "Is it David? Did he ask you to do this?"

"No," Mac said, "David didn't ask me to put all this in motion. I consider you my friend, and I hate to see my friends have their dreams shattered by circumstances that are no fault of their own. You were in law school and on your way to becoming a lawyer when a car accident turned your world upside down. I'm in a position to help you realize that dream through a job as a paralegal with flexible hours to allow you to go to law school, through paying your tuition, and through a nice place for you and Molly to live in."

"You know I can't pay you back."

"I don't expect you to."

"Like maybe by getting together with David?"

Mac chuckled. "That's Archie's dream." He shrugged. "Hey, if having you here in Spencer with David driving you and Molly around will help to spark a little romance, so be it."

"What if it doesn't?"

Mac could feel her light blue eyes boring into his face. "What if it does?"

Standing up straight, she stuck out her chin. "I don't need or want a man. It's nothing against David. We've become good friends since all this happened with Riley. I've forgiven him for what happened back when we were in school—but that's it—nothing more. We're never going to be anything more than friends, and I wouldn't be surprised if David felt the same way."

The lady doth protest too much. Mac lifted his head to look at her. Her ivory cheeks were bright pink. Her pale coloring made it very difficult for her to hide the blush that happened when David was around or the topic of him came up.

Hearing the door open and shut, they both looked up in the direction of the doors leading in from the back deck.

"Okay," they heard David say into his cell phone, "I'll be there in an hour." Dressed in his uniform and jacket, David jogged up the steps from the drop-down dining room. He slipped his cell phone into its case on his utility belt. "Good morning, Chelsea. You look great this morning. I always thought you looked pretty in turquoise."

"Thank you." Her smile contradicted her claim that she and David could never be more than friends.

"I see you're finally rested up from your trip," David said to Mac while retrieving Chelsea's coat from out of the closet.

"It's a wonder what fourteen hours of sleep can do."

"I'm going to run Chelsea in to Fleming's office." David held her coat open to help her slip into it. "Doc called with the autopsy results. She wants us to meet her at the morgue. Would you like to meet me there?"

"Sure." Mac sat up from where he was lounging. "What did Doc tell you?"

David shook his head and shrugged at the same time. "She said it just keeps getting weirder and weirder."

"I hate being an imposition." Chelsea buttoned up her coat.

"You're not." David picked up her briefcase and held it out to her. "I like driving you and Molly."

"But you have to go to the morgue to find out about Khloe Everest's murder."

"I'd have to do that anyway, whether I was taking you into work or not." When she didn't take the briefcase, David continued to hold it out to her.

"Yeah," Mac said. "He'd have to go to the morgue anyway."

"How about if after the morgue I swing back over to take you to lunch?" David offered while shaking the briefcase in hopes that she would notice it.

She gazed at him without answering. Mac could see her yearning to say yes, but holding back.

"My treat," David added.

She opened her mouth to answer, but fear refused to let her form the words.

"Think about it on the way." He took the strap of the briefcase and draped it over her shoulder. He then took her hand and wrapped her fingers around the strap and held them there until she took hold of it. "There," he said after observing that the case was secure. "That will work." Taking her by the arm, he ushered her to the door. "Come along, Molly."

Reminded of her duty as Chelsea's service dog, Molly stopped licking Gnarly's ears to scurry to her mistress's side and go out the door with her. It was only because David quickly closed the door that Gnarly didn't follow them. Unable to accompany the white German shepherd, Gnarly ran to the window and jumped up to place his front paws on the sill and watch them leave in David's cruiser.

"Don't you feel ashamed, lying here warming yourself by the fire while your girlfriend goes off to work?" Mac joked.

As if to respond to him, Gnarly turned his head to look back at Mac from over his shoulder.

"No more than you do when your girlfriend stays up working until after midnight while you're sawing logs in a nice warm bed," a feminine voice replied from the stairs behind him.

Mac sat up to respond only to be pulled back by two soft hands on his shoulders. Once he had fallen back, she further restrained him by wrapping her arms around his shoulders. Her rosy scent surrounded him before she laid a kiss on his cheek next to his ear. "Good morning, handsome."

He took her hands into his. "Good morning, my love. Did you make headway on that book before you came to bed?"

"Some. This one is brutal. Talk about butchering the English language."

"Why did the publisher accept it if it's so bad?"

Archie smiled. "Because she's a has-been teenybopper singer. The publisher is betting that her fans read and will buy the book even if it is trash." She sighed. "Publishing isn't like it was back when your mother started out. Then publishers cared about great literature. Now it's only a business focused on the bottom line."

Keeping his hand in hers, she came around the sofa to sit next to his legs. He saw that she was naked under her bathrobe. "Speaking of butchers…I was really out of it last night, so I didn't catch everything you were telling me about Khloe Everest getting murdered. Her body was dismembered?"

Mac nodded his head. "And I've got to go shower and leave. Doc Washington finished the autopsy." He swung his legs off the sofa and put on his slippers.

"Do you think Khloe knew her killer?"

"Hard to say right now," Mac said. "No sign of a break in. But then, people like Khloe…"

"I did a look at her social media sites before I went to bed last night," she said. "Khloe was making a big deal that she had some big news that she was going to drop in her interview with E-Entertainment. She referred to it as a 'bomb.'"

"Did she drop any hints about what made up this bomb?"

Archie shook her head. "Not a clue. All she said was that it was going to make a big blast."

Mac gazed at her. "Almost sounds like keeping her from making that announcement could be the motive for her murder."

"That's what I thought."

He leaned over to press his forehead against her. "How about doing me a favor?"

"You want me to dig deeper into Khloe's social media sites and the media to see if I can figure out what her news could have been."

He kissed her. "You're my girl."

"I know." She grinned.

Mac stood up, only to have her pull him back down onto the sofa. She wrapped her arms around his shoulders. She pressed her lips against his mouth. "You know you're going to owe me for this."

He stroked her cheek and drew his fingertip down her throat to her chest. "Have you ever known me not to pay up?"

Their lips were barely touching. "Never."

"Then what's the problem?"

She brushed her fingers down his chest to his stomach. "I think this time I want you to pay up front." Grasping the belt of his bathrobe, she pulled him in closer.

Taking in a deep breath, Mac murmured, "I guess I can be a little late."

"You don't have to walk me in," Chelsea told David while he walked her into the county prosecutor's office in Oakland.

"I don't have to, but I want to." David held the door open for her and Molly. Once inside the office, Chelsea took off Molly's leash. The white German shepherd curled up in her bed in the corner behind Chelsea's desk.

David set Chelsea's briefcase on her desk. Seeing the county prosecutor in his office, he called out, "Good morning, Ben."

"David! Morning!" Ben got up from behind his desk and rushed out of the office. His pace told David that he wanted to talk to him before he had a chance to leave. "What's this I hear about Khloe Everest getting murdered yesterday?" Spotting his assistant, he greeted her with a nod of his head. "Nice to see you, Chelsea."

Seeing the prosecutor dressed in khaki slacks and a blue sweater, the police chief surmised he didn't have any court appearances scheduled for the day. "Khloe wasn't murdered yesterday," David said. "She was murdered five days ago. I found her body yesterday."

"Bogie told me that her house appeared to have been searched." Ben folded his arms across his chest. His furrowed brow put a crease in his forehead. His blue bloodlines and privileged upbringing had taught him how to handle difficult situations with grace. A furrowed eyebrow on Ben's face was uncommon.

"I think so," David said. "It's hard to say because the place was trashed anyway."

"Too bad," Ben said. "Ed Willingham, Florence's attorney, is coming in from Washington this morning. Can we meet with you this afternoon?"

"What about?"

"We may have some information that will help you with the case."

"I'll appreciate anything you can give me." David refrained from giving into his curiosity and asking for that information up front.

"Now the bad news." A playful curl came to Ben's lips before he bent over to pet Molly.

"Of course you would have bad news." David shot a glance at Chelsea who had taken her seat behind her desk.

"Bevis Palazzi is revving up to stick his nose into your case," Ben said, "and he's got enough juice that he may be able to do it."

"Bevis Palazzi as in Senator Harry Palazzi?" Chelsea asked.

"Bevis was friends with Khloe," David said. "He's also an arrogant jerk."

"Keep this under your hats," Ben said. "The governor is planning to retire at the end of this term. He hasn't announced it yet. Since it seems like Senator Palazzi is never going to retire, Bevis decided to start his political career as governor. He's using whatever means necessary to get his name in the headlines, and how better than by playing the victim's advocate for his dead friend? Since his father is a United States Senator, he is not without influence."

"So I may be forced to have him under foot like a bad piece of chewing gum," David said.

"Exactly," Ben said. "Now here's the good news."

"What? You have some good news?"

"The governor is not Bevis' biggest fan," Ben said. "He's a friend of mine and Catherine's. Off the record, he calls Bevis a degenerate and is not thrilled with his party grooming him to take over as governor. He's told me that it's enough to make him want to not retire. That's pretty bad. He only supports Bevis publicly because some big backers in his party think Bevis can carry on his father's legacy. If that pain in the butt gets too bad, give me a call and I'll ask the governor to reel him in."

"That's why I have you on speed dial."

With a smile at Chelsea and David, Ben went back into his office.

David leaned over her chair to whisper into her ear. "What's your answer about lunch?"

In spite of her effort to prevent it, a coy smile came to her lips. "It sounds like your day is already planned."

"I can fit you in," he replied. "I'll swing by before going back to Spencer after meeting with Doc."

Lauren Carr

"You don't give up." She watched his back on his way out the door.

"Never."

50

CHAPTER FOUR

"Sorry I'm late." Mac practically ran through the door in his rush into the medical examiner's office. He found David and Dr. Washington standing over the examination table that was covered with a white sheet.

"No problem," David said.

"Are you okay?" Dr. Washington asked Mac with concern. "You look flushed."

Mac ignored David's grin. "I guess I had the heater up too high in the car when I was running late."

"Oh, is that all?" Her lips curled into a smirk. "I thought it was something a little more intimate."

While David burst out laughing, Mac said, "Can we get on with this?"

The medical examiner turned serious. "Cause of death was stabbing. I counted forty-six stab wounds with the concentration in her stomach and some strikes in her chest."

"Was there any sign of sexual assault?" David asked.

"You had to ask me that." The medical examiner looked at him for a moment before shrugging her shoulders. "Can't be conclusive because of the extent of the mutilation. I did find semen—enough for a DNA sample. However, the bruising and tearing could be due to the attack that resulted in her murder, and not rape. The sexual activity could have been completely consensual."

"And then things went bad afterwards," Mac said.

"In addition to the dismemberment, he gutted her from the ribcage down to the pelvis and took her uterus."

"Her what?" David asked.

"Uterus," Doc Washington repeated the word. "Her female organ."

While David gazed at her in shock, Mac asked, "Could she have been pregnant? Archie said Khloe was making a big deal on her social media sites about a huge announcement in that interview. Maybe she was going to announce that she was pregnant, and the father wanted to stop that. So he killed her and took the uterus with the fetus."

"That's sick," David said.

"We already know our killer's sick," Mac said.

The medical examiner was shaking her head. "According to the blood tests, she wasn't pregnant."

"Does it look to you like the killer had medical training?" Mac asked her. "Did he know what he was doing when cutting her?"

"No," she said with a firm shake of her head. "The cuts were frenzied. Sloppy. Not precise. I saw a lot of rage in them. He basically hacked out the uterus when he took it."

David asked both the seasoned detective and medical examiner, "Have you ever seen something like this before? A killer who guts the woman and takes the uterus?"

Mac was staring down at the sheet under which Khloe Everest's dismembered body rested. "I have seen similar cases. Usually it's a man who hates women, plain and simple. I once caught a killer who didn't care who the woman was—he would hunt them like animals and butcher them because he simply hated their sex." He grinned. "But we got this guy's DNA from his semen. Is it in the system?"

She smiled. "Oh yes."

"Great," Mac said. "Then this can be an easy case."

"No, not that easy," she said. "The same DNA was found on two other bodies listed in the database, but the donor has never been identified."

"That means this guy has killed two other women," Mac said.

"The first one is Amber Houston."

"Where do I know that name from?" David asked.

"She disappeared the month before Khloe staged her abduction," Mac said. "Her body was found in a garbage bag in a motel dumpster."

"Like Khloe, her body was dismembered, and her uterus taken," the doctor said. "There's no way this is a copycat, because the dismemberment and uterus were never made public."

"So it's the same guy," Mac said. "The DNA matched for a third victim?"

"Los Angeles," she said. "Twenty months ago. Tiffany Blanchard. She was a model. Her body was found in a garbage bag dumped over a hillside on the beach. Dismembered with her uterus missing. In all three cases, the killer had sexual relations with the woman before stabbing her to death, mutilating and dismembering her bodies, and then taking her uterus."

"We have a serial killer," David said.

"Yep," Mac said, "the worst kind."

In the upscale resort town of Spencer, Maryland, where many of the town's residents were listed in "Who's Who," the small police station resembled a sports club. Its fleet of police cruisers was top-of-the-line SUVs painted black with gold lettering on the side that read "SPENCER POLICE." Located along the shore of Deep Creek Lake, the log building that was home to the police department sported a dock with a dozen jet skis and four speed boats. For patrolling the deep woods and up the mountains trails, they had eight ATVs. Like the cruisers, all of the vehicles were black with gold trim.

The conference with Ben Fleming and Ed Willingham, the attorney for Khloe's late mother, turned into a luncheon meeting. Ben brought Chelsea along to take notes during their meeting. Whether she liked it or not, she was eating lunch with David.

They met in David's office, which was located on the second floor with a view of the lake. Ben had ordered Chinese takeout from the one restaurant that dealt with it on the lake. While dealing out the food around the conference table, Ed Willingham, a prestigious lawyer and senior partner of one of the largest law firms in the Washington, DC, area, tried to talk business to Mac about a producer wanting to purchase the movie rights for Robin Spencer's last three Mickey Forsythe books.

In spite of the obscene amount of money the producer was offering, Mac balked. "No cast approval, no rights."

"He's not going to let you have say in the casting of the movie." It was difficult to tell if Ed thought, or rather hoped, that Mac was joking in his request.

"Mickey Forsythe was my mother's creation," Mac explained. "I'm not going to have his image tarnished by the casting of some degenerate to play him on the screen, or maybe by someone who decides to make him more sensitive or more like a boob."

"Or maybe select a neutered German shepherd to play Diablo," David said.

"That's right," Mac agreed. "Gnarly would be in a snit for a year if that happened. Have you ever seen Gnarly when he was in a snit about something?"

"It's not pretty," David said.

Mac pressed the top of his finger against the tabletop. "No cast approval, no rights. That's final."

"I guess these movies won't get made," Ed said in a firm tone, as if the decision had been his.

Mac picked up an egg roll with a shrug of his shoulders. "Fine with me."

After everyone's plates were made, Ben Fleming took the lead in the meeting. "As you know, close to a month ago, Florence Everest passed away, which started a whole mess with Khloe coming back to town and expecting to collect an inheritance, only to discover that her mother had been serious when she said she was disinherited."

"Knowing Khloe," Ed said, "she thought that since she was an only child she would get it all no matter what. Big surprise when her mother left it all to charity to help women victims of violent crime."

"Which Khloe then became," Mac noted the irony.

"Khloe managed to find an attorney to file a suit against Florence's estate and fight the will," Ed said. "No way was she going to win that. In the meantime, she took up residence in the house and refused to leave."

David urged them to continue. "What information do you have that can help us find her killer?"

Ben looked across the table at Ed. The lawyer got up and closed David's office door. On his way back to the conference table, he took a microcassette recorder out of his pocket, turned on a button, and placed the recorder in the middle of the table.

A woman's voice came from the speaker with the smooth, cultured tone that had belonged to Florence Everest.

"I said no!"

Slap!

"Oh, I forgot how you like it rough," a male voice said. "If you want it like the last time—"

"Last time was not rough! Last time was an attack. I said no—"

"Of course you said no. They all say no, but they don't mean no."

"You pinned my hands down and you raped me!"

"You call it rape, I call it playing rough."

There was a sound of movement followed by the man yelling, "What the hell is that?"

"Don't you recognize it?" the woman's voice replied with laughter. "It's called a gun! You come near me again and I'll shoot your balls off before shooting you dead."

"You shoot me and you'll spend the rest of your life in jail—in a federal prison. Shooting a sheriff is a federal offense."

"But you'll be dead, and this tape will be on the national news!"

"Damn, bitch! You set me up!"

"Damn straight!" she said. "And you're going to live with what you've done for the rest of your life because I'm pregnant now and you're going to pay for it. Oh, and don't even think about doing anything to me because copies of this tape will be all over—anything happens to me, and the whole world is going to know that Sheriff Harry Palazzi is a low-life, common rapist!"

"Oh, man," Mac muttered.

Ed snapped the tape off. "Oh man is right."

"She said copies of that tape were all over. Obviously you had one." David noticed Mac glaring at the recorder like he wanted to shoot it.

"It was in a sealed envelope that was only to be opened upon her death," Ed said. "She gave it to me when she came to me pregnant with Khloe. All these years, Florence has been getting a direct deposit of ten thousand dollars into her account every month. I assumed it was from Khloe's father, who wanted no emotional part of her."

"And here she was, the product of rape," Chelsea said.

"Did Khloe know?" David asked.

"No," Ed said with certainty. "When I encountered this tape I took it to Ben, and we've been trying to decide what to do."

"The man is a rapist." Mac grabbed the recorder and shook it. "He's a sexual predator who has been raping women for years and getting away with it. Don't you think it's time to stop him?"

"This victim is dead," Ben said.

"She's not the first rape victim that Senator Palazzi got rid of," Mac said.

"Mac," David said gently, "Florence's death was an accident. Pure and simple. It was investigated. What other victims has Palazzi gotten rid of?"

Mac felt all of their eyes on him. "It was back when I was working the special victims unit in Washington, before I went to homicide." He gritted his teeth. "One night, I got called to the hospital where this woman had been dumped at the ER. Her name was Dee Blakeley. She had been beaten up and raped. When I finally got her to speak to me, she told me that she was a lobbyist who had gone to meet with Senator Harry Palazzi to talk about an upcoming bill. He poured Dee a drink. They sat in his office to talk about the bill, and suddenly, he raped her. When she fought him, he beat her up. Then, his assistant and driver arrived to take her home. When she passed out in the back of the limo, they literally dumped her at the ER and drove off."

"Why didn't you arrest him?" Chelsea asked.

Mac shook his head. "His people circled the wagons. The assistant and driver who knew the truth insisted that she was drunk when she showed up for the meeting and they saw her put the moves on the senator, who swore it was consensual and she was lying about the rape for her own personal gain. They all claimed afterwards, when she was leaving the senator's office, that she had tripped and fallen and hit her face on the desk. Because she was so drunk, they refused to let her drive. When they discovered that she was bleeding from the fall, they dropped her off at the hospital. The victim told me that her cat disappeared and she had received a visit from an intimidating man saying that the same would happen to her. She wanted to withdraw her complaint and said she wouldn't testify, but I talked her into doing it. The morning that she was to appear at the grand jury, I went to her apartment to pick her up and…" His voice trailed off.

The room fell silent.

Ben broke the silence. "What?"

"She was dead," Mac said in a voice barely above a whisper. He looked across the table at David. "Stabbed to death—multiple stab wounds."

"Like Khloe," David said.

"She wasn't dismembered, and her body hadn't been mutilated, but that was about twelve years ago. Killers usually escalate. He may have just been getting started back then."

"Did you have any proof that Palazzi was behind it?" the prosecutor asked.

"Come on, Ben," Mac said. "It was the night before she was to testify to the grand jury about him raping her. That night, of all nights, a maniac breaks into her apartment and stabs her to death?"

"Was she raped during that attack?" David asked.

"No," Mac said. "No sexual assault."

"Since Palazzi has never been charged—" Ben started to say.

"Yes, he got away with having Dee Blakeley killed," Mac said. "I tried to make a case, but my boss put pressure on me because he got orders from people above him to let it go. I know the senator had that girl killed."

"Leak the tape to the media," Chelsea said. "Even if he can't be arrested, his reputation can be ruined. He claims to be a proponent for women's rights, and here he's a sexual predator."

"Khloe's announcement," Mac said. "Florence said these tapes were going to be all over. Khloe could have found a copy of the tape and decided to play it during the interview."

"Knowing Khloe," the estate attorney said, "I would not put it past her trying to blackmail Palazzi. She had nothing. Her bid for fame fizzled. She thought she was going to inherit a fortune from her mother and had gotten cut out. As a matter of fact, after that stunt, the mysterious monthly payment stopped coming. I asked Florence about it—knowing nothing about it being from Palazzi or this recording. Florence said that the benefactor had paid in full and nothing was coming in from him anymore."

"Florence was so mad that she cut Khloe loose completely," David said.

Ed nodded his head. "And Khloe was furious when she found out it was real."

"So she decided to squat in the house and search for something that she could use to her advantage and found the tape," Mac said. "Then, she tried to blackmail Palazzi. She was doing a countdown on the social media sites. She was giving him time to squirm and think about it. Only instead, he had her killed."

"Nah," David said. "The M.O. for the murder doesn't fit."

"Unless the contract killer purposely made it look like a crazed serial killer," Mac suggested. "I've run into that. A contract hit that was made to look like the victim had run into a maniac. Only in this case, we have DNA that matches two other murders."

"Then maybe it wasn't Palazzi," Ben said.

"Don't tell me that you're friends with Palazzi," Mac said.

"I never said I was friends with the man," Ben said. "Nor am I surprised by this. I learned a long time ago that the apparent character of a person, especially someone who is a public figure, is nothing like what it is behind closed doors."

"Does Palazzi know you have this tape?" Mac asked him.

"He has to know someone has it," Ed answered. "He did invite me for drinks soon after Florence's death. He knows I'm her lawyer. I could tell he was feeling me out and trying to determine if we had anything on him. I gave him nothing. He's nervous."

"Are you going to move to prosecute?" David asked Ben.

"We don't know any of the particulars," Ben said. "The victim is dead—not killed by the suspect."

"So you decided not to move forward," Mac said. "Palazzi got away with it again."

"It's a very weak case, Mac," Ben said. "If Florence was still alive, we'd have a chance."

"Not only is there the matter of the rape," Ed said, "but I can also see Khloe deciding to make a claim as Senator Palazzi's daughter."

"That would make Bevis' day," Ben said in a tone heavy with sarcasm. He even chuckled at the thought.

"Which makes Bevis a suspect," David said. "Now that makes my day."

"Unless Khloe didn't find the recording," Mac said. "We need to dive heavy into what she has been doing since getting to Spencer and moving into that house."

This case is going all over the place.

Mac made himself at home at David's laptop while he walked Chelsea out to Ben's car after lunch. *The man never gives up … as well he shouldn't.*

Meanwhile, Mac was logging into the police database to bring up what information he could on Amber Houston's murder. Her body had been found in a small rural town outside Pittsburgh. The case was being handled by the Pennsylvania state police.

Tonya buzzed the intercom into the police chief's office. "Hey, Mac, Bevis Palazzi is on the phone for the chief. He wants to talk about Khloe Everest's murder, and he wants to talk to someone in charge. I could make him sit on hold until the chief comes back in, or would—?"

"I'll talk to him." He grabbed the phone. "Mac Faraday here."

"I want to talk to your so-called police chief."

"You got me."

"That's unacceptable," Bevis Palazzi said before launching into a tirade. "I specifically told that bitch that I wanted to talk to the chief of police about the status of locating Khloe Everest's killer. She was a very good friend of mine, I might add. I specifically told that idiot—"

"That lady is a sergeant with the police, and she can beat the snot out of your fat little nose."

"Are you threatening me?"

"It's not a threat," Mac replied, "It's a statement. Sergeant Tonya is an experienced police officer who deserves to be treated, and spoken about, with respect."

"Whatever!" he uttered a loud scoff. "She's still a bitch."

"You have three seconds to ask your question before I hang up," Mac said, "because while I'm here on this phone listening to your foul mouth, I could be tracking down a killer."

"Do you know who I am?"

"Yes, I know exactly what you are," Mac said. "You're a spoiled brat who needs to grow up and learn some manners. Call me when we can have a civilized, grown-up conversation." Hanging up the phone, he resumed studying the information listed under Amber Houston's murder.

The name of the lead investigator caught his eye: Pennsylvania State Homicide Detective Cameron Gates.

I know her.

The phone rang again.

"I'll get that," David announced while hurrying into the office. Pointing a finger of accusation at him, he said, "You've been a bad boy." He snatched up the phone. "Police Chief David O'Callaghan here." He grimaced while listening to Bevis' outrage, which Mac could hear all the way over on his side of the desk. "If you would calm down, Mr. Palazzi, we could discuss this rationally like two adults."

"You need one more adult to make that happen," Mac said.

"Well," David said, "if you want to know what I think about your involvement in this case,—" Without another word, he slammed the phone down on the base.

His eyes wide, Mac chuckled. "What did you just do?"

"We got cut off," David said. "That's how you hang up on someone. What are we going to do about him?"

"He's a suspect," Mac said. "We have legitimate cause to keep him and his father out of the investigation." He pointed at the laptop screen. "You'll never guess who the lead investigator is in the Amber Houston murder. Detective Cameron Gates."

"You mean that detective with the cat? What was his name?"

"Irving," Mac said, "but, if he likes you, you can call him 'Irv.'"

"Big devil that looks like a skunk," David recalled. "She takes him everywhere."

"Because he has issues," Mac said.

The intercom buzzed again. "Chief, now it's the governor."

"I'll take it." Mac picked up the phone.

Relieved, David gathered up his laptop and turned on his heels. "I'll go call Irving's mother."

Downstairs, David took his laptop to a vacant desk in a corner of the squad room. After looking up Cameron Gates' number on the police report, he placed the call to her office in Pennsylvania.

"Hello, Police Chief David O'Callaghan," she greeted him with her low sexy voice.

"How's Irving?" David asked with an equally husky tone.

"Still has issues," she said. "How's Gnarly?"

"Still a kleptomaniac."

"How about his uncle?" she asked.

"Uncle?" David laughed. "You better not call me his uncle in front of Mac. He swears he did not sire that dog."

"Josh is the same way about Irving."

"Speaking of Josh," David asked, "how is he?"

"My silver fox," she said. "He's better than fine. He's downright fantastic. He's prosecuting a case right now against a young man who tried to hold up a bar with an automatic handgun shortly before they closed. Unfortunately for the guy, he walked into a retirement party for a sheriff's deputy and pulled his gun out while standing in the middle of a bar filled with cops. Josh has like twenty police officers for eyewitnesses."

"I wish they could all be that simple."

"So do I, sweetheart."

The two of them shared a good laugh.

Recalling that Cameron had taken a stab wound in the shoulder during their case together, he asked, "How's your shoulder?"

"Fine," she said. "Yet another badge of courage. So tell me, are you still on the market?"

"Market for what?" David asked her.

"I'm taking about ladies," she said. "A good looking piece of beefcake like you has to have a lady, or are you still shopping around?"

Thinking of Chelsea, he replied, "I'm working on it."

"Don't give up. She'll come around."

"I hope." He settled into the reason for his call. "Amber Houston."

"Tragedy." The humor had left her voice. "What about her? Tell me you've got a lead."

"We have a young lady who got stabbed and butchered," David said. "Her uterus was taken. Plus, we got DNA that matches with the DNA left in your victim. Would you call that a lead?"

"That means our guy hit again," Cameron said. "That's three hits. I got a call last year about a woman in LA who got killed. The perp used the same M.O. What have you got?"

"Tell me about Amber?"

"I'll do better than that," she replied. "Does Mac Faraday still own the Spencer Inn?"

David grinned. "Will you bring the case file?"

"I'll show you mine if you show me yours."

"Deal."

CHAPTER FIVE

"Are you ready for some television viewing?" Mac asked Bogie and David when they came into the police chief's office. There was a big bowl of popcorn in the middle of the conference table and the television was set up with the Blu-ray player.

"You seem to be making yourself kind of comfortable here," David noted.

"The killer placed Khloe's body in front of the television with her reality show playing," Mac said.

"And it was set to re-loop one particular episode."

"Why that one episode?" Mac asked. "I looked it up. Khloe's show had shot twelve episodes." He pointed at the set with the remote. "Why this one? I think he's sending us a message."

"We need to watch that episode to see if we can find that message," Bogie said.

"Can I delegate one of you to watch it?" David asked.

"You found the body." Bogie poked David in the shoulder with his finger. "In this department, the responding officer who finds the body takes the lead in the investigation. Your daddy's rule. This is your case, so you need to watch the hour-long cat fight between four material girls who wanna be stars."

Mac held up the bowl to offer them. "Popcorn, gentlemen?"

David took a handful of popcorn. "I need a beer, too."

One corner of his lip curled when Mac shook his head. "Sorry, man, you're on duty. You need to watch this sober."

While David took three bottles of water out of his portable fridge for them to have with the popcorn, Bogie asked Mac, "Tonya said the governor called to request we let Bevis in on the investigation. What did you tell him?"

"No," Mac said.

"You said no to the governor?" Bogie shook his head. "You're either the bravest man I know, or the stupidest."

Seeing the arch in Bogie's eyebrow, Mac added, "I also told him that I would present to him a weekend getaway at the Spencer Inn for his birthday if he kept Bevis away from this case—on account of him being a suspect. That was when he said okay."

"Which proves it pays to have friends in high places." After giving Mac a high five, Bogie slipped into a chair at the table.

Sitting across from him, Mac said, "You seem to know a lot about Khloe's show. Have you ever watched it?"

"Only one episode out of curiosity," he confessed. "It was everything I thought it would be."

David set a bottle down in front of the deputy chief. "What was it you imagined?"

"Stupid," Bogie said. "It was a stupid show about stupid women who couldn't stop acting stupid with each other and everyone in their lives. Reality? Bah! I can't believe real people could be that stupid."

"I really want a beer," David muttered.

"When you're off duty." Mac hit the play button.

The show opened with the sun rising on a sprawling home in the Hollywood hills. The first several minutes had the four roommates making cutting remarks to each other while fixing their breakfasts and checking their emails and texts. Bogie paused and introduced each of the three women who lived with Khloe.

"That's Rain Drop," Bogie said when a leggy redhead came into the kitchen. "She and Khloe hated each other."

"She was the woman Khloe was fighting with on the show when I found her body," David said.

"Rain Drop is a singer, and a good one," Bogie said. "She's the only one out of the four to make anything of herself. Probably because she's the only one who had any talent for anything besides back-stabbing. Khloe was so jealous of her that she couldn't see straight. Rain Drop saw Khloe for what she was, and she would call her on it."

The show progressed, and Khloe and Rain Drop bickered during the course of the day about a singer in Rain Drop's band being interested in Khloe. The fighting escalated into a knock down drag out fight in which the two women brawled until their two roommates had to pull them apart.

David recalled that was the scene he heard when he had come into the bedroom to find Khloe's body. The show went on to end later in the evening with Khloe tearfully drinking a glass of wine with a young man, Nick. In a sidebar, she told the audience that Nick was her best friend. A homosexual, he seemed to really understand her, and to love her unconditionally.

"He's got a hundred times more talent than Rain Drop," she told the camera. "I met him while he was singing at a club that my friends and I went to for my twenty-first birthday."

Mac sat up. "Didn't Khloe turn twenty-one the month before her so-called abduction?"

"Yes," David said. "Five weeks before she disappeared."

"Do you recall interviewing that guy?" Mac pointed to the television screen where Khloe was dissolving into tears. Her friend was an extremely slender young man. His face was so gaunt looking that his high cheekbones and sunken eyes made him resemble a skeleton.

"Nope," David answered.

"No one could possibly understand," Khloe sobbed on the show. "They don't care about what I've been through. No one believes me—the police in Maryland are trying to have me arrested."

"For what?" Nick asked.

"For getting kidnapped," Khloe said. "They know I lied after I had escaped, but they don't understand. Even if they did, they wouldn't care. No one cares." She reached for his hand. "You're the only one who cares about what happens to me, Nick."

"Tell me what happened." Nick patted her hand. "I'll believe you."

Almost knocking his chair over backwards, Mac went to David's desk to retrieve the case file for Khloe's murder. He tossed it onto the table and opened it.

"I was kidnapped," Khloe said. "I really was. I had been talking to this guy on the beach at the lake and he wanted me to spend the night with him, but it was getting late and I was tired. I was going to my car, and suddenly he grabbed me and threw me into the trunk of his car. Then, for the next four days—" She wailed. "We were in a motel. That part was true. But he had made me his sex slave for four days."

"You poor girl," Nick said. "Then what happened? How did you escape?"

"I crawled out through the bathroom window," she said. "I thought he was going to kill me. I was afraid that if I told the truth that he would come after me and kill me, or worse, my mother." She sucked in a shuddering breath. "I was only trying to protect my mother, but instead of being grateful, she turned on me like everyone else."

"That's bull!" David said when Mac paused the disc. The frame froze with Nick's image on the screen. "She wasn't raped."

"She's not a good actress," Bogie agreed. "No wonder her career in Hollywood went nowhere."

Mac went up to the television screen and held up the sketch drawing next to the Nick's image. "Gentlemen, does this face look familiar to you?"

David and Bogie leaned forward in their seats to compare the image of Nick, Khloe's homosexual best friend and confidante, to the drawing of the man Khloe had been seen speaking to on the lake before her disappearance. While the image of the man on the beach had a hairless face and long hair, Nick had shorter hair and a goatee. But the facial features, including the pointy nose, high cheekbones, and sunken eyes, were a match.

"Khloe said that the guy she was talking to on the beach abducted her and made her his sex slave," David said. "But, according to that sketch, that's the same guy she's telling this story to."

"We need to have a talk with Nick," Mac said. "Even if he didn't kill Khloe, he obviously knows something about that faked kidnapping."

"It was a publicity stunt," Bogie said.

"We all know that," Mac said.

"Khloe wouldn't have known the truth if it had bit her in the butt," David said. "She was a pathological liar."

"Which is why we need to talk to those close to her to find out what was really going on," Mac said. "This..." He waved the picture in front of the image on the television screen while trying to recall his name, "Nick was seen with her the night she'd disappeared. Khloe claimed she spent four days in a motel having sex with a boy."

"You're thinking that boy," David said.

"Whoever it was, he was in on the fake kidnapping, and we have yet to find him," Mac said. "This guy matches the sketch. Do the math. The kidnapping was three years ago. This was shot almost two years ago. They'd been together for over a year at the time this was filmed—that makes it more than just a fling in a motel."

"Does that mean he's not Khloe's gay best friend?" Bogie said.

"It's not really reality," Mac replied in a loud whisper.

Bogie's mocking frown pushed his mustache up into his nostrils. "I'll call the show's producers and get the scoop on Nick, the fake gay guy."

Mac realized he was being optimistic in hoping that Lily Carter, Khloe's ex-best friend, would be of any help in identifying the murderer in their case. After the charade in which Khloe pretended to have been abducted, Lily immediately ended their friendship. While Khloe went off to Hollywood, Lily attended two more years of graduate school at West Virginia University. After receiving her master's in business administration, she went to work at the Spencer Inn. In a year, she had worked up to assistant manager in the resort's event planning department. It was her job to coordinate between guests and clients for special events, like wedding receptions and conferences, which took place at the Spencer Inn resort.

Lily was coming out of a staff meeting with the inn's manager when Mac nabbed her before she had a chance to go back to her office with a stack of folders. She looked as simply pretty as she had three years before. When she saw Mac, her face beamed. "Hello, Mr. Faraday."

Upon hearing Mac's name, Jeff Ingles, the inn's manager, rushed out. He tried to be nonchalant about looking toward the floor for any sign of Gnarly, the bane of his existence at the resort. When Mac directed his attention toward Lily, the rest of the hotel management team moved on to their respective jobs.

"Do you have a couple of minutes?" Mac invited her to join him in the lounge for a drink.

"What's this about?" Her expression was one of confusion.

"Khloe Everest."

Lily stood rooted in her tracks. "Khloe and I aren't friends anymore."

"Considering how she was murdered, I don't think it's a friend we're looking for."

Lily's mouth dropped open.

Seeing that this was not hotel business, Jeff Ingles turned and went in the opposite direction toward his office.

"Would you like me to buy you a drink?" Mac offered.

"Depends," she replied.

"On what?"

"Are you going to arrest me?" she asked.

"Depends," he replied.

"On what?"

"Did you kill her?" Mac asked her.

"Would you believe me if I told you no?"

"You haven't lied to me yet."

He led the way to the inn's lounge where Lily ordered a root beer float after Mac had told her to order anything she wanted. He ordered a Brandy Manhattan. After some small talk in the corner booth, Mac eased his way into his interview with her. "When was the last time you saw Khloe?"

She seemed to think for a short time before answering. "Last week. She and her friends had been coming in fairly regularly since she came back. I knew her mother had disinherited her. I stayed tight with Florence after what Khloe had pulled. I was surprised by how furious she was, but do you blame her?"

"No, not at all," Mac said. "Thinking someone is hurting your child is the worst thing that a parent can go through. To find out that it's a joke…" His voice trailed off when he saw a flicker of something in Lily's eyes. *I wonder if she's talking about something else.*

"You mentioned her friends," Mac said.

"Khloe was coming in with a guy," Lily said. "She had introduced him to me. His name was Nick, but I don't know anything about him. I'll admit, she and I had words after she started showing up here."

"What about?"

"She was putting her stuff on her mom's account," she said. "She expected Florence's estate to pay for it. So, I told Jeff. Next time she came in, Jeff went to her table and told her that they had to pay cash or put it on a credit card—no hotel credit. Well, without any hesitation, the guy she was with pulled out a credit card. Only the name on it was some woman—Sheila. Now he didn't look like any Sheila. So Jeff told me to check into it. Sure enough, the card was legit and not reported stolen. So we let them use it—and man! They did. They were doing the spa, happy hour, dinner—everything."

"Did you get the last name on that card?" Mac asked.

"I have it written down in my office," she said. "But anyway, after Jeff cut them off, Khloe came to my office and called me all types of names. She said I was jealous because she didn't take me to Hollywood and make me a star. 'Really? Is that all you've got?' I told her. 'You're a joke,' I said. 'You're a pathetic pathological liar and a joke.' Then I had security remove her from my office."

After a pause filled with pride for what she considered a winning moment, she added, "But I didn't kill her." The ice cream in her float was gone. From across the booth, she leaned toward him. "I forgot to ask. How did she die? I mean, how was she killed?"

"She was stabbed to death."

Lily shuddered. "You know, knowing Khloe the way I did, being friends from back when we were kids, I knew she wouldn't live to an old age. She lived too fast and hung out with—" She shook her head. "Like that guy that I saw her talking to that night at the lake. I never did get a clear look at him, and it was dark, but I had a bad feeling about him—like he would only lead her into trouble. But then, she wasn't kidnapped." She cocked her head at Mac. "I wonder who he was."

Mac wanted so much for her to confirm that the Nick that Khloe had come into the inn with was the same man she had seen her talking to the night that she faked her disappearance. "Have you ever seen that man since that night?" he asked while studying her face for a reaction.

Lily stared into her float for a long moment. "To tell you the truth, since it all ended up being a lie, I never looked for him. I mean, he didn't end up being a killer or anything. Why?"

"Well," he replied, "she did end up spending four days in a motel with him." He shot her a grin. "They must have been friends. Maybe you've seen him around—hanging out with her and her crowd."

"You know that was so long ago and it was dark when I saw him..."

They finished their respective drinks. His brandy drained, Mac asked, "Did Khloe come in with anyone else besides this Nick?"

"Bevis Palazzi."

Mac sighed. "Really? I thought he was *your* friend."

"Are you kidding?" she replied. "I never did like him. He had latched onto Khloe, or rather Khloe's theater friends." She shook her finger when a thought came to her mind. "That guy could have been one of her theater friends— playing the role of a crazed kidnapper and all."

"Maybe." Mac tucked her suggestion away in his mind. After all, Nick was playing Khloe's gay best friend on her show. It was a good suggestion, the more he thought about it. "Tell me more about Bevis and Khloe."

She sighed. "Bevis was a theater groupie."

"Are you kidding? Bevis was a groupie?"

Lily nodded her head. "He would do volunteer stuff for the local theater groups. You do remember that Khloe was big on the local theater in Morgantown and other groups around here? I worked backstage as stage manager and assistant director. Bevis played the big shot by throwing money around to help support the groups. So they would let him hang around no matter how big of a jerk he was."

"Was he a closet wannabe star?" Mac couldn't envision Bevis being a thespian.

She shook her head. "He never performed on stage. It was backstage stuff that he would do in order to hang out with the theater crowd. Khloe may have been a lousy actress, but she did have this star quality that attracted guys—even some gay guys would hang around her all starry eyed. Sort of like she was Liza Minnelli or something. Bevis had it bad. I mean, he was ten years older than us and was a spoiled jerk. But he had money and was generous with it, as long as Khloe and her entourage let him hang with them." She added, "Florence couldn't stand the air he breathed."

Realizing why, Mac nodded his head. "I can imagine."

"Bevis and Khloe stayed tight," she said. "When she went to Hollywood, he made regular trips out there to see her and rub elbows with celebrities to drum up support for when he ran for national office. As a matter of fact, I hadn't seen him in years when he came in with her—and he was in here with her more than once."

"Did they seem to get along?" Mac asked.

"It's hard to tell with Bevis Palazzi," she said. "He's never happy with anyone except himself."

Mac was taking the garbage out with Gnarly close behind him to scoop up anything good that might fall out of the container when David drove his cruiser between the two stone pillars that marked the entrance into Spencer Manor. Spying Molly peering out at him from the rear passenger window, Gnarly forgot about the garbage and raced after the cruiser to greet her. The two dogs ran off to frolic in the gardens.

After releasing Molly, David opened up the back of the SUV to reveal bags of groceries and boxes of new dishes and cookware.

"Someone has been shopping," Mac said.

"Spoken like an ace detective," David said. "Grab a box and put it in the garage."

"I tossed out my old dishes and cookware when I moved out here," Chelsea explained. "They were over thirty years old—used to belong to Mom. So I splurged with my first paycheck from my job and bought new." She showed Mac the picture on the box. "They're square. How do you like them?"

"They look familiar." Mac peered at the image of square white dinner dishes. "Who do we know that has dishes like these?" he asked David.

"The lounge at the Spencer Inn," David said.

"Yeah, that's where I know them."

"I am not copying the Spencer Inn." Seeing their doubtful expressions, she turned around. "I'll go show Archie. She'll tell you."

"Spencer Inn," David mouthed.

With a laugh, Mac checked the contents of the grocery bags while David put the cookware in the garage. "Do you want my help in moving Chelsea into the condo after they're done remodeling it?"

"It isn't like she has that much to move," David said. "The new furniture will be delivered there. All she has is her clothes and towels and linens and household stuff." Seeing Mac examining the steaks, enough for two, he snapped the bag shut and yanked it out of his hands. "Why? Do you and Archie have plans for something else you'd rather do?"

"No," Mac said, "but if you'd like for us to disappear, I can arrange that. Chelsea's first night alone in her own place… with you. After spending the whole day doing heavy lifting for her, maybe she'll want to give you a massage to relax your tired muscles…" His voice trailed off into a chuckle.

"In my dreams," David said. "Now you're beginning to sound like Archie."

"You know what they say about couples," Mac said. "You hang around each other long enough, and you start to think and act alike." Seeing David's lack of humor, he asked, "You two are coming along, aren't you?" He pointed at the boxes in the garage. "You're shopping together."

"Because I drove her." David picked up the rest of the grocery bags. "Frankly, this is getting old. I've been sucking up to her for weeks, and…" He lowered his voice to a whisper. "She won't even let me kiss her. Everyone tells me not to give up, but I'm getting close to the point that I'm about ready to. What happened in the past is ancient history. I cheated. I broke her heart. I told her I was sorry and I meant it." Gesturing for Mac to get out of his way, David slammed the back of the SUV shut.

Mac watched David looking down at his feet with the grocery bag hanging from one of his hands. A slow smile came to Mac's lips when he said, "You know what I think? I think you never had to work this hard for a woman."

His eyes narrowed, David cocked his head at him.

Mac chuckled. "You haven't, have you? Every woman you've ever wanted just fell into your lap after you flashed a smile and winked at her. But Chelsea's different. She knows you inside and out. She knows how you play. She knows your tells. She's not like other women because you can't get around her. That's what's driving you up the wall."

David whirled around on his heels. "I'm going to go have a beer." He climbed the steps to the walkway to take him back to his cottage.

"This is really fun to watch," Mac called to him.

"Don't make me shoot you, Mac."

The dining room table was set for two when Mac came back into the house. It had been set for four when he took out the garbage. His assumption about the steaks had been right.

Archie was lying out across the sofa with her laptop resting on her knees.

"Is Chelsea eating at the guest house?" Mac asked her as she sat up to make room for him to sit down next to her.

"She and David are celebrating her first paycheck from her new job," Archie said. "She's cooking dinner for him over at the cottage. I guess they're having a date night." After setting the laptop aside, she slipped his arm around her shoulders and cuddled up next to him. "Which means we're getting a date night." She gazed up at him with a wide grin.

"Date nights are always good." He kissed her. One kiss turned into two and then three, until they heard a throat clear.

Looking awkward about walking in on them, Chelsea stood at the bottom of the stairs. "I was going to sneak out, but…"

"That's okay," Archie assured her.

"What are you cooking for your chauffeur?" Mac asked her. "I saw steaks in the grocery bag."

"Steak Diane,"' she said. "It's one of David's favorite foods. I'm also serving roasted potatoes and grilled asparagus."

Mac asked Archie, "What are you cooking for me?"

"Salmon and rice pilaf."

"I'd rather have steak." He asked Chelsea, "Can I crash your dinner?"

"Behave," Archie ordered. "It will be hard enough to keep Gnarly from crashing it."

"Gnarly won't be any trouble," Chelsea said. "You talk like he's a devil dog."

"You don't know Gnarly," Mac said. "If he gives you any grief, tell David to bring him back home."

"He never gives me trouble." She started for the doors leading to the back deck.

Calling out, Mac stopped her. "Hey, Chel?"

She turned to them. "Yes?"

"How are things going with David?"

"Fine," she replied. "Why?"

"Well," Mac drawled. "You're cooking dinner for him. He's helping you move. He drives you to and from work and takes you to lunch."

She placed her hands on her hips. "Are you asking about a return on your investment?"

"Actually," Mac said, "my question is, are you leading him on?"

"I would never do that," Chelsea said. "What kind of woman do you think I am?"

"The type of woman who would be straight with a guy." Mac turned back around. "I just wanted to be sure."

Chelsea slammed the door on the way out. When she stepped out onto the deck, Molly and Gnarly sounded like a herd of stampeding horses escorting her back to the guest cottage.

"What was that about?" Archie asked him.

"Exactly what it sounded like," Mac said. "I don't want her hurting David by leading him on. He's got it bad for her."

"And she's got it bad for him," Archie said. "She's been playing touch-don't-touch for weeks. She wants him, but then she's afraid that he'll hurt her again, or she'll give up her independence, which she has worked hard for. It isn't that she doesn't want him. It's that she wants him so bad that she's scaring herself."

"I know exactly what she's going through," Mac said. "I'm afraid that if she doesn't make up her mind soon, she'll lose her chance with him."

"David's not going anywhere," Archie said. "It'll do him some good working to win her back. Make him appreciate her more."

"Sounds like you've been thinking about this."

"And you haven't?" She sighed. "She wouldn't be cooking Steak Diane for him if she didn't care. Women don't cook for men they don't want."

"You cooked for me from day one," Mac recalled.

"I wanted you from day one," she said with a smile.

"And you're still cooking for me."

"The day I stop cooking for you is the day you should start worrying." She tapped the keys on her laptop to take it out of sleep mode. "Here's another show of my love for you. I took a break from my editing to research Khloe's communications, including her cell phone records."

"Bogie's still waiting for those records."

"Well, I didn't wait for any to get sent over," she said, "I just hacked in."

"That's illegal."

"So arrest me." She closed the lid to her laptop. "I guess you don't want—"

Mac opened up the lid. "Tell me what you found out."

"You're curious." She giggled. "Lucky for us, Khloe and her friends operate with text messages, which are easy to follow because you actually know what they're saying."

"If you can decipher the shorthand language."

"I know how to decipher the shorthand."

"That's why I love you." He squeezed her shoulders.

She gazed up at him. Anxious to find out what she had learned, he gestured to the laptop. With a start, she resumed. "Another break for our side is that all of Khloe's friends have registered cell phones, so that made it easy for me to identify who she was talking to. For the last month, she was texting almost a hundred times a day." She added as a sidebar, "No wonder she didn't have a job. She couldn't take time off from texting."

"Tell me about it."

"Anyway, ten days before her body was found, she makes a phone call, which was a red flag for me. Not only was it a call, but a call to a land line phone. Guess who she called."

"Who?" Mac asked.

"The phone number was Senator Harry Palazzi's office in DC."

Mac grinned.

"You know something?" she asked.

"Senator Palazzi is her birth father," Mac said. "Ben and Ed met with David and me today to reveal that Florence had left a recording of her confronting Senator Palazzi about raping her—"

"Rape?" Archie sat up straight.

"Palazzi admitted to it on the tape, and Florence held it over his head all these years. Ed didn't even know, and he was her lawyer. She had left the tape sealed for him to find upon her death. She said that there would be more than one tape. Ed didn't tell Khloe, but she was living in that house."

"So she found the tape," Archie said. "That's why she called Senator Palazzi's office. That makes sense with this pattern of calls."

"What pattern do you see?" Mac asked her.

"Her first call to the office was only a couple of minutes long," Archie said. "Six days before she was killed. The next day, she receives a call on her cell phone from the senator's office. That call lasts close to twenty minutes. Less than an hour later, Khloe receives another call from a landline phone, which lasts twelve minutes. That number belongs to a law office in Washington, DC."

"What law firm?"

"Samuel Brooks and Associates," she said.

"Palazzi's attorney," he said.

"For the next four days," she reported, "there's a series of phone calls between Khloe and this law office—three or four a day. Then, communication ceases. Minutes after the last call, Khloe texts Bevis Palazzi. This text reads, 'Hey, bro, guess what I just found out.' Later, Bevis replies with 'Whats up?' She replies, 'Did you know you had a sister?' He responds, 'Wouldn't surprise me. Who is it?' She responded, 'ME.'"

Mac chuckled. "Bevis did know that Khloe was his half-sister at the time of the murder."

"Obviously, she and the senator could not reach an agreement," Archie said.

"How did Bevis take the news?"

"Don't quite know," she replied. "He called her from his cell. It was a very long conversation. After that call, Khloe started scouting for media outlets to take her story to. I found emails in her sent folder. She said she had big news that was going to shake Washington to the core." She added in an ominous tone, "Her last posting was on her Facebook page on Sunday afternoon: 'be sure to catch my interview on E-Entertainment Thursday when I'll make an announcement that promises to rock this country. You won't be disappointed.' That must have been when she was killed."

"Harry Palazzi is a senior senator," Mac said. "He's got a lot of juice. If that tape was made public—"

"He's a rapist."

"I know that," Mac said. "I've known it for years, but his friends and the media, who agree with his politics, have protected him all this time."

"Are you thinking he had Khloe killed? She was his daughter."

"I've met Senator Harry Palazzi," Mac said. "Nothing means anything to him except his own personal gain."

"This means both Senator Palazzi and his son could be suspects in murdering Khloe to keep her quiet about the rape and being his illegitimate daughter."

"The house was searched," Mac said. "I wonder if whoever killed her got the copy she had found of the recording. We still have the copy Ed has."

"I hope it's in a safe place," Archie said.

"So do I," Mac said. "Palazzi's people will stop at nothing to get what he wants." He glanced around the house. A wicked grin crossed his face before he squeezed her shoulders to bring her in closer. "Guess what I just realized."

"What?" She set her laptop aside.

"We're all alone."

"Date night!" She grabbed him by the front of the shirt and dropped back to pull him on top of her.

Giggling like teenagers with the house alone, they groped at each other and kissed long and hard in anticipation of a lust-filled evening—until the deck door in the dining room flew open.

Lying across the sofa, they were unable to see who came in.

"Gnarly ate my shrimp cocktail!" they heard David yell.

The door slammed shut.

Before Mac could recover, Gnarly jumped over the back of the sofa to land on top of them. The three of them fell to the floor in a mangled pile of arms, legs, fur, and paws.

"So much for our evening alone," Mac grumbled.

CHAPTER SIX

The height of ski season was the busiest time at the Spencer Inn—especially on the weekends. The inn was packed with guests. Some would be into the skiing. Some would take advantage of the spa's amenities—have a massage or go in the hot tub—and others would simply camp out in front of one of a dozen roaring fires while enjoying the view of the skiers and snowboarders outside. Everyone, it would seem, was enjoying the food and drink in the restaurant and lounge.

Sometimes the inn would be so packed that Mac avoided it. It was simply too hard to elbow his way through the mob to get where he wanted to go.

But he had a murder to solve, and this was an opportunity to question a suspect who would otherwise not be available.

Senator Harry Palazzi was guest of honor at a fundraising event being held in the Spencer ballroom. Ben Fleming's wife, Catherine, was a power broker in the senator's party. Being a multi-millionaire, Mac's pockets were deep enough to earn him an invitation.

Archie had taken a break from editing to be Mac's date. She even consented to putting on shoes. After a quick tour of the room in which she was introduced to most of Garrett County's political movers and shakers, Archie welcomed the opportunity to sit down with the prosecutor's wife to enjoy a glass of champagne.

A stunning blonde, Catherine Fleming was an honest-to-goodness debutante, which many people believed were extinct. Having grown up in prestigious private schools, with summers spent overseas, she came from old money on both sides of her family and married an impressive lineage in Ben Fleming, whose ancestors had been friends with the Spencers, the town's founders. Catherine had more social and political power in her little pinky than any of the women in Deep Creek Lake. While you could see it in her dress and regal bearing, you would never know it in her girlish laughter when she got together with her favorite gal pal, Archie Monday.

Ironically, Catherine Davenport Fleming had married into the opposing political party. As much power as her family held, Ben Fleming's family was equally powerful on "the other side of the aisle." Catherine had confided to Archie that all her husband had to do was give the word, and his party would clamor to appoint him to run for Maryland governor—and, as the proud and supportive wife, she would throw her full support behind him.

Luckily for Garrett County, their prosecutor preferred Deep Creek Lake to Annapolis.

"Why did you decide not to go to the Governor's Ball?" Archie asked Catherine after they had completed their first round of champagne.

"Same reason you decided to close up your laptop for the evening and put on shoes," Catherine said. "What fun is a fiasco when you aren't there to witness it first hand?"

"Mac has come a long way since he first moved to Deep Creek Lake," Archie said.

"I'm not talking about Mac," she said. "I'm talking about Palazzi. It isn't every day he has to face someone who knows exactly what he is and has the guts to tell him to his face."

"Is he really that arrogant?" Archie asked.

"He's the worst." Catherine craned her neck to see around a group who had gotten between them and the bar where Mac and Ben were waiting to ambush the senator. "He was tough on crime and had an impressive record as sheriff. That got him elected to the senate. When his wife disappeared, that got him the sympathy vote that seems to have held him in office ever since. Anytime anyone questions his ethics, he trots out his dead wife and sobs about how much he has sacrificed for his fellow Americans."

A wave of sympathy swept over Archie. "What exactly happened to his wife?"

"It was during his first term as senator." Catherine shrugged. "I don't know how old Bevis was—maybe he was a teenager. Barbara and her best friend were kidnapped from the Palazzi home. The place was wrecked. Police narrowed it down to a guy who the senator had put away for robbing a convenience store back when he was sheriff. The guy had been released only the month before." Her disgust gave way to pity. "They never did find their bodies. The friend was married and had a daughter. Last I heard, her husband drank himself to death."

"Garnished Palazzi a lot of sympathy, huh?" Archie said.

"'I was quite young when all that happened," Catherine said. "And one would assume that all that tragedy contributed to Palazzi's and his son's character, but I was raised to believe that there is no excuse for being rude. Of course, some would say that's old fashioned."

"Of course."

Catherine's mouth turned downward into a frown. "I used to be really excited about my folks' role in politics. I even had aspirations of running for political office—back when I was young and idealistic."

"What changed your mind?"

"It's nothing like it used to be," Catherine said with a shrug of her shoulders. "Priorities have changed. No longer is it, 'what's best for the county?' Now it's 'what's best for the party?'" She gestured at the well-to-do guests filling the room. "Everyone here knows that Harry Palazzi is an arrogant, lying SOB, whose number one question about any political issue is 'what's in it for me?' Those who offer him the most political favors, win his vote. Yet, would any of them think of making moves to run someone else for the senate seat in the next term? No." She shook her head. "Not as long as he can get enough votes to keep the other party from winning his seat. He can sell our country to China for all we care—just don't let the other guy win."

"I find that hard to believe," Archie said. "Don't tell me that if Mac had proof that he was a rapist and a mur—"

"You mean admit that we had made a mistake by backing him in the first place?" Catherine laughed. "That would mean taking responsibility." A flash of anger crossed her face. She tapped one of her manicured fingernails on the tabletop. "Somewhere along the line, we've turned into a couple of street gangs in designer suits. All anyone—in both parties—cares about is winning that next rumble against the folks on the other side of aisle. If the conclusion turns out great for the country, so much the better. If not—well, it's not our fault. It's the fault of the other gang. Unfortunately, our country is falling apart while we're behaving like upper-class street thugs."

"Divide and conquer," Archie said.

"Exactly," Catherine said. "Who divided us, I don't know or care. The fact is that it's happened, and every time someone stands up to say enough is enough, the media hunts down his Achilles' heel and rips him apart while the people watch and do nothing." She sighed. "It's sad." The corners of her lips curled when she caught sight of Archie looking at her out of the corner of her eye. With a smile, she took a sip of her champagne. "That's the end of my speech."

Archie didn't return her grin. "Do something about it."

Catherine laughed. "Like what?"

Archie smiled. "Catherine Davenport Fleming, this is your party. You can change the playlist to set the theme for whatever you want it to be. How about setting it to the tune of common sense and mutual respect for your fellow country-men ... or women?"

In silence, Catherine gazed at Archie while trying to determine if she was serious or not. "Do you really think I could do that? I'm only one person."

"Why not?" Archie said. "It took only one person to get prayer yanked out of our schools. Why can't one person do something right to turn our country around?"

"You do have a point, Archie Monday." Seeing some action across the room, Catherine let out a laugh filled with glee. "The show is about to begin."

"Did you bring your gun?" Ben asked Mac while signaling the bartender for another round of drinks.

"I'm never without my gun." Mac was still nursing his first drink. He declined Ben's offer for another. He wanted to be sober when he faced Harry Palazzi.

"I wish you hadn't."

"Don't worry, Ben." Mac flashed him a grin. "I haven't shot anyone so far this week."

They watched the guests swarm toward the entrance. The guest of honor was arriving. Men dressed in black and wearing security earpieces pushed back the guests to make way for the senator.

Worry creased Ben's brow for the second time that week.

Mac eyed the heavy-set man with a square jaw taking the position of honor among the sea of bodyguards coming toward them. He was next to a tall, reed-thin man. "Of course, the week is still young."

"Maybe this was a bad idea," Ben said.

"I've come a long way since I first moved to Spencer."

Ben looked Mac up and down. Gone was the faded navy-blue t-shirt with "POLICE" emblazoned across the back and faded jeans and flip-flops. He was dressed in a tailored black suit with a blue shirt and a matching blue tie. "Yeah, Mac, you have come a long way."

"Good evening to you, Ben!" The senator broke from the crowd and took the prosecutor's hand in a firm handshake. "Great to see you again. It's been a while. When was the last time? We knocked back a couple of drinks at that lounge in DC after that reception for—"

"It's been at least two years," Ben said.

When the slender man stepped up to take his hand, Mac recognized him as the same lawyer the senator had represent him when he had been interrogated about Dee Blakeley's rape and subsequent murder. Samuel Brooks had the reputation of representing the slimiest of the scum. It was no surprise to Mac that he had conversations with Khloe shortly before her murder. With their hands in a firm grasp, Samuel Brooks' eyes locked on Mac's. It took only seconds for recognition to set in.

"Harry, I want you to meet a friend of mine." The sound of Ben's voice coming closer jolted Mac out of his glare with Brooks. "Mac Faraday."

Mac turned to face the senator, who backed up a full step upon hearing Mac's name. He froze when he saw the former homicide detective. "Mac—" he stuttered out.

"Faraday." Mac offered him his hand, which the senator refused to touch.

"Is this some sort of joke, Ben?" the senator accused the county prosecutor. "Of course! You would invite this man to our fundraiser where I am the guest of honor. I'm going to have a word with your father-in-law about you inviting this—this—"

"I think the word you're looking for is homicide detective," Mac said.

"Bastard is a better word for it."

"If you've lured the senator here to trap him in some sort of interrogation about some incident in which you have no jurisdiction…" Samuel Brooks was in legal mode.

"What incident would that be?" Mac asked. "Are we talking about Florence Everest, who you raped while you were sheriff, or Dee Blakeley, who you raped after you became senator? Or maybe the murder of your daughter, Khloe Everest? That we do have jurisdiction over."

"Who let him in here?" The senator turned to the political party's event coordinator. "I want this man removed from this hotel. Call security!"

The pretty young woman who didn't look old enough to drink stammered without uttering any intelligible words.

"Don't just stand there, you morons!" The senator raged to his security personnel. "Call the manager. Call hotel security! They're supposed to be sure riffraff like these people don't get in! I'm a senator, for God's sake. Has anybody checked to make sure this man isn't armed?"

One of the senator's bodyguards stepped forward to take Mac by the arm. Another approached from his other side. Mac turned sideways to throw a kick into the gut of the one guard, which made him double over and drop to his knees. Simultaneously, Mac grabbed the hand of the bodyguard who dared to grab his arm and twisted it around. Digging his thumb into the pressure point of the guard's palm, Mac brought him down onto his knees.

While holding the guard down with one hand, Mac drew his gun out from where he had it concealed behind his back and aimed it at Senator Palazzi's face. "Order them to back off or you're going to get what you should have gotten twelve years ago!"

With an arrogant grin, Senator Palazzi took on a calmer tone. "Hold on, men! Let's just wait. Hotel security and the police will be here any minute, and Detective Faraday will be escorted out." Smoothing his hair, he turned to the cameras of the news stations following the fund-raising event. "I learned long ago, back when I was sheriff, that sadly, sometimes members of our law enforcement go over the edge. It's brought on by the stress of the job. You have to be understanding and sympathetic to them. I'm sure that, after some in-depth counseling, Detective Faraday will become emotionally well again. Hopefully, even find a job in a less stressful field."

Squaring his shoulders, the senator added, "Right now, my concern is for the safety of the hotel's guests. But I am sure the management here at the Spencer Inn will be able to peacefully remove this sick man without incident."

Ben covered his mouth with his hand to conceal his smirk.

Releasing the guard, who scurried away while massaging his aching arm, Mac laid his gun down on the bar. "While we're waiting for security to come throw me out, Mr. Brooks, can you tell me about the numerous conversations you had with Khloe Everest on the days leading up to her murder?"

"Have you ever heard of client-lawyer privilege?"

"So she was your client?" Ben asked. "Now she's a dead client."

"Did those conversations have anything to do with a recording her mother had left her in which your client, Senator Harry Palazzi, confessed to raping her mother and getting her pregnant?" Mac asked. "I take it you couldn't reach an agreement for her silence, which is why right after your last conversation, she texted the news to Senator Palazzi's son, Bevis."

"Who happens to be planning a bid to run for governor," Ben interjected.

"Khloe then proceeded to contact various media outlets to break the story and play the tape," Mac said.

"He's lying!" Samuel Brooks yelled before telling Mac, "You're opening yourself up for a defamation of character suit, Mr. Faraday!"

"Do you have that tape now?" the senator asked.

"We do," Ben said. "We've heard it. We also know that you were paying ten thousand dollars a month to Florence Everest for child support and her silence."

"That was a retainer for her services as a decorator," the senator said.

"Suppose what you said is true?" Samuel Brooks said for the benefit of the media present. "Mind you, this is just speculation. Suppose Khloe Everest did find the recording and wanted to make a deal for her silence? What makes you think we didn't come to an agreement?"

"Because she started shopping around to make an announcement," Mac said.

"Do you know for a fact that she was going to reveal the recording?" Brooks asked. "Did it ever occur to you that we came to an agreement and it was some other news that she was going to announce?"

"What other type of news?" Mac asked.

Seeing Jeff Ingles, the Spencer Inn's manager, and Hector Langford, the inn's chief of security, the senator said in a loud voice, "It's about time. What type of place is this that you let anybody in?"

"What do you mean?" Jeff asked.

"This man is harassing me!" the senator yelled while pointing a finger at Mac. "He's spreading vicious lies about me in a campaign to ruin my reputation."

Many of the guests gasped and stepped back.

"He has been harassing me for years, accusing me of crimes I didn't commit, which I was never even charged for, and now he has crashed this private event in order to unfairly accuse me in a conspiracy to damage my reputation. I demand that he be thrown out of the Spencer Inn and he be barred from ever coming back."

Jeff Ingle's already pale face grew paler.

Hector Langford, a bald-headed Australian, laughed out loud.

"This is not funny!" the senator shouted at the chief of security.

"I suggest you do as the senator says," Samuel Brooks told them. "He's worked hard serving the people of this state. All he asks is that he gets the respect he deserves without being accosted by the riffraff. You would think that your inn security would be aware of that."

"What did you call Mr. Faraday?" Jeff mopped his face with his handkerchief.

"He called me riffraff," Mac said while leaning against the bar. He signaled to the bartender for a second drink. The poor young man's eyes looked like they were about to pop out of his head.

Not seeing any movement on the part of hotel security, the senator raged, "Why aren't you doing what I told you? Are you people deaf, or just dumb?"

"There's a small problem with trying to throw this man out of the Spencer Inn." Hector held up his finger and thumb to show a small amount.

"What problem is that?"

"It's my inn." Mac grinned at the sight of the senator's face growing redder than before. "That means they can't throw my riffraff butt out, but I can certainly throw your lying butt out—even if you are the guest of honor at this event. Sure, your people will be upset about all the money they have paid the inn, but I'll be happy to cut a check to cover the money they have lost. It will be worth it to me to see you tossed out with the rest of the garbage."

There was an audible gasp from the guests crowded in the ballroom. At a table in the corner, Catherine Davenport Fleming was enjoying the scene so much that her laughter bounced off the walls.

"H-how?" Samuel Brooks asked.

Jeff explained, "Robin Spencer, the famous novelist who owned the inn, left it to her son, who is Mac Faraday."

"Mr. Faraday," Hector asked, "is the senator bothering you? Would you like me to throw him out with the garbage?"

Mac leveled his gaze on the senator. "I may not be a senator, but I certainly have the power to have you tossed out of this inn in front of all these people."

"Robin Spencer?" Senator Palazzi ran his finger across his plump lips. A wicked grin came to his face. "I should have known the first minute I met you that you were of some relation to that rude stuck-up bitch. Thought she was too good for me—me!"

Samuel Brooks grabbed his client by the shoulders. "Senator! Calm down! Don't say anything more. Let's just leave."

The senator jabbed his thumb into his own chest. "What I wouldn't have given for an opportunity to give her a taste of what being with a real man was like by giving her a proper attitude adjustment." He made a gesture of a backhanded slap.

"The senator is naturally upset!" His lawyer tried to block the view of the cameras. "Stop recording—now!"

Mac grabbed the senator by the front of his shirt with both hands. He felt his fingers dig into the senator's flabby chest. While journalists closed in to get a closer view, Ben and Hector jumped in to pry Mac off him while the senator laughed.

Jeff Ingles fainted.

"I'm going to get you for what you did to Dee and Florence and all the other women you've been allowed to abuse at will all of these years," Mac said in a low voice. "You're going to pay for it. If it's the last thing I do, I'm going to make you pay."

"She wanted it!" the senator laughed while his lawyer pulled him away. "She would have loved it!"

"We need to leave, Senator," Samuel Brooks said. "Now! Don't say another word."

"Get Senator Harry Palazzi out of the inn and off of the resort grounds," Hector order the lawyer. "Both of you! I recommend that you not come back, if you're smart." He went on to tell the organizer for the fundraiser, who looked like she was going to throw up. "This event is now over. Call my office on Monday and we'll issue you a refund. We will not be hosting anymore events for your senator here at the Spencer Inn."

The organizer was equally displeased. "We wouldn't dream of giving the Spencer Inn any of our business."

Ben held Mac back while they watched the senator laugh while his bodyguards and hotel security escorted him out.

Out in the hallway, Mac saw Lily Carter watching the senator being escorted out. Her eyes were wide. Mac couldn't tell if it was disbelief at him coming unglued, or at the senator's outburst. When the young woman's eyes met Mac's she broke into a run and disappeared into the crowd.

After giving Mac his second drink, the bartender tended to Jeff Ingles, who was finally coming to. After learning that none of what had happened was a dream, the manager needed to be helped to his feet and back to his office where he had his therapist on speed dial.

After the crowd dispersed, Ben shook Mac by the shoulders. "What's wrong with you? You were supposed to be in control. You let him get to you."

"He's crazy," Mac muttered. "He's a sexual predator and homicidal maniac and his people and friends in power let him get away with abusing women. Khloe was twenty-four years old. He's been doing this for at least twenty-four years, and I'm willing to bet he's still preying on women. When they stand up to testify against him, he has his people kill them."

"We'll stop him, Mac," Ben said. "Before, you didn't have the power to stop him. Now you have the power and the people behind you to stop him, and we'll do it. All of us together. I promise."

Chapter Seven

"What happened?" Catherine asked after they had moved into Mac's private booth in the corner of the Spencer Inn's lounge.

"Mac lost control." Ben shook out his napkin with a snap and dropped it into his lap. "You think Senator Palazzi circled the wagons before." He shot a glare at Mac. "Now they're really going to be circled, and circled tight."

"What happened, Mac?" Archie grasped his hand and squeezed his fingers. "You don't usually lose control like that. I thought you were going to break his neck."

"I wanted to." Mac resisted the urge to order a scotch and make it a double. "He brought up Robin. He called her a bitch and said he wanted to give her an attitude adjustment—with the back of his hand. She was my mother." He shook his head. "It was strange. I had met her only once for one day and never knew until after she had died—but the rage I felt when he talked about her like that—I never expected to feel that way about her."

"You've gotten to know her," Archie said, "through her journal, through us who did know her, through living at the manor and here at the inn. Even though she's been gone, she's become a part of you, and when he talked about her like that, your protective instincts took over."

"Are you sure he wasn't jerking your chain?" Catherine asked.

"Of course he was jerking Mac's chain, and it worked," Ben said. "I'm sure he met Robin, but knowing her, she would have put him in his place real fast if he tried anything with her. She had good instincts, too. She would have sensed him for what he was."

"You know who would know if Palazzi had tried something with her?" Archie sat up in her seat.

"No one who's alive," Mac said. "She would have told Pat O'Callaghan. He's dead."

"And if Pat was going to tell anyone, he would have told Bogie, his best friend," Archie said.

Anxious to find out what Bogie might know about his mother and Senator Harry Palazzi, Mac and Archie abandoned dinner to rush over to the police station. When they got there, they found the deputy chief and David eating their dinner of a takeout pizza while pouring over the forensics reports from Khloe's murder.

"Hey, have you eaten?" Bogie offered them some of the pizza.

Realizing how hungry she was, Archie dove in while David reminded Bogie, "They just came from the Spencer Inn where Mac was rubbing elbows with Senator Harry Palazzi at a fancy shindig."

"Actually, the fancy shindig ended up being an all-star wrestling match when Mac tried to kill him." Archie plopped down at an empty desk with a slice of pizza. In her sequined cocktail dress, she looked overdressed for her dinner.

"You never were suited for high society," David told him. "What happened?"

"He brought up Robin," Mac said.

"What about her?" Bogie's bushy gray eyebrows knitted together.

"He wanted to give her an attitude adjustment with the back of his hand," Mac said. "He called her a rude bitch."

"Robin couldn't stand the air Palazzi breathed," David said.

"For good reason," Bogie said.

"Did he attack her, too?" Archie asked.

Bogie nodded his head. "Oh, yeah." Chuckling, he sat down behind his desk and started working the mouse on his computer. "He was a junior senator then. Robin had met him at a Washington, DC, fundraiser. He offered to give her material for her books by telling her about some of his cases from when he was sheriff."

In the search engine for images, Bogie typed in the senator's name. "They were supposed to go to a dinner party, and the senator had asked Robin to come to his apartment in DC. She had picked up bad vibes from him, but thought that he had been a sheriff, which meant he had respect for the law. However, when he came into the living room wearing only his bathrobe, she realized her vibes were right. He put the moves on her and she tried to leave, but he blocked her way to the door."

"He did say she was rude," Mac said.

Bogie laughed. "That's putting it mildly."

"I never heard about this." David didn't know whether to be amused or concerned about Robin's encounter with Senator Harry Palazzi.

"Remember," Bogie said, "all Palazzi was wearing was his bathrobe. When he got in Robin's way, she planted the pointy toe of her stiletto pump right in the family jewels. She said not only did he land on the floor, but also that it was a full body slam. She ran for the door. Now, we can't forget that this guy was a trained law enforcement officer. He managed to grab her by the ankle and pull her down to the floor."

"Oh, my," Archie said. "Tell me Robin got away."

"Well," Bogie gestured for them to come around to see his computer monitor. "After it was over, Robin didn't have a scratch. You can't say the same for Senator Harry Palazzi."

The picture on the monitor was of a younger Senator Harry Palazzi with his arm in a cast, a broken nose, and a black eye. The headline for the news article read that the junior senator had been injured playing football with some of his security officers.

"Robin did that to him?" David asked.

"Yeah," Bogie chuckled while admiring the picture. "Never mess with a murder mystery writer who takes her research seriously."

Mac wasn't so amused. "We need to put a stop to him. He's raped more than just Dee Blakeley and Florence Everest, and he tried to attack my mother. I'm convinced that the same guy who killed Dee killed Khloe and those two other women. He's had plenty of time to escalate, and it can't be a coincidence that both Khloe and Dee had connections to Palazzi that made their deaths beneficial to him."

"Problem is," David said, "we can't find any connection between Senator Palazzi and the woman in Hollywood, or the woman in Pittsburgh."

"Listen," Mac said, "We know this. The senator isn't the type to get his hands dirty. So these murders weren't committed by him, but for him. If he uses a paid contract guy, he could be taking on contracts for other people, but using the same M.O. Maybe the other two women weren't for Palazzi, but for someone else."

"Now we're talking about a pro, Mac," David said. "A pro wouldn't leave his semen behind. He'd know that, if he ever got picked up, his DNA would directly connect him to these murders. So what is it? A professional hit for Palazzi, or a maniac?"

Frustrated by the logic in David's point, Mac paced the squad room to sort out his thoughts. Bogie went into his office to answer the ringing phone on his desk.

"Is Senator Palazzi's DNA in the system?" Archie asked Mac.

"Yes," Mac said. "We were able to get it with Blakeley's case."

"Is it a match for the semen left with Khloe and these other two women?" she asked.

"No," David said with a shake of his head. "No match at all."

"Was there any evidence left behind at the Blakeley murder?" Archie asked.

"Nothing to trace back to Palazzi," Mac said. "I didn't expect there to be. The creep even had a solid alibi for the time of the murder. He spent the whole evening playing chess with his son, Bevis."

Bogie came out of his office. "We got some luck. That gay friend of Khloe's that she was spilling her guts to? His name is Nick Fields. He used to be a singer with a rock group. According to the producer for Khloe's show, it was like a package deal when they signed on Khloe. She insisted that he be on the show, too, so they had him in a scene or two every couple of shows and he made some money."

"Then she knew him before the show," Mac said. "Like while she was living here and he helped her to pull that stunt."

"He went to Hollywood with her," Bogie said. "He came from Smithfield, Pennsylvania, not far from here."

"Do you have a current address for him?" David asked him.

"Potomac, Maryland." Bogie handed a slip of paper with the address on him. "I'll run a background check."

"Mac," David said while studying the address, "looks like you and I are going to take a road trip."

"Can we do it Monday morning?" Mac asked. "There's an angle I want to check out."

"Are you going to keep me in the loop on that angle?"

"If something comes of it."

"Fair enough," David said. "Monday would work better for me, too. I've got a meeting tomorrow afternoon."

"With anyone we know?" Archie asked with a wicked grin.

"As a matter of fact, yes," David said. "But not who you think."

CHAPTER EIGHT

In her office off of the morgue, Dr. Dora Washington was shrugging out of her lab coat when Mac, with a manila folder tucked under his arm, came in. The unexpected visitor made her jump. "You scared me," she giggled while patting her chest.

"Considering where you work, I wouldn't expect you to scare easy." Mac followed her to her desk where she sat down to slip off her flats and put on a pair of red stiletto heels. "You're on your way out."

"As a matter of fact, I am." She took her purse out of the bottom drawer of her desk, set it on top, and opened it. "I don't usually work on the weekends, but there were some things I didn't want to let go until Monday. I have a minute for you. I'm not meeting my date until one o'clock."

"Saturday afternoon date?" Realizing he didn't know very much about the medical examiner's personal life, he asked, "Someone special?"

She grinned up from the mirror in her compact where she was checking her lipstick. "As a matter of fact, he is." She gestured at the folder. "Is that for me?"

"Yes, but I don't expect you to look at it now." He shrugged. "It's my copy of a case file from when I was in Washington. The young woman was a rape victim. The night before she was to testify before the grand jury, she was stabbed to death. It was a viciously violent attack."

"Like Khloe Everest's murder," the doctor said. "Was she dismembered, too?"

"No,'" Mac said. "And her uterus wasn't stolen, either. But this happened twelve years ago. Obviously, Khloe's killer is deranged. I'm wondering if this attack could have been an earlier attack by the same—?"

"Killer, before he had time to escalate to where he is today," the doctor said.

"If you look at the stab wounds in Dee Blakeley's murder and compare the specifics about that attack to Khloe's attack, do you think you could tell somehow if they were done by the same person?"

"Do you mean like comparing handwriting samples?" she asked. "The words may be different, like the victims, written years apart, like these two attacks, but if you compare the thrusts, angles, and characteristics that would be unique to this attacker, we might be able to determine if they were committed by the same person."

"That's what I'm hoping," Mac said.

"Never know until we try." She laid the case file in the center of her desk. "Who is Dee Blakeley, anyway?" She stood up and went over to the coat tree in the corner of her office where she had a dress encased in a garment bag. Taking the bag with her, she stepped into the bathroom and closed the door. "She must be important if you kept a copy of her case file after retiring," she called through the door to him.

"She didn't want to testify against Senator Harry Palazzi," Mac raised his voice for her to hear him through the door. "His people warned her against doing it. Her parents told her that it was a losing battle. I talked her into doing it. When she was murdered, her parents blamed me."

"And you blame yourself," she said.

"Yes, I do."

Stepping out of the bathroom, the medical examiner revealed herself to be transformed. Her skin-tight short red dress hugged every sensuous curve of her body. Her red high heels revealed a pair of long legs that seemed to go on forever.

"You like?" she asked.

"I like," Mac said. "That's enough to make a man forget how brilliantly smart you are."

"Exactly."

"Where are you going to lunch?"

"The Cornish Manor." She took him by the arm, grabbed her purse, and escorted him out of the office. "But I will take a look at that file first thing Monday morning."

"I'd appreciate it."

On his way out of town back to Deep Creek Lake, Mac followed her red Porsche out of the parking lot and through Oakland for a mile before she turned right to go down the short road to where the Cornish Manor was located in a sprawling country setting. Mac continued driving his sports car on the road to the lake. On the other side of the intersection where the medical examiner had turned right, he spotted a Spencer police cruiser with its left turn signal on, waiting for Mac to clear the intersection before following Dr. Washington's Porsche.

"It's a beautiful day," Chelsea told David during the drive from her condo where they had spent the morning hanging curtains. "Would you like to go snowmobiling before dinner?"

"I'd love to, but I can't," he said. "I'm meeting a homicide detective from Pennsylvania to compare notes from one of her open cases against Khloe Everest's murder."

"How long will that take?" she asked.

"All afternoon," David said with a sigh. "We need to go over every detail of both cases to see if we can find a pattern for this guy. Plus, there's a case in California that fits our guy's M.O., too. She has a copy of that case file."

"That's okay," she said. "I understand."

"I guarantee there'll be weekends that I'll be spending alone while you're working a case after you become a prosecutor." He saw Molly gazing back at him in the rearview mirror. "Is Molly ready for law school?"

"Molly can handle anything I throw at her," she replied. "I was hoping we could spend some time together now before I start law school this fall. It's going to get really busy then. We'll be lucky if we can ever find time to be together."

"And we don't spend time together with my driving you everywhere?" He pulled the cruiser in through the stone pillars marking Spencer Manor.

"You know what I mean," she said.

"Actually, I don't." David turned off the car engine.

The cruiser was filled with silence. She peered over at him where he sat staring straight ahead in the driver's seat before reaching over to lay her hand on his. "I'm sorry about the other night."

"I know you are." He shrugged. "You still don't trust me."

"I do."

"No, you don't." He turned to her. "I cheated on you fifteen years ago and broke your heart. I get that. Maybe if the shoe was on the other foot, I'd have just as much trouble trusting you. But I've been here for you for all these weeks. When you ask me for anything, I'm there, day or night, no questions asked. I think that should count toward some level of trust."

"I do trust you."

"Then prove it. Kiss me. Here. Now. Not a sisterly kiss, but like you really mean it."

Her eyes wide with fear, she gazed at him. Her mouth opened slightly while she stared at him. "I…"

"I didn't think so." David popped open the door and slid out of his seat.

Her heart beat so hard that she thought it was going to pop out of her chest while she watched him open the back door to let Molly out. The German shepherd ran around the front of the cruiser to wait for David to yank open her door.

Chelsea gasped.

"I need to go." He handed her purse to her. "I'm expecting to get home really late. So I'll see you in the morning. Good-bye, Chelsea."

He went around to climb back into his cruiser, turned on the engine, and sped around the circle to head back out of Spencer Manor and down the point.

You blew it, Chelsea. She kicked at a stone in the driveway. You want him. He wants you. Why can't you trust him? What is it that scares you so much?

The manor's front door opened. Gnarly barged down the steps to greet Molly, and the two of them took off to the yard rolling down to water.

"Has David left already?" Archie called to Chelsea while slowly making her way down the ice-covered steps in her bare feet.

"Yeah," she said.

"Rats!" Archie stomped one of her feet. "I had a message for him. Cameron called from the Spencer Inn. She's starving and wanted to know what he wanted from room service."

Cameron? Spencer Inn? Room service? "That lying snake in the grass! I knew I had good reason not to trust him! And here he made me feel so guilty for not trusting him! Oh, when I get my hands on him!" She dropped her purse in the drive-way. "I'm…where's the keys to your car?"

"You can't drive," Archie argued.

"Oh, yes I can," Chelsea said, "It's just that the police don't want me to."

"Chelsea, I think you should calm down."

"Don't tell me to calm down!" Her hands were curled up into tight fists wishing that David was there to punch with them. "I'm going to the Spencer Inn to catch that little liar red-handed! And if you don't drive me, I'm stealing your car and driving myself."

"Nick Fields," Cameron repeated the name while staring at the composite drawing and the publicity picture they had re-ceived from the television studio. "That name sounds famil-iar." She dug through her case file. They were sitting next to each other on the sofa with their reports, crime scene pictures, and case files spread out across the coffee table. In compar-ing the three murder cases, they had littered the suite's sitting room with crime scene pictures of the three women and their dismembered bodies stacked up in garbage bags.

Anxious to share their information on the cases, David and Cameron spent minimal time catching up on their personal lives before getting down to work. Though she did take time to take his late lunch order and call it down to room service.

"He's a singer?" Cameron brushed her cinnamon-colored bangs out of her greenish brown eyes. Her hair fell in shaggy, wavy layers down to the bottom of her neck. For the drive from her home in West Virginia, across the border from Pennsylvania, near Pittsburgh, she was dressed in worn jeans and a heavy sweater, which matched with her casual nature.

"According to the reality show," David answered her question. "They don't have much credibility in my book."

"Mine either." She let out a gasp. "I knew it." She handed him the witness list. "I questioned him in Amber Houston's disappearance. He was a male stripper at the club that Amber and her friends went to a few weeks before she went missing. They had gone for a bachelorette party for one of her friends."

The loud knocking on the door kept her from finishing her train of thought. Instantly, her focus shifted to lunch.

"Her friends said she had struck up a hot and heavy friendship with him." She handed the list to him while getting up to answer the door. "Room service must be anxious for their tip."

David studied the list. "He wasn't on our list. But Khloe said on her show that she had met him when he was singing at the club that she went to for her twenty-first birthday, and that was only a few weeks before her supposed disappearance."

Cameron peered through the peephole. "I don't think that's room service." She backed up and reached into her handbag for her gun.

David got up to peer through the peephole. "Chelsea?"

"Your girlfriend?"

"I wish." He opened up the door.

"Why do you look so surprised?" Chelsea barged into the room.

Her fury was so great that Molly stuck near the door after coming in. His face filled with amusement, Mac followed close behind.

"I told you I wasn't the same naïve little girl I was back in school." With both hands, she shoved him in the chest and knocked him one step backwards. "You actually thought you could get away with it again. I should have known. You acted the same way when you took off to have your fling with Katrina. I knew you didn't change."

"How did you know I was here?" David looked over at Mac.

"I didn't tell her."

"Your cheap slutty girlfriend called the manor to ask what you wanted her to order you from room service," Chelsea said.

"Who are you calling cheap?" Cameron asked. "I'll have you know, I can be very expensive."

Chelsea strolled around the sitting area in the suite. "Oh, I can imagine how cozy you two were planning this rendezvous here with no one to disturb you—just you two and—" She caught sight of the crime scene pictures spread out across the coffee table. She then looked up to see the gun that Cameron was holding in her hand. The detective held up her badge to show her.

"Yes," Mac said, "just David and Detective Cameron Gates from the Pennsylvania State police and cozy pictures of murdered women."

"Not only is she the homicide detective I told you I was meeting," David said, "but she's a married homicide detective."

Cameron held up her hand to show Chelsea her wedding ring. "For one whole month. I'm a newlywed."

"And you didn't tell me?" Chelsea accused them.

"I did tell you," David said.

When Chelsea looked at Mac, he shook his head. "I wanted to tell you, but I learned long ago to never argue with a woman."

"You did this on purpose," Chelsea told David. "If you had told me that you were meeting a woman detective—"

"You would have assumed what you did assume," David said, "which is why I didn't tell you that Cameron was a woman. This proves it. You don't trust me, and you probably never will."

"Chelsea, would you like to stay for dinner?" Cameron offered. "I can order anything you want. Mac's buying."

Seeing the hurt and disappointment in David's eyes was more than Chelsea could bear. *Maybe he's right. Maybe there's no hope of me ever trusting him again.*

She tried to run from the room but the room service cart was then coming in through the door. Not wanting David to see her collapse into a puddle of shame, she ran into the bedroom and slammed the door shut.

"Oh, great," Cameron said. "Now we have a crying woman in my bedroom."

A scream came from inside the room.

"He's a cat!" Cameron yelled to the woman in the room. "Not a skunk! A cat!"

A cat wailed from inside the room. The door opened for a second for the twenty-five pound Maine coon with the identical markings of a skunk to dart from the room. Seeing the cat that resembled a skunk, Molly scurried into the room before Chelsea had time to close the door.

Once out of the bedroom, the cat stopped and shook himself. Equally disgusted by the intrusion into the room where he had been sleeping, Irving trotted over to Cameron. Picking up the cat, Cameron said, "Irving doesn't like crying women, either."

"Someone needs to go in to talk to her," Mac said.

Aware of their gaze on her, Cameron paused in stroking the cat to shake her head. "She's not my girlfriend." She pointed at David. "It's you that she has trust issues with. You go in there to talk to her, and you better work it out because I didn't leave my husband to come to the Spencer Inn to sleep on a sofa."

"What about my lunch?" David asked.

Mac slipped a generous tip to the server. "I'll take care of it." He picked up the bottle of beer meant for David and poured it into the frosted glass.

"I'm sure you will." David went over to knock on the door. "Chelsea, we need to talk."

"Go away!" she said in a blubbery tone.

"No, it's time," he said in a firm tone. Seeing Mac sit down to his dinner of lamb chops à la Spencer, served with a special cabernet sauce created for Robin Spencer, he managed to kick his mood up a notch. "We should have talked weeks ago when you came back to Spencer. We've been dancing around our feelings for too long. Now if you don't open this door, I'm going to kick it in."

"Jeff won't like it if you go breaking his doors." Mac mixed the sour cream and chives in with the potato.

"His doors or your doors?" Cameron was diving into a sixteen-ounce slab of prime rib seared on the grill.

"They're my doors," Mac explained, "but Jeff Ingle, the inn's manager, is as protective of this resort as he would be of his own—which is a good thing."

"Chelsea," David snapped, "I'm coming in." He stepped back to kick in the door. "I'm giving you until the count of three."

"It's been a long time since I've been to a dinner and a show," Cameron said to Mac in a low voice. "All of this makes me wish Josh was here."

"Three!" David drew up his leg to kick in the door only to hit air when Chelsea threw it open. The momentum of the kick sent him into the room. With nothing to break his fall, he landed on his face inside the bedroom.

"Oh, David, are you okay?" Slamming the door shut, Chelsea rushed to where he landed on his chest on the floor. "Did you hurt yourself?"

The air knocked out of his lungs by the fall, David took a moment to catch his breath and regain his dignity before rolling over. "I'm okay," he gasped out. He stretched out flat on his back. Above him, he made out Molly's white face. Up on the bed, the dog cocked her head all the way to the side while gazing down at him with curiosity.

Chelsea's face then came into view. Her eyes were red and her face moist with tears. He reached up to wipe her tears from her cheek. "I never like to see you cry."

"I know," she whispered.

"I hurt you a long time ago," David said, "but in all the time that we've been together, the times I didn't hurt you outweigh the times I did, don't they? Don't those times count for anything?"

Unable to form the words, she nodded. Tears filled her eyes again.

"Why do I scare you so much?"

"Because..." she started again, "I'm afraid of..." her voice trailed off.

"What?"

"Of going back to who I was before," she finally said. "That insecure little ninny whose whole identity was wrapped around her boyfriend who she had to check with before getting her hair cut."

David sat up on his elbows. "I never told you to check with me before getting your hair cut."

"You didn't, but I did," she said. "I let you become my whole world, and when it ended, my world was gone. I had to rebuild it from the foundation up."

"And now you have your world," he said, "and I want in, and I want you to be a part of my world."

She looked down at her hands.

He placed his hand into hers. "Neither of us is the same as we were back in school. We're both stronger now.

There's no reason why we can't have our own separate lives together."

"Don't you think I know that?" she asked. "But every time I'm with you, I feel myself going back to that insecure teenager—like what just happened out there. That's wasn't me now, that was me fifteen years ago, living out the scene that I wish I could have had when you sneaked off to be with Katrina."

He grinned. "Now that that's out of your system, I doubt if it will ever happen again."

"Certainly not with an armed homicide detective playing the role of Katrina." She smiled through her tears.

Rolling over onto his side, David stroked her face. "Here's where we are. We have feelings for each other. You're here and going to stay. I'm here and I'm not going anywhere. What do you say to taking a leap of faith and giving this thing a try?"

"I…"

He moved in to touch her lips with his. He could feel them trembling with his touch. When she pulled away, he assumed that once more, she gave in to her fear. Her light blue eyes were filled with uncertainly that melted away before she wrapped her arms around his shoulders. As she covered his mouth with hers, David rolled over to take her into his arms.

Chapter Nine

Nighttime had fallen on Spencer Manor.

Archie had spent the day in frustration. The author whose book she was editing had made major changes before she was done and sent her a new draft. She was practically starting over.

Well, he's going to pay for it. At least I'll make a lot of money on the deal. But will it be worth the frustration?

With Mac and Chelsea out, she worked as long as she could on the manuscript before turning in to bed with a headache. Even Gnarly seemed more subdued. Archie surmised it was because he missed Molly, who had become his best friend. She wondered how he would do after Molly moved out with Chelsea.

To Gnarly's gentle snore from under the bed, Archie had drifted into a pleasant dream of being on a cruise of the Pacific with Mac. It was only Mac and her alone on a yacht—except for Gnarly. The weather had abruptly turned rough. With the waves tossing the yacht about, her cries for help were drowned out by the roar of the storm and the crash of the waves over the bow.

The sun rose the next morning to find them washed ashore onto a desert island. With a note for help attached to his collar, Gnarly swam out into the ocean.

Then she was alone with Mac, who was clad only in a loincloth. With the sun setting on the other side of the ocean, with love in his eyes, Mac whispered those words Archie so loved to hear—

"Help!"

No, that doesn't sound right.

"Help me, please!"

With the call for help invading her dream, Archie stirred awake.

No, not now! I don't want to wake up. Take me back to the island. What was Mac about to say?

Hugging her pillow to her chest, she tried to return to her dream and Mac in his loincloth about to tell her that he loved her.

"Help! Someone help me please! Anybody!"

Archie threw back the covers. The moon poured in through the skylight to bathe the room in a dim light. The manor was quiet. Has to be part of my dream. Dropping back down onto her bed, she closed her eyes.

"Help me!" Now the call sounded weak and hoarse.

Nope, not part of any dream. Archie sat up again. Seeing that the bedroom door was open, she realized something was missing: Gnarly's snoring.

"Gnarly?" she called down to under the bed.

"Someone help me!"

"Gnarly!" Throwing on her bathrobe, Archie hurried out into the hallway and peered over the banister to the entryway below.

Upon discovering the curtains torn down from the front window, the Oriental rug askew, and furniture overturned, Archie surmised the night's events in Spencer Manor had been as chaotic as her dream during the storm that wrecked her cruise.

"Somebody! Somebody come and help me! Please!" the call came again.

It was coming from the lower level of the manor.

"Gnarly, where are you?" Archie took the three steps down into the sunken dining room to find the chairs pulled out from the table, which was pushed up against the wall. The crystal vase centerpiece had been smashed on the floor.

Archie wondered if Gnarly's not answering her call was a sign that something horrible had happened to him. She called for him again and quickened her pace through the kitchen to the stairs leading down to the ground floor, which contained the home theatre, study, and laundry room.

The kitchen was more of the same. The contents of the canisters covered the floor. The usually smooth surface felt like sawdust. The pantry door was open. The room looked like the scene of a food fight. The plants that decorated the top of the fridge had even been thrown to the floor, the potting soil mixing with the flour, sugar, coffee, and tea from the canisters.

Upon hearing Gnarly's bark from the direction of the laundry room, Archie felt a sense of relief that lifted a heavy weight from the pit of her stomach. Running down the hall to the laundry, she caught sight of the study, where books were scattered across the floor.

"Can you hear me? Help!" The call sounded strained.

When Archie saw a black bag that she didn't recognize on the floor in front of the desk, she concluded that whoever it was in her home calling for help had not been invited.

At the room at the end of the hall, Archie threw open the door to find the visitor cowering on top of the washer and dryer. His tattered black clothes, pale face, and trembling demeanor evidenced his participation in the events that had wrecked Spencer Manor during the night. It was his luck that he wasn't much bigger than she was. Otherwise, he wouldn't have been able to fit on the giant-sized twin washer and dryer units that stood five feet tall, leaving only a space of four feet open between their tops and the ceiling.

Gnarly was pacing in front of his catch like a guard on duty.

The burglar pointed a finger at Gnarly. His hands were clad in black leather gloves. "Call off your dog," he demanded.

Seeing the finger pointed in his direction, Gnarly jumped up with a snarl as if to try to snip the finger off. Shrieking in a high-pitched voice, the burglar drew back his hand and clutched it to his chest.

With a cocky grin, Archie asked in a calm tone, "Excuse me."

As if he didn't believe Archie's lack of action to call off the dog, the burglar replied, "What?"

"What did you just tell me?"

The pleading tone was replaced with agitation. "Call off your dog."

"I don't think so."

"Hey, lady!" The burglar sat up on top of the washer and dryer to display his arms bare from having the sleeves shredded up past the elbows. "Your dog bit me! Not just once, but– I'm going to sue!"

Letting out a round of barks in response to the threat, Gnarly jumped up and almost caught an ankle. When the burglar jumped back from the edge of the washer he momentarily lost his footing, which threatened to send him plummeting into Gnarly's jaws.

"Good boy, Gnarly." Archie patted the dog on his head. The touch of her hand caused the dog to wag his tail. "Hold him there." She left the room to go in search of the phone to call Mac.

First, I need a pot of coffee.

"Aren't you going to call off your dog?" the burglar called out to her. "I have rights! I'm calling my lawyer! I'll sue. Vicious dog attack, physical and emotional torture, and mental distress."

Maybe, I'll eat some toast before I place that call.

"The name is Nick Fields," Cameron was reporting on her cell phone. "He had made appearances on a reality show that was taped in Los Angeles called Four New Girls in Town." The news she was getting from the detective on the other end of the line excited her enough to make her stand up from where she had been sitting on the sofa. She turned to Mac, who was in the middle of sipping his cognac for an after dinner drink, which contrasted with the hot fudge sundae Cameron had brought up by room service. "Was there a model on that show by the name of Melissa Kincaid?"

"I have no idea," Mac responded.

"Never mind." Cameron plopped back down on the sofa and searched the Internet. "I'll look up her name in the search engine. If she was—" With a squawk of delight, she pointed at the screen. "Yes, she was one of the four girls."

Mac was unsure if she was talking to him or the detective on the other end of the line.

He got his answer when she swung around on her seat. "Khloe Everest's co-star, Melissa Kincaid, was a model, and she was questioned by police when Tiffany Blanchard was murdered. The last time Tiffany Blanchard was seen alive was at the cast party for Four New Girls in Town when it was cancelled. Melissa had invited her to that party."

"Khloe's best gay friend, Nick Fields, was also on the show, so he must have been at that cast party, too," Mac said. "He very well could have met Tiffany Blanchard there."

"Do you have Nick Fields on the list of witnesses at the party?" Cameron asked the detective at the other end of the phone line.

"Fields wasn't on my list to be interviewed," the investigator noted when she answered that Fields hadn't been questioned. "I'll go through our records to see if anyone can place him at that party."

After Cameron disconnected the call, she picked up her hot fudge sundae and sat back with a sense of satisfaction. She held out her ice cream bowl in a toast. "Here's to closing three murder cases and getting one more creep off the streets. Amber Houston was killed in my jurisdiction first. That means I get first dibs when we nab him."

"I haven't forgotten how it works." Mac reached for the cell phone vibrating on his hip. "We get him after Los Angeles. Assuming they can get a case together, we get him third." He checked the caller ID to see that it was Archie. "Hey, hon, what's up?"

"Gnarly caught a burglar."

Mac jerked upright to sit up straight. "Are you okay?"

"Oh, I'm dandy," she said, "but this lousy burglar interrupted a totally lovely dream I was having. Can you and David get here before I shoot him? He's making all kinds of racket in the laundry room screaming for his lawyer and threatening to sue us. I'm afraid I won't be able to get back to my dream. Have you ever thought of wearing a loin cloth?"

Mac hung up the phone and banged on the bedroom door. "Time to go, Lover Boy! We need to go to the manor. Gnarly found a burglar and Archie has lost her mind."

Chapter Ten

Unable to resist a good time, Cameron insisted on accompanying them back to Spencer Manor. She rode with Mac in his SUV, which followed David's cruiser, carrying Chelsea and Molly as passengers, down the mountain to Spencer Point.

Coming from across the lake, Bogie's cruiser fell in behind them when they turned onto Spencer Lane to take them to the Point. When they climbed out of their vehicles, Mac sauntered back to where Bogie was getting ready to climb out of his cruiser. "Did you have a nice afternoon at the Cornish Manor?"

"You're not going to tell anyone, are you?" Bogie peered down at him from beneath his bushy eyebrows.

"Why don't you want anyone to know?" Mac asked. "You're not married, and Doc is a gorgeous, intelligent woman."

"She's also twenty-five years younger than me," Bogie whispered.

Mac chuckled. "Another reason to shout it from the mountaintops. You should be proud, Bogie. I know I'd be."

Bogie chuckled. "She's hot and she's crazy about me. At least I guess she is, since it was her who asked me out."

"She asked you?" When Bogie nodded his head, Mac let out a breath. "Wow. Don't let her get away."

When Mac stepped away, Bogie clasped his shoulder. "You're not telling anyone, are you?"

"Not if you don't want me to," Mac said. "I'll keep it all to myself."

"And when you tell Archie, you'll tell her to not tell anyone?"

"Of course I will, Bogie."

Inside, they found that David had rescued the burglar from the laundry room and handcuffed him to a dining room chair. As vocal as the thief was about being trapped by Gnarly, one never would have known that he was the one committing a felony.

"What? Another one? You have another German shepherd?" he yelled when he saw Molly in the dining room. Based on his hysteria, one would have thought she was as big as Gnarly and chewing on his leg. "You people are insane. You have no right to have two German shepherds. No right!"

"But you have a right to break into my home?" Mac asked.

"Breaking into your house?" He looked at each one of them. When he noticed David and Bogie's police badges, his eyes grew wide. "Now, wait a minute. Are you here to arrest me? I thought you were here to save me from these crazy people who sicced their vicious dog on me."

"That's a crock of malarkey," Archie said.

Mac laughed. "You broke into my home."

"Your home?" he shouted. "This is your house? Why … I am so sorry." He giggled. "Now I know what this must look like."

"What does it look like?" Cameron asked.

"Like that maybe I had broken in and was trying to steal something," He giggled again. "But that isn't what happened."

"What did happen?" David asked.

"It's all a big misunderstanding. You see, I thought this place was a restaurant and bar."

"Do we look stupid to you?" Archie asked him.

"It's true," he said. "I came here to have a nice martini on the lake, and instead I got attacked by your vicious dog."

"Gnarly is not vicious," Archie said.

"What do you call this?" He held out his legs with shredded cloth hanging from them. "Not only is he vicious, but that dog is a sadist," the burglar insisted to the police chief. "Look at him." Unable to point with his hands cuffed behind his back, he nodded with his head from where he had been plopped down in a chair.

Gnarly was making grunting noises while wiggling on his back to scratch just the right spot between his shoulder blades. Seeming to sense every eye in the room on him, he stopped to look up at them from his upside down position. He didn't seem to have any shame about his hind legs being spread out to display his masculine parts to all of them.

"I see." David studied the identification he found in the wallet they had taken from the suspect during their search after rescuing him. Archie and Mac made no pretense of reading the driver's license from over the police chief's shoulder. The name on identification read Otto Grant. He was from Baltimore, Maryland.

"You're a long way from Baltimore, Otto," Mac said. "That's quite a drive to get a martini."

"I'm on vacation."

"Let's start this from the beginning, Otto," David said. "You're on vacation. You decide to go have a martini lakeside and you see this house, with no sign out front, and assume that it's a bar."

"You also find all the doors locked," Archie pointed out, "so you break in."

"Finding no servers, you decided to help yourself," Mac finished.

David handed the wallet to Bogie to check for background information on their perpetrator. The deputy chief went to work entering the information from the driver's license into his computer tablet.

"Can't you see I've been terrorized?" Otto claimed before stomping a foot. "Look at my pants. These are brand new. This is the first time I've worn them, and look at what that dog did to them." As if they had failed to notice before, he stuck his legs out straight to show them his tattered pants. "What that dog and woman did to me was worse than any simple B & E."

"I didn't do anything to you," Archie said. "I was sound asleep and having a totally luscious dirty dream about Mac in a loin cloth."

"Archie, TMI," Mac said while making a cutting gesture with his hand across his throat. "That's too much information."

Feeling hot, he pushed the mental image of what she could have been dreaming from his mind, which was difficult since he had noticed the red silk from her negligée under the hem of her robe. In that particular nightgown, she always made his heartbeat race.

"Don't forget to get every detail of her dirty dream down in her statement," Cameron leaned over to whisper into David's ear.

Smiling, David asked, "Do you think I should have a sketch artist make up a composite of Mac in a loin cloth?"

"Email it to me," she replied.

"That's enough." Mac was torn between joining them in their laughter and leaving the room.

"Hey!" Otto stomped both of his feet. "Remember the man handcuffed to the chair!" He turned his attention back to Archie. "Don't tell me you didn't hear all this." He gestured with his head at the wrecked room.

Giving into her curiosity, Cameron asked, "What happened?"

"That demon dog from hell is what happened." When Archie laughed out loud, Otto glared at her. "I wouldn't be surprised if she was in on it. She probably has a closed-circuit television and was watching me run for my life all night while being stalked like an animal by her trained killer."

David plopped the black bag that Archie had found in the study down on the floor at Otto's feet. "And what's this? Your suitcase that you carried in when you checked into the house of horror."

Otto looked away. "I never saw that bag before in my life."

"Then I guess I won't find any of your fingerprints on it or anything inside." David leaned over him. "We have you for breaking and entering and vandalism."

"Vandalism?" Otto squawked. "I didn't break anything when I broke in."

The police chief gestured around him at the broken furniture.

"I didn't do that," Otto claimed.

David asked, "Then who did?"

"I told you already. That demon dog!"

As if he had been wounded by the insult, Gnarly climbed his front legs up into Archie's lap, hid his face under her robe, and let out a whine.

Otto uttered a crazed laugh. "You may have convinced them that you're a nice, cute, pretty puppy dog needing comfort from your pretty little mistress there, but I know what you're really capable of."

Bogie came back from where he had been looking up Otto's background on his computer tablet. "Well, Mac, it looks like Gnarly snagged a pretty big fish. There's three outstanding warrants on Otto Grant in Maryland, Virginia, and Washington, DC."

"What about the one in Pennsylvania?" When he realized his goof, Otto said, "You can't use anything I say. I'm traumatized. That's a mix-up. There's another Otto Grant who has a police record and is wanted for breaking and entering, but that isn't me."

Mac wanted to know, "How did you get past my security system?"

Showing his tattered legs again, he replied, "I didn't!"

Archie said, "He meant the electronic security system."

"According to what I found here," Bogie said, "Otto has been breaking into some of the most secure estates on the east coast. He's a retrieval expert for hire. His known associates are private investigators and lawyers who don't mind bending the rules. They hire him for work they want done under the radar."

"I told you already," Otto said. "That's not me."

"Clearly, it's not you," Cameron said, "I mean, if you were such a professional, you wouldn't have gotten snagged by a simple dog. No, you're not any Otto Grant, retrieval expert. You're just a simple everyday common burglar who doesn't know how to get past any house with a dog. Only an expert would know how to do that. Of course, it's not you."

"Hey! I've broken into hundreds of homes with dogs," he retorted. "Big dogs. Little yip-yaps. Nice dogs that showed me where the family silver was hidden. Vicious dogs that would kill you on sight. I've gotten past them all."

Archie squinted at him. "But you didn't get past Gnarly."

As if he was agreeing with her, Gnarly uttered a single bark.

One of Otto's eyes twitched while he glared at the German shepherd. "Because he's a sadistic psychopath." Sitting back in his seat, he said by way of an insult, "I wouldn't be surprised if he was gay."

"What?" Mac was insulted.

Equally offended, Molly exploded with a round of barks in the burglar's direction and wouldn't quit until Chelsea ordered her to stop.

"Unneutered German shepherd," Otto said. "It works every time. I brought a towel soaked in urine from a bitch in heat and left it out by the dock. He smells her, scratches at the door. I had bypassed the alarm and he took off for the dock while I slipped in—no problem. I closed the door behind me so even if he got finished early, I'd be in the clear. I had five minutes to collect the merchandise and get out and off the property before the dog had his way with the towel and returned to find me and sound the alarm."

Mac asked, "What was the merchandise?"

"A recording," Otto said. "My client was paying me twenty thousand to lift it. Ten thousand up front. Ten thousand when I delivered the recording. My client didn't know where it was, but that was okay. I had only started searching in the desk in the study when—wham!"

Everyone jumped.

"It was like some bear trap had been released on my ankle." With the tone of a child who had lost a game, he asked, "Do you know how many houses I have broken into with dogs?"

"No," David said, "tell us."

"Hundreds," Otto said. "Dogs are supposed to growl and bark to give you some sort of warning before they attack." He glared at Gnarly. "But not this one. He sneaked up behind me without making a sound and clamped onto my ankle and wouldn't let go." He yelled at Gnarly, "Which is not fair—not fair at all! You weren't even supposed to be in the house."

"If Gnarly had given you a warning bark, he wouldn't have been sneaking," Cameron said.

"There are rules in nature." Otto jerked his head in Gnarly's direction. "He broke the rules. That's not playing fair. Therefore it is only right that you release me now."

"So you can have a do-over?" Mac asked. "I don't think so."

Recapturing his dignity, Otto sat up. "I'm a professional. Even when he was ripping the skin from my body, I didn't make a sound. I knew that if I bided my time and kept a cool head I could outsmart him. After all, he's a dog, damn it. Then, things really got weird."

Cameron's interest was captured. "They got weirder?"

"He winked at me."

"Winked?" Bogie's salt and pepper eyebrows went halfway up his forehead.

Otto nodded his head. "He let go of my ankle and sat down and got all quiet like he was going to let me go. So I went for the safe to finish my job and he bit me in the arm. I managed to get loose and ran for the door. He actually leapt over the sofa and landed on my back and took me down. Then he let me go again. It was like he was playing some game—like he was some giant cat in a dog suit playing with a human mouse. Every exit I went for, he'd cut me off and take me down—I never knew where he was hiding. He was stalking me like some wild animal." His voice went up in pitch as he claimed, "It was a nightmare." He turned to the police chief. "I'm suing. That dog violated my civil rights."

"We'll discuss your lawsuit after you tell us what recording you were after and who hired you to steal it," David said.

"And why did you think it was in this house?" Mac asked.

Otto said in a firm tone, "I want a deal."

"Sure, we'll talk about a deal," Mac said. "We'll all step into the kitchen to talk about what kind of deal we can offer you. You don't mind if we leave Gnarly here to guard you, do you?"

Otto almost jumped out of his chair when Gnarly rose to his feet. "It's a PI in Washington. I don't know who hired him, but I know he's got some big name clients."

"Do you mean like senators?" Mac asked him.

"Politicians." Otto nodded his head. "Politicians are my bread and butter."

"How were you supposed to know which tape was the right one?" Mac asked. "Someone had to have told you what was on it."

"I don't know who was on it," Otto said. "Only that it was a man and woman, and she was accusing him of raping her and telling him that he got her pregnant."

With a toss of his head, Mac gestured for David and Cameron to follow him into the kitchen. "We know what recording he was after," he said once they were in the kitchen.

"I don't," Cameron said. "What have you not told me?"

David explained, "Khloe's mother, who passed away a few weeks ago, left a recording of a conversation she had with Senator Harry Palazzi, in which he admitted to raping her and getting her pregnant."

"Senator Harry Palazzi?" Cameron said with a gasp. "Why am I not surprised? I always thought he was slimy."

"At the time of the recording," Mac pointed out, "he was a sheriff in Maryland."

"Why is his butt not in jail?" Cameron asked David.

"Because the victim is now dead—a true accidental death," David said. "Without any solid details about the rape and the victim not available to testify, the county prosecutor decided not to press charges. It doesn't even say on the tape where the rape took place, so our prosecutor may not have jurisdiction."

"According to the recording," Mac said, "Khloe's mother had more than one copy of the tape, and in the event of her sudden death, it would make its way to the proper authorities. Her lawyer had one copy."

"Khloe was staying at her late mother's house," David said. "It did show signs of having been searched. For all we know, the killer found the tape."

"We have evidence that Khloe was in contact with Palazzi's lawyer shortly before her murder," Mac said. "We have every reason to believe she was going to reveal that the senator was a rapist."

"And her murderer found the tape," Cameron said. "So where does that leave our psycho singer-slash-stripper-slash-gay best friend?"

"He could be a hired killer," Mac said, "who decided to up his price when he found out what a gem he had."

With her arms folded across her chest, Cameron peered at Mac. "Why did Palazzi think you had the tape?"

"Because I called him on it," Mac said. "This proves he's scared."

"Maybe he has reason to be," she replied. "You say the house where your victim was killed had been searched. The prosecutor and lawyer aren't doing anything with their copy. Palazzi must know they have it. Yet he sent someone to break into your house for a copy of the tape."

"She's right. Why would Palazzi send someone to steal it from you if he had it stolen when he had Khloe killed?" David asked.

"Everest didn't say on the tape exactly how many copies she had," Mac said. "The killer Palazzi hired could have gotten the copy Khloe had and gave it to him. When I called him on

it, Palazzi must have assumed I got my hands on yet another copy."

"Or your senator didn't kill Khloe," Cameron said, "and my psycho singer-slash-stripper-slash-gay best friend killed her, stole her copy of the tape, and decided to add extortion to his resume."

CHAPTER ELEVEN

"If Otto Grant says he's working for me, he's lying," Private Investigator Kevin Cooper said with a laugh when Mac, David, and Cameron confronted him upon arriving at his office the morning after Otto's failed break in.

They had decided to use the element of surprise. Since the court system was closed for the weekend, Otto had to spend the rest of the weekend in jail before Bogie could book him for criminal trespassing and breaking and entering.

Otto was fortunate in that he had an alibi for the day of Khloe Everest's murder. Williamsburg police in Virginia had him on a surveillance video breaking into a bank's safety deposit vault. The evidence against him for breaking and entering into a bank also eliminated him as a suspect for murder-for-hire.

First thing Monday morning, David, Cameron, and Mac left in the police chief's cruiser to go to Washington, DC. On the off chance that she was going to be gone for a long time, Cameron had left Irving with Archie to care for, much to the relief of the hotel manager, Jeff Ingles. When two members of the hotel staff had gone up to move Cameron into another suite, they ran screaming from the room after catching sight of the twenty-five pound skunk cat.

Driving without stopping, they quickly made it to Old Town Alexandria, Virginia, and Kevin Cooper's brownstone office, which, Mac noted, with its view of the Potomac River, was the high-rent district.

Before they left, Archie did a quick background check, which revealed that Kevin Cooper had been a police officer whose career was speckled with disciplinary charges, until he had abruptly quit twelve years ago to start his own private investigative practice. Based in the historic district of Old Town Alexandria, his service had a staff of six investigators working under him.

"That's pretty good for a private investigator starting out on his own," Mac noted when Archie reported her findings.

She looked up from the screen of her laptop. Her emerald green eyes, their hue deepened by the red in her robe, sparkled. "He's got a pretty good bank account and a couple of off-shore accounts with over a million dollars in both of them."

"He's dirty," Mac concluded. "He's Harry Palazzi's clean-up man." Struck with a thought, he asked, "When did you say he left the force?"

"Twelve years ago."

"What month?" Mac asked.

She flipped through some screens before finding the answer. "In a couple of months, it will be thirteen years."

"Dee Blakeley was murdered twelve years ago. In April, it will be thirteen years." Mac peered closely at her report. "Kevin Cooper was a uniform. There was no sign of forced entry. Dee had let her killer in. She would have let in a uniform officer the night before her hearing."

"He may be your killer," Archie said. "He got a big payday for killing the woman who was going to ruin Palazzi's career and life, and he started his own business doing dirty work for bad guys."

"Which could explain the other women's murders," Mac said. "They were hits for some of Cooper's other clients."

Mac's suspicions were further compounded when he called a detective friend who was still working in the department. Kevin Cooper had been on duty at the time of Blakeley's murder; plus, he had been patrolling her area.

"What's it like?" Mac asked Kevin Cooper after the investigator invited them into his office. In response to the private investigator's questioning gaze, he explained, "Working with criminals like Otto."

"I don't work with criminals," Kevin Cooper said. "I never hired him. He's lying." He was a tall, broad-shouldered man with a weak jaw and thick, wavy ash-blond hair. The combination of a dark tan and deep wrinkles gave his face a worn look.

"How do you know him?" David asked.

Seemingly unengaged in the conversation, Cameron was taking in the expensive décor, which consisted of original paintings and a Tiffany lamp on his antique cherry desk. It was not your typical PI decor.

"I busted him once breaking into my office," Cooper said. "Because I have a heart, I didn't have him arrested, and I sent him on his way with a warning. I guess implicating me in this job was his idea of revenge."

"Revenge for what?" Mac asked while looking him up and down. "If you didn't send him to jail, he should have been grateful." He tried to envision Kevin Cooper, dressed in a police uniform, stabbing Dee Blakeley to death while she begged for her life.

"Crooks don't think like you and me." Practically knocking David out of his way, he ordered Cameron, "Don't touch that."

Cameron stopped in the middle of adjusting the thermostat. "I'm sorry." She proceeded to fan herself with her hand. "Hot flash. I was trying to turn the temperature down a bit. I'll step outside to cool off." She went out into the hallway.

Seeing Mac's and David's startled looks, Kevin chuckled. "I have a devil of a time keeping control of the heating bill around here with people changing the temperature up and down to meet their own personal temps."

Mac folded his arms across his chest. "Do you remember Dee Blakeley?"

"Should I?"

"You were on patrol in her area the night she was murdered. One month later, you resigned from the police force to start this company."

"Now I remember." Kevin grinned. "Pretty young woman. She was a lobbyist. Stabbed multiple times by some maniac."

"Why do you say maniac?" Mac asked.

"Like you said, I was with the force then. I know all about the murder. Multiple stab wounds. It had to have been a psycho."

"I was the lead detective on that case," Mac said. "She was scheduled to testify before the grand jury the next day about Senator Harry Palazzi raping her, but she ended up dead. You were on duty that night. One month later, you had the bucks to start this PI firm. Last night, Otto Grant told us that you sent him to retrieve an audio recording on which Senator Palazzi confessed to raping another woman. Does he by any chance have you on retainer? I guess after Blakeley's murder, he knows he can trust you."

The private investigator stood up to his full height. "What are you suggesting, Faraday?"

Mac stepped forward to look him in the eye. "I'm not suggesting, I'm saying. Your name has come up twice in connection to the senator, and both times the situation involved cleaning up this sexual predator's messes. Now's your chance to be one of the first rats off the ship that I'm going to personally sink."

"Obviously, you have no idea who you're dealing with," the private investigator told him. "If you had any proof of a connection between me and Grant or Palazzi, then we wouldn't be talking here. You'd have me in the police station."

"Oh, but we will," David said. "That recording has gotten a lot of people interested in Senator Harry Palazzi and his dirty dealings. It's only a matter of time before the rats start jumping ship and cutting deals. There's only a limited supply of deals to go around. If I were you, I'd cut one while there were still some to be had."

"Good luck with that." Kevin plucked a business card from his desk blotter. "Now I have a breakfast meeting with a governor at the yacht club. I suggest you leave, and the next time you want to speak to me call my lawyer." He held out the card to David.

Outside the office, David allowed a smile to come to his lips.

"What?" Mac asked him.

David handed him the card. "Check out the name of his lawyer."

Mac chuckled at the name: Samuel Brooks. Kevin Cooper had the same lawyer as Senator Harry Palazzi.

Out on the street, they found Cameron Gates sitting on the front stoop.

"How's your hot flash?" David asked.

She smiled at them. "Once a woman claims to be having a hot flash, men stop all questioning. Notice he didn't even walk me out, which left me free to snoop around."

"What did you find?" Mac asked.

"That thermostat was a fake," she said. "I spotted it right away. It's a hidden camera and mic. Cooper apparently records his meetings. I also found that his administrative assistant listed a meeting between him, your Senator Palazzi, and a Brooks guy Saturday morning. It was called suddenly, because I saw where she had to scratch out a couple of meetings for him to make that one, which was noted with a red pen and starred. We could be assuming things, but it looked important."

Noting that the sidewalk was becoming busy with people out and about, David gestured for them to head for the cruiser that he had parked at a meter down the street.

Mac fell into step to walk with Cameron. "Suppose your theory is right. Suppose the killer wasn't working for Palazzi. One of Khloe's friends got wind of what her announcement was going to be about and decided to cash in without Khloe. He killed her, found the tape, and used it to blackmail the senator."

"And then after your encounter with Palazzi Friday night," David said over his shoulder as he was leading them to the cruiser, "he assumed it was you who had the tape when he was contacted by the blackmailer. So Cooper sent Otto to search your house."

"But you don't have it," Cameron said. "We know our stripper-slash-rock singer-slash-gay best friend is connected to Khloe, which would have given him access to her house, so he may have it."

"That's our next stop." David punched the button on his keychain to unlock the door.

Luckily, morning rush hour traffic was lightening up. They went up the Washington Beltway to cross into Maryland until they came to Potomac, which was where they exited.

"Potomac is quite a ritzy neighborhood for a gay reality show actor," Mac noted.

Cameron was equally impressed by the brownstone townhomes and luxury houses. "Not the neighborhood I was expecting. Are you sure you're in the right town, O'Callaghan?" She checked the caller ID on the phone vibrating on her hip. "Hey! It's that producer from Hollywood."

Doubtful himself, David checked the address on the GPS. "Yes, I'm in the right neighborhood, according to the address we have in his file."

Cameron was too busy talking on the phone to listen. "What have you got for me?" She put the producer on speaker.

"I got it from a very reliable source. Tiffany Blanchard was involved with Nick Fields," came the sultry voice from the phone.

"What reliable source?" Mac asked.

"Tiffany's modeling agent," was the answer. "Who are you?"

"He's Mac Faraday," Cameron said. "He's the homicide detective on the case for Khloe Everest's murder."

The producer's voice deepened. "Well, Mr. Faraday, you have a very sexy voice. Does your body match?"

David laughed.

"My name is Shelby," she said. "Maybe you'd like to come out to the West Coast. We could do lunch…or dessert…or what not."

"Focus, Shelby," Cameron said. "Tell us about Tiffany Blanchard and Nick Fields."

"She didn't tell her agent about Nick," she replied. "Remember, Nick was supposed to be gay on Khloe's reality show. Everyone thought he was for real. But then one weekend shortly before Khloe's show got cancelled, Tiffany's agent went to a resort in Malibu where a lot of people in the industry go to hook up with people they aren't supposed to

138

be hooking up with. Why they all go to this place, I don't know. If someone really doesn't want people to know who he's hooking up with, then he should go someplace where no one knows him. But this is Hollywood."

"Maybe it's because they do want to be seen there," Cameron said.

"Maybe," she replied. "The paparazzi practically live there. Anyway, Tiffany's agent ran into her and Nick Fields. Tiffany begged her agent not to tell anyone because she said Nick was up for another gig and if word got out about him and her, it would ruin it."

Mac and David exchanged glances.

"In other words, if word got out that he was straight," Cameron said, "his career would be over."

"Which is what happened," she replied. "Word got out. I don't know who spread it. Her agent said that Tiffany was ga-ga over Nick and devastated when his career was ruined and he had to move back East."

"Maybe she forced him out of the closet," Cameron said. "Though from where I come from, it isn't the straight guys who are in the closet."

"Whoever leaked it, ended Nick's Hollywood career," Shelby said. "A month after her agent ran into her at that resort, Khloe's show got the ax. The last time Tiffany was seen alive was at the cast party. She got murdered, and Nick high-tailed it out of town." She gasped, "Oh, but guess what."

"What?" Cameron asked.

"You know that resort I was talking about? Tiffany's body was found on their beach. Do you think that means something?"

"Sounds significant to me," Cameron said.

The cruiser was now nearing the end of a cul-de-sac that was home to two houses. Seeing that they had arrived at Nick's home, Cameron thanked her.

"Hey, Mac," Shelby called out, "Cameron has my number. Call me sometime. I could listen to your voice all day long."

David and Cameron laughed at the blush that came to Mac's cheeks while she disconnected the call and placed the phone in its case on her utility belt.

Outside a white stone home, a woman was helping three small children build a snowman. According to a sign in front of the house next door, a yellow Colonial-style house with white shutters, it was the address they were looking for.

David pulled the cruiser up in front of the house and parked in the street. Seeing the police cruiser, and David in his uniform and police jacket, as well as Cameron and Mac, who were wearing their police shields and weapons on their hips, the children and woman stopped playing.

The three of them offered smiles to the family. David tipped his hat. "Morning."

The woman's smile was weak. "Good morning." She continued to watch them file up to the front stoop of the yellow house. Reaching the door first, Mac stopped and held up his hand for them to stop. He leaned sideways to press his ear to the door. "Do you hear that?"

David stepped up next to Mac to listen. "What is that? Sounds like a woman screaming."

"That's what it sounds like to me."

Her hand on her gun, Cameron stepped between them to listen. Abruptly, the scream became louder and higher in pitch. All three of them reached for their guns.

"I think we got our guy, and he's got another victim," Cameron said.

"I'll go around back." Stepping off the stoop, Mac saw the woman and children still watching them. Seeing them unholster their weapons, the woman pulled the children close. "You need to go inside," Mac ordered in a loud whisper. He didn't have to tell them twice. The woman practically shoved the children inside and slammed the door shut.

Mac ran around to the back, climbed up the steps to the deck off the kitchen, and tried the back door. It was unlocked. As he was coming in, he heard David kick in the front door. "Police! Nick Fields, you're under arrest. Come out with your hands up!"

The scream became louder.

Their weapons drawn, David and Cameron ran up the stairs in the front while Mac raced up the back staircase. In a line, they charged into the master bedroom at the end of the hall, where the screaming reached an unbelievable pitch.

When the officers barged in with their guns drawn, the woman on the bed suddenly kicked out her legs and tried to sit up, but the naked man on top of her, in the throes of an orgasm, pushed her back down. "Not yet, baby, I'm just about to come! Come with me, baby! Come with me!"

"Nick! We—" she gasped, "We have company!"

With the moment gone, she shoved him off the bed, gathered the covers, and ran wailing into the bathroom where she slammed the door. The naked man climbed up onto his knees from where he had fallen out of bed and brushed his long hair out of his eyes. "Who the hell are you?"

"We're the police." David lowered his gun, but he was prepared in case the young man pulled a weapon out from under the bed clothing. "Are you Nick Fields?"

"Depends," he shot back. "What do you want? And why didn't you knock? You can't just come busting into a guy's house."

"We did knock," Cameron lied. "But you couldn't hear us over the screaming."

"Police do have the right to break in if they believe someone is in danger," Mac said. "Your girlfriend was screaming. We thought she was in trouble."

141

"Katelyn can be pretty loud." He smiled broadly while running his fingers over his thin mustache and goatee.

The bathroom door flew open. Dressed, Katelyn came rushing out. "I'm out of here!"

Unashamed of his nudity, Nick stood up to give chase. "Baby, wait!"

She whirled around. "The police busting in on us is bad enough!" She pointed toward the bathroom. "Now I find a whole dressing room filled with makeup and enough women's clothes to clothe a third-world country! I knew something smelled funny with you, Nick! You're married!"

"No, I'm not!" Nick insisted. "All that stuff belongs to my sister. She stays here some—"

Not sticking around to listen, she stormed down the stairs and slammed the door. Mac, David, and Cameron exchanged glances. "Married?" David mouthed to Mac.

Cameron excused herself and went outside while David and Mac moved in on their suspect.

"Now look at what you did." Nick turned to the men who had interrupted his fun.

"Sorry," Mac said while holstering his gun. "Would you mind getting dressed?"

"Is this going to take long?" Nick asked with a sigh filled with disgust.

"Pretty long," David said. "We have a lot of questions."

"About what?" Nick still did not move to put on any clothes.

Mac stepped up to him. "Amber Houston, Tiffany Blanchard, and Khloe Everest."

Nick's eyes widened.

"They all have two things in common." Mac's breath feathered his face. "One, they all knew you, and you had relationships with them. And two, all three of them have been murdered." His voice hardened. "Now get dressed."

Nick's face grew white. Staring at Mac as if he feared what he would do, Nick moved to the bed, bent over and felt around the floor in search for his clothes.

Outside, Cameron saw that the woman had run halfway up the block to a blue sedan, jumped inside, and sped off, but not before the detective memorized and jotted down the license plate. It had Virginia plates. When she turned back around to go inside, she saw the woman next door peering out the window at her.

I hope this is one of those nosey neighbors. Cameron sauntered up to the stoop and knocked on the door.

The woman opened the door as if she had been waiting for her. "Is everything okay?"

"We're taking in your neighbor for questioning," Cameron said.

"About what?" She opened the door to invite Cameron into the foyer of her home. In the living room, Cameron heard a children's program on and saw the three preschoolers roughhousing on the furniture.

"I can't really say." After introducing herself and showing her police identification, Cameron asked her for her name.

"Sandy," the neighbor answered with a toss of her head that propelled her shaggy dark hair out of her face. "Sandy Patton."

"How long has Mr. Fields lived here?"

"Something like a year and a half." Folding her arms under her bosom, Sandy let out a giggle.

"What's so funny?" Cameron asked.

"I never knew his name until now," she said. "He never says anything to anyone. I guess he travels, because he'll be gone for days at a time. His wife certainly travels a lot because I'll only see her on the weekends and maybe a couple of times during the week. When she's around—" She held up her hands. "Let's just say that my children and I steer clear when she's in town. That was who I thought you were here to arrest."

"Why did you expect her to be arrested?"

"With her temper, I wouldn't be surprised if she killed someone." Seemingly grateful for the opportunity to get her frustration about her neighbors off her chest, Sandy went on, and Cameron didn't stop her. "The day after they moved in, she came over here and screamed at me about my children's play set being on their property." Sandy pointed toward the back of the house. "The neighbors who used to live there were friends of ours. When we got the play set, they invited us to put it on the most level part of the backyard, which put one corner on their property. It was there for years. Then they sold the house and went into assisted living. But when that couple moved in, the wife was over here banging on my door before the moving van had even left. She wouldn't stop screaming at me long enough for me to say I was sorry and that we would dismantle the whole thing and move it, which is what we had to do. She kept on saying how unacceptable it was and that there were laws and she had legal recourse if my family or I trespassed again."

Sandy shook her head. "That was my introduction to her. She never lets me get a word in edgewise—even to apologize—and if I do apologize, she's so busy screaming at me that I know she hasn't heard it. Last summer, the kids were playing in the swimming pool on our property, but they were squealing and making kid noises, and she said it was too loud. Her husband has never said a word to me. It's like he doesn't even know we're here. Nor has she or her husband ever said a word to my husband. It's always me that bitch—excuse my language—is screaming at. For some bizarre reason, she hates me. Maybe she's afraid I'm going to steal her husband."

Scratching her head over Nick's marriage and the discovery of a dressing room filled with women's clothes, Cameron asked, "Do you know for a fact that they're married? Maybe they're only living together—or she's his sister."

Sandy shook her head. "She refers to him as her husband. She doesn't even call him by name. Only 'my husband.' She's very proud of it." A smirk crossed her face. "With her attitude, she must know it's a miracle that she was ever able to snag a man."

"Well, if that's what she calls him…" Cameron asked, "Do you know her name?"

"No," she giggled. "Only that she is very aware of her rights and what rights I don't deserve—like having five children and a big dog."

"You have no right to have five children and a dog?"

"That's what she said—her exact words—when she was screaming at me about the kids making too much noise in the pool." Sandy screwed up her face. "She's obviously a socialist. That must narrow down your search some. You're looking for a fat, ugly, female socialist with a nasty attitude."

"Who is more territorial than a junkyard dog," Cameron said. "Do you know anything else about her?"

Sandy laughed at her comparison. "She certainly has the disposition of one." Her eyes lit up. "Oh, yes, there is something else that can help you."

"What's that?"

"She's got huge breasts."

"Breasts?" Cameron asked.

"Humongous." With a wicked grin, Sandy indicated by waving both of her hands in front of her own bosom.

"Okay," Cameron laughed. "We're looking for a nasty, ugly, fat socialist with huge breasts. Should be easy to find."

After a moment of thought, Sandy said, "She must have a really good job. She drives a red jaguar convertible. He drives a black Ferrari."

Cameron made note of her information.

"I guess I wasn't much help," Sandy said.

"Actually, you've been very helpful."

As soon as Cameron was back outside, she was on her cell phone to the Spencer Police department. She could have called her own, but since this was David O'Callaghan's show, she thought it best to run the information through Bogie.

"How's it going, Cam?" Bogie greeted her.

Cradling the phone against her shoulder, Cameron pushed through the front door of the yellow house. She could hear Mac's voice, forcibly demanding something, coming from the kitchen in the rear of the house. "Bogie, I need you to find something out for me—or maybe Archie. Who owns the house that Nick Fields lives in?"

CHAPTER TWELVE

After assuring Cameron that he would look up that information immediately, Bogie disconnected their call and turned his attention back to Archie, who was going over her statement about the burglary before signing it. While reading, she was sucking on the top of the ballpoint pen. Noticing her furrowed brow, the deputy chief sat back in his chair behind his desk and crossed one long leg over the other. "What's the matter, Ms. Monday? After all these years, you suddenly decided you don't trust me."

"Haven't you ever heard about the woman who was married for over twenty years, sleeping every night with her husband who would get up in the morning, kiss her goodbye and then, carrying his briefcase, go off to work?"

Bogie nodded his head. "She had no idea she was married to a professional hit man who killed close to a hundred people during the course of his career."

"Proves you never really know anyone." She leaned over toward his desk and signed the statement. "I have no idea what you do after you leave this station at night." Shooting him a wink, she slid the statement across the desk toward him.

"Now don't you go spreading that around."

"I don't know what you're ashamed of, Bogie," she said. "Doc Washington is a young, vibrant woman. She's certainly smart enough to know a tremendous catch when she sees him. You deserve to be happy. Enjoy it."

"I think women hate seeing men who aren't attached."

"No, I just want everyone to be as happy as Mac and I are," Archie said.

"You have had a special glow about you since coming back from your cruise," he said, which brought a broad smile to her face.

"Where's O'Callaghan?" a loud voice with an arrogant tone demanded from the reception area.

Gnarly erupted in a round of loud barking at what he considered a foe. He was right.

Bogie's mustache rose up into his nostrils in response to the snarl that came to his lips. His eyes narrowed. He pushed back from his desk and stood up.

"Amazing how fast a pleasant moment can turn ugly," Archie said. "Usually with the introduction of nasty."

But Bogie didn't hear her. He was on his way to the reception area.

"He's out investigating a murder." Tonya had lived on the lake her whole life. Many suspected the long hours the desk sergeant put in at the station were an excuse to not go home, to which two of her three grown children had returned with their offspring after a short time spent in the outside world.

Tonya was a huge fan of every dog. Sometimes, Mac felt like she was simply going through the paces while making small talk until they arrived upon the topic of Gnarly and his latest escapades. She had three dogs of her own that she doted on more than her kids. The dogs were more self-sufficient.

"He's the chief of police," the man replied. "Why isn't he ever in the office?"

Bogie's booming voice drowned out that of the town councilman. "Because the work that needs to be done is out there. You got a problem with that, Clark?"

The displeasure was doubled with the chubby man at Bill Clark's side. When he didn't get results through the county prosecutor and governor, Bevis Palazzi had gone to the chairman of Spencer's town council, who was more than happy to throw a snag into Police Chief David O'Callaghan's operations.

"I have a lot of problems with how this department is run," Bill Clark replied. As chubby as Bevis Palazzi was, Bill Clark was slender from spending most of his days on the golf course cutting political deals. "Number one is a lack of communication. Mr. Palazzi's good friend, Khloe Everest, was killed almost a week ago, and your department refuses to give him a status report on how close you are to catching her killer."

"Mac Faraday went ape on me when I asked him about it," Bevis said from a safe position behind Clark. "When I tried to talk to O'Callaghan, he hung up on me—me, a taxpayer who he had been hired to serve. It's a disgrace, the trouble I had to take to ensure that this police department respected my rights. It makes me wonder how the little man who has no connections gets treated."

"Maybe if you grew some manners the police department would be more willing to cooperate with you," Archie said.

Bevis charged forward with his hand raised. "You're opinions are uncalled for, bitch!" He found himself face to chest with Bogie, who had stepped in between them.

His hackles up, Gnarly cut off Bill Clark, who tried to intervene on Bevis' behalf. Seeing the snarl on the German shepherd's lips, Clark decided to back up to take shelter behind Tonya, the desk sergeant.

"You have nothing to worry about, Clark," Tonya said to the town councilman. "Gnarly doesn't eat garbage."

"Bevis lost a very good friend," Bill Clark said while eying Gnarly glaring up at him. "We're here to demand some action."

"You want action? I'll give you action." With a wicked smile, Tonya stepped aside.

When Gnarly moved forward, Bill Clark turned and ran. Enjoying the thrill of the chase, Gnarly galloped after him. With a high pitched shriek, the councilman hopped up onto Tonya's chair and then on top of her desk.

The bad man put away, Gnarly whirled around and seemed to hitch his rear end up in Clark's direction before trotting back to Tonya, who tossed him a doggie biscuit, which the dog caught in mid-air.

"Looks to me like you have a temper, Mr. Palazzi," Bogie said in a low voice.

"Eighty percent of murders are committed by friends or relatives of the victim," Archie said. "Sixteen percent are actually committed by family members." She added, "Also killers often follow the police and use whatever connections they can to get inside the investigation, or to get the media to keep tabs on how close the police are to catching them." She leaned around Bogie to ask, "Bevis, is that why you've been calling in all of your political favors to get a status report on Khloe's murder? Because you're a psychopath, and you want to know how close we are to catching you?"

With a roar, Bevis tried to reach around Bogie to grab her. "You—" He exploded with a string of obscenities while trying to reach Archie. Bogie held him back for as long as he could before finally picking him up, body slamming him down onto the floor, and pinning him there with his knee in his back.

Standing over Bevis, Gnarly's barks sounded like cheers of approval for Bogie's quick action.

From where he was seeking safety on top of Tonya's desk, Bill Clark knelt with his mouth hanging open. When he found his voice, he stammered. "You're all insane! This is totally unacceptable. Do you have any idea who this is?"

"From what I see, he's a murder suspect," Tonya replied.

"This is Senator Harry Palazzi's son! He's going to be senator one day." He pointed at Archie. "She provoked him."

"Which makes him trying to physically attack me okay?" Archie said. "I guess in your book, if he killed Khloe, it was perfectly okay because she had to have provoked him in some way."

With Bevis handcuffed, Bogie dragged him up to his feet. "You want a status report, Clark? Here it is. I'm about to question a suspect in Khloe Everest's murder."

"Don't just stand there, you moron!" Bevis said to his friend, the councilman. "Call my father!"

"I'm confused." Mac closed in on Nick, who was then dressed in baggy, low-cut jeans and handcuffed to a chair in his formal dining room.

After getting Nick dressed and downstairs, Mac finally got a look around the house that their suspect called home. The décor did not fit with its occupant—at least not with Nick Fields. The dining room furniture was cherry. Except for dirty dishes in the sink that they assumed belonged to Nick, the counters were spotless. Teddy bear-shaped canisters were lined up along the counter. Homey pictures of fruit hung on the wall. Any minute, Mac expected to see his mother, wearing an apron and high-heels, walk in with an armload of groceries.

David opened up a folder and laid out crime scene pictures of each of the women. Closing his eyes, Nick turned his head. His prominent cheekbones looked like they had been chiseled onto his face.

"Three woman," Mac said, "who you associated with, are now all dead, all stabbed to death and dismembered. Now, explain to me how that happens?"

"Just lucky, I guess," Nick giggled.

Cameron grabbed him by the hair on the back of his head and whipped him around to make him look at the images of the butchered women. "Look at them, Nick! Not only were these women stabbed to death, but someone also slit their bellies open and gutted them like cattle. The only thing they all have in common is that they knew you. Now, are you going to lie to us and tell us you didn't do this?"

Nick shook his head.

"I know how it can be sometimes, Nick." David straddled the chair across from him. "Sometimes, stuff happens. There can be a series of events that, to those on the outside looking in, point to one thing, when really it's something else. I know that. I've seen it happen. So, it may just look to us like you, being the only common denominator, killed these women for whatever reason. But really, maybe that's not what happened. That's why we're here. We want you to help us by telling us what you know about them that can lead us to their killer."

They sat in silence. Nick stared across at David, who appeared to be his only friend. David abruptly reached inside his coat. "Oh, and to help you to prove your innocence, you can give us a sample of your DNA to prove you weren't there when these women were killed."

Any appearance of cooperation dissipated. Nick shook his head. "No way."

"Yes, way," David slapped a warrant down on the table. "We have a warrant. Open your mouth."

Mac's phone vibrated on his hip. When he read on his caller ID that it was Archie, he stepped into the kitchen to take the call. Knowing that he was out collecting a suspect, she wouldn't have called if it hadn't been important.

"How's it going?" she asked.

"He's not admitting to anything," Mac said. "What's up?"

"Cameron called Bogie to ask him to check on something, but he's a little tied up right now, so I checked for him. She wanted to know who owns the house Nick Fields is living in."

"Did she tell you why?" While normally Mac would have been offended about being left out of the loop on something involving a case, he sensed that Cameron knew better than to interrupt the interrogation for something that might not lead anywhere.

"She asked Bogie, not me," she replied. "But I think she's on to something. That house is owned by a Sheila McGrath. She lives at one-zero-seven-one-eight Potomac Tennis Lane in Potomac, Maryland. Not only does she own that house, but for close to two years, Nick Fields has been receiving an allowance of several thousand dollars a month from a trust she had set up for him."

"Interesting timing," Mac noted. "That's about how long ago Khloe's show was cancelled. I wonder if after Nick lost out on that one gig, he decided to take this one." The wheels in his head were turning. "Could this Sheila have had something to do with outing him and making him lose that gig?"

"What are you talking about?" Archie asked. "Outing him? He was already out of the closet."

"We're talking about a different closet," Mac said. "Nick was up for an acting gig in Hollywood, but—talk about twisted—his image was that of a gay man, which he isn't. Somehow, word got out that he was really heterosexual and having an affair with a woman—Tiffany Blanchard, who was one of the three woman killed. After losing out on that gig, it looks like Nick happened into this set up."

"Which is one sweet set up," Cameron said from where she had been listening in from the kitchen doorway. She jerked her head in the direction of the house next door. "House. Sports car. Generous allowance. The lady next door said that there's a woman who lives here on the weekends and visits a couple of nights a week. She claims to be his wife. But his background check doesn't show him as having ever been married."

"Nick has a sugar momma," Mac said. "But he's also got a problem. He can't keep his zipper shut. When a girlfriend threatens to blow the whistle on him, he does what he has to do to keep her quiet."

"We just found his motive," Cameron said.

"We're taking him back with us to lock him up." With a quick good-bye to Archie, Mac disconnected their call.

Cameron stopped him on his way out of the kitchen. "Remember, Pennsylvania gets him first."

In the dining room, Mac shoved a chair aside, causing a loud scraping noise across the hardwood floor. "Get up, Fields! You're going for a ride. We're taking you in for questioning."

Nick grabbed his cell phone. "I'm not going anywhere before I call my lawyer."

"He does have a temper," Archie whispered to Ben Fleming as if Bevis Palazzi could hear her talking from where he sat in the interrogation room. The prosecutor had rushed over as soon as he heard that Bevis insisted on having his father called. It went without saying that his father would call in his lawyer, none other than Samuel Brooks.

"I know that," Ben said. "Catherine can't stand to be in the same room as Bevis. Brooks is having a busy day today. This morning he was at Grant's arraignment."

"He's defending the cat burglar?" One of Archie's eyebrows was arched. "Interesting."

"That's not the only thing that's interesting," Ben said. "Bevis is junior partner at a large legal firm in Rockville, Maryland, with an excellent reputation for criminal defense. So why call in his daddy's lawyer and not one of his own?"

"Double interesting." Seeing Bevis pick up his cell phone to answer a call, Archie nudged Ben with her elbow. "I guess that's Brooks telling Bevis that he's going to be late."

"What the hell have you done?" Bevis cursed.

"Bevis isn't happy," she smirked over at Ben.

"Bevis is never happy about anything," Ben said with a sigh.

"No," Bevis ordered. "I can't come right now. I'll send someone. Don't say anything to anyone." He disconnected the call and then pressed another button. Seemingly aware of the mirror, he turned his back to them and lowered his voice.

"What's that all about?" Ben asked.

"You've got me," she replied.

"Why would a straight guy pretend to be a homosexual in a reality show?" David asked Mac loud enough for Nick to hear him in the back seat of the cruiser where he was riding with Cameron. "I mean, wouldn't all of his friends then think that he was gay?"

"You don't know how many women love the idea of straightening out a homo," Nick called up to the front seat before Mac could respond.

"So you lied," Cameron said.

"How do you know I lied?"

"We saw you with a woman with our own eyes," Cameron said. "We know about you and Tiffany Blanchard spending time at the resort in Malibu. You didn't want anyone to know about it because you didn't want anyone to know you were straight."

"Since when is being straight something you want to hide?" David asked.

"Since gay is in right now," Nick said. "It's all the rage in Hollywood—especially on these reality shows—which is my market. If they knew I was straight, I'd be back working the strip clubs in hick towns in Pennsylvania."

"Isn't that what happened?" Mac asked. "Didn't word get out about you being straight? Maybe you thought Tiffany had forced you out of the closet, and that's why you killed her."

"That isn't what happened," Nick said.

"Then why aren't you in Hollywood right now?" David asked. "What are you doing back here?"

"I'm on hiatus," Nick said. "I'm working on a CD. It's coming out next year."

"Weren't you working as a male stripper when Amber Houston met you?" Cameron asked.

"Stripping, singing, reality star," Mac ticked off. "I guess you're still trying to find yourself, huh, Nick?"

"A guy does what he has to do to get ahead," Nick said. "All I have going for me is my looks. I was never one for schooling. College was out of the question. When I was stripping and singing in the clubs, I discovered that I have a talent for being whatever I need to be for those who can give me what I want."

"Who do you have to be to live in a big house in a ritzy neighborhood?" Mac asked.

"Wouldn't you like to know?"

Mac turned to look back at him. "I do want to know."

"Who were you to Amber, Tiffany, and Khloe?" Cameron asked.

In the rearview mirror, Mac could see a wicked grin cross Nick's face. "It was the other way around for them. They became who I told them to be. It was sweet."

Turning back around, Mac glanced at David. "Role playing."

"How does your wife feel about you having other women role playing for you?" Cameron asked him.

Nick's mouth drew tight. While Mac and Cameron watched him in the rearview mirror, his cocky grin fell from his face. Nick turned to look out the window at the passing countryside off the expressway.

Watching Nick in the rearview mirror, Mac almost regretted the decision to take Nick back to Deep Creek Lake. Since they had picked him up, they were unable to visit Sheila McGrath, the woman who was apparently keeping Nick in the lifestyle to which he had become accustomed. Clearly, with as much money as she was spending on him, she would have had reason to fly into a rage and kill his mistresses.

What type of woman spends thousands of dollars a month keeping a slimy snake like Nick Fields for a lover? A desperate, lonely, and jealous one—the type of woman who commits murder.

Chapter Thirteen

"That bitch provoked me on purpose!" Bevis Palazzi jumped out of his chair to tell Samuel Brooks as soon as he stepped into the interrogation room. "Of course, they're all on her side because she's Mac Faraday's whore."

"Sit down and shut your mouth!" the lawyer ordered.

In the observation room, Mac, David, and Cameron were watching the lawyer instruct his client in a low voice. Down the hall, Nick Fields was waiting for Mac and Cameron to resume questioning him.

"The senator and all his people have trouble," Mac said. "Someone has a copy of that tape proving Harry Palazzi is a rapist. That person, who may or may not be our killer, is blackmailing the good senator. Obviously, Palazzi's cleanup team doesn't know who the blackmailer is. Otherwise, why hire a cat burglar to break into my house to look for the tape?"

"We didn't find a copy in the Everest home," David said. "So it could be the same copy that Khloe was blackmailing Palazzi with. It could very well be the motive for her murder. Now who outside of Senator Palazzi's inner circle had knowledge of the tape and opportunity to commit the murder and steal it?"

They all looked in the direction of the hallway and down the hall to the other observation room. "He is Khloe's best gay friend."

Mac and Cameron stepped out into the corridor at the same time that the interrogation room door opened and Samuel Brooks stepped out. "My client and I are ready to meet with you now."

Over his shoulder, Mac saw David coming out of the observation room. Deciding Nick Fields could wait, he followed Samuel Brooks in to meet with Bevis.

Since the Spencer police had gotten the warrant for Nick's DNA, Cameron had to wait for the Maryland lab to process the evidence. "I should go call my silver fox anyway," she told them. Whipping out her cell phone, she sauntered down the hallway in the direction of the squad room.

In spite of his lawyer's warning, Bevis didn't try to contain his disgust. "Well, if it isn't the big bad David O'Callaghan, the big man in Spencer. After my father and I are through with you, you won't be able to get a job as a garbage collector. I guarantee it, you'll learn some manners."

"You have to know some manners before you can teach them." Mac folded his arms across his chest and leaned against the wall.

Sitting across from Bevis, David said, "Tell us about Khloe." He placed a yellow notepad on top of the case file.

"You already know about Khloe," Bevis said through a scowl. "We were friends."

"How good of friends?" David asked him.

"Let's cut the crap," the lawyer said. "For some bizarre reason, you think Bevis killed one of his closest friends when he had no motive for killing her."

The lawyer turned to Mac. "A few days ago you publicly accused his father of killing Khloe. This is clearly some witch-hunt instigated by a bitter ex-cop who thinks he has a score to settle with the senator. Since you can't touch the senator, you're going after his son. Well, we can save you a lot of time and embarrassment. When was Khloe Everest murdered?"

"Sometime Sunday night," David said. "Right after she had set up a television interview. She was planning to make a big announcement that promised to rock this country." He looked across at Bevis. "Do you know what that announcement was about?"

"Yeah," Bevis said. "I know exactly what it was about."

"Care to share it with us?" Mac asked.

"She was leaving Hollywood and going into business," Bevis said. "She was going to take over her mom's company."

David was doubtful. "How would that news rock the country?"

Bevis' eyes grew big. His plump lips stretched across his face to make him look like a clown. He threw his hands up in the air in an exaggerated shrug. "Khloe was delusional about her importance and fame. She thought people actually cared what she was doing every minute of every day."

Samuel Brooks cocked his head at his client and narrowed his eyes. "Do you remember where you were the night Khloe was killed?"

Bevis answered quickly, "Of course." He smirked. "I was at my father's house playing chess until after midnight. Since it was late, I slept in my old room."

Mac pushed off the wall. He gritted his teeth to keep from saying anything that would give away his disbelief and fury.

"You and the senator were playing chess?" David said. "All evening?"

"All evening."

"And you never left the house?" David asked. "Not even to run an errand?"

"My father and I were together all evening."

"Playing chess?" Mac replied. "When did the match start?"

"Right after dinner," Bevis said. "We ate dinner together. Sunday dinner. We cooked it together. It's a tradition since my mother was killed."

"How sweet," Mac said with a note of sarcasm.

"Was anybody else at the house to verify that you were there?" David asked.

"Isn't the word of a United States Senator good enough verification?" Samuel Brooks asked.

"With all due respect," David said, "the word of the United States President wouldn't be good enough for me without verification."

Samuel Brooks stood up. "We're through here. Come along, Bevis."

"Yes," Mac said. "Go along, little Bevis."

Bevis thrust his finger in Mac's face. "You just wait. You have no idea who you're messing with."

Mac narrowed his eyes and took in the finger. "Remove that finger or lose it."

The two men locked their eyes on each other.

With Bevis close to him, Mac's attention was diverted by the space above the suspect's eyes, around his eyebrows. Mac spied bits of new hair growth and the perfect shape of his eyebrows. *Plucked eyebrows? Seriously?* Mac's intense glare changed to one of curiosity.

"Come, Bevis," the lawyer ordered for him to fall in behind him.

Mac leaned out into the hallway. He waited to hear Bevis and his lawyer leave the police station before turning to David, who was smirking at him. "Did you see that?"

161

"Yes, I did," the police chief replied.

"What kind of man plucks his eyebrows?"

"That wasn't what I was talking about," David chuckled. "It's not that strange. Believe it or not, a lot of men I know have their eyebrows cleaned up—Ben Fleming, for one."

Mac exhaled. "You're kidding. I never noticed that about Ben. I've known him for three years and—are you sure?"

"He and I have our hair done by the same stylist," David said. "You aren't supposed to notice it. You have to understand, many of the men here in Spencer are in high-profile positions—politicians and CEOs. Physical appearance is a huge thing, and it can have an indirect connection to their success or failure. Bevis is a junior partner at a big law firm in the Washington, DC, area. He's trying to start a career in politics. Those waxed eyebrows as just as important in creating his image as that Porsche he drives." With a shake of his head, he gestured in the direction of the parking lot outside where Bevis' sports car had been parked when they pulled in.

"I respect the Porsche more than I do the eyebrows," Mac said. "They're arched like a woman's."

"I admit Bevis does go further with his eyebrows than most men I know who have it done," David said. "At the salon Ben and I go to, some men will have their backs and shoulders waxed." A wicked grin crossed his face. "Haven't you noticed by now? Spencer is a whole different world. I can give you the name of Ben's and my stylist."

Mac waved his hand at him. "No, thanks."

"Maybe you'd like to have your brows done."

"Forget it."

"Suit yourself," David said with a shrug of his shoulders. "Back to the case. Did that alibi sound slightly familiar to you?"

"Very familiar," Mac replied. "You remembered I told you that the senator gave the same alibi the night Dee Blakeley was murdered. The senator had dinner with his son, and they played chess the whole evening until late into the night. No one was at the house to verify his alibi then, either."

David rubbed his hands together. "Two women. Both women have the ability to ruin the senator and his reputation—"

"Not only would he have been run out of office, but Senator Palazzi also would have had to stand trial, and he could have gone to jail if Dee had testified against him," Mac said.

David added, "If Khloe had made her announcement in that interview and played that tape, she would have ruined his reputation. Other women he'd raped throughout the years may have felt compelled to come forward."

"Both women end up murdered," Mac said, "and both times, the senator and Bevis were playing chess at the time of the murder."

"Do they think we're stupid?" David sounded offended. "Why use the same alibi?"

Mac laughed. "Kind of reminds me of something my adoptive mother used to tell me. The worst thing about lying is that you have to remember the lies you tell. Otherwise, you're bound to slip up because you forgot something. The advantage of the truth is that you never have to remember it to keep it straight because it's the truth. It's been twelve years since Dee Blakeley's murder. They forgot they'd used that lie already." Mac jerked his thumb toward the interrogation room down the hallway. "Ready to go tackle another liar?"

"Cameron will sic Irving on us if we exclude her," David said. "I think she's back in the squad room." Seeing Mac studying his face, he added, "To answer your other question—no, I do not have my eyebrows waxed."

"Thank you for telling me that." Mac turned to head down the hall to the squad room. "I feel much better."

David fell in behind him. "But I do have my nails buffed."

"I wish you hadn't told me that."

They found Cameron in the squad room sitting next to a desk where Archie was using her laptop to research the major players.

"Hello, beautiful." Mac gave Archie a quick kiss on the top of her head.

Casting a sideways glance in Cameron's direction, Archie swooned. "Oh, Mac, say that again. I could listen to you talk all day long."

"You had to tell her," Mac said to Cameron.

Kicking back in her seat, the detective laced her fingers behind her head and laughed. "Some things are too good to keep to yourself."

"It's going to be years before I live this down." With a sigh, Mac asked Archie, "Have you found anything interesting on our suspects?"

"I've been digging a little deeper into the life of Nick's sugar momma," Archie said. "According to what I've been able to uncover, Sheila McGrath is fifty-six years old and isn't employed. Her money is inherited from her husband, Richard McGrath, who was killed in a multi-vehicle accident on the Capital Beltway almost four years ago. He was a CEO of a computer company. He left Sheila a twenty million dollar estate. Since she's been widowed, she's been spending her inheritance like water. Trips out of the country. Spa treatments. Cosmetic surgery. Jewelry and expensive clothes."

"And keeping a man," Cameron said.

Struck with a thought, Cameron and Mac exchanged glances. When Mac turned around, he saw the same question on David's face.

Archie voiced their question. "If she's widowed, then why hide Nick? Why not just move him in with her?"

"Maybe she has children who would disapprove," Mac said.

"No children," Archie said.

"She doesn't live there all the time." Cameron scratched her ear. "And her home address is someplace else. That says she's hiding something." She asked Archie, "Did you say she was fifty-six years old?"

Archie nodded her head. "Which could explain the shopping spree and cosmetic surgery and shacking up with a younger man. I mean, she's middle aged and recently widowed. She's having a mid-life crisis and trying to regain her youth. Take a look at all the cosmetic surgery. Nose job. Tummy tuck. Liposuction. Lip implants."

"Lip implants?" Cameron asked. "What do you implant in your lips?"

"Silicone implants," Archie said. "Made of the same stuff that women have implanted to make their breasts larger."

"Why?" the detective asked.

"To make their lips plumper," Archie replied.

"Again, I ask why?"

"Because…" Archie responded with a shrug.

Mac cleared his throat to draw their attention back to the case. "Cameron, did the next-door neighbor say anything about Nick's quote-unquote-wife being older than him?"

"None," Cameron replied. "I think she would have if she had noticed."

"If she's having a mid-life crisis," David said, "that could explain her flipping out and killing her romantic rivals for Nick's attention. After all, she's paying him to be her lover."

"But they have only been living there for eighteen months," Mac noted. "Nick has only been getting an allowance for that long. Amber Houston was killed well over a year before Nick hooked up with Sheila McGrath."

"Before becoming Sheila's gigolo, Nick was pursuing a Hollywood career," Archie said.

"That's right," Cameron snapped her fingers. "Remember what the producer said? He was up for a part, but when it got out that he was straight, he lost it and his career was over. That was when he took this set up."

"Nick's career flop was Sheila's beefcake gain," Mac said. "Makes me wonder who outed him in Hollywood."

"Maybe Tiffany Blanchard, who was murdered at the same time," Cameron said.

"Sheila McGrath clearly benefited from the outing and Tiffany's murder," Mac said.

"This case is going in ten different directions," Cameron said with a groan. "We have the rapist senator, the spoiled son with anger management issues, the has-been gay reality star turned straight gigolo, and now the millionaire widow suffering from a mid-life crisis getting stuff implanted in her lips. I say let's choose a psychopath and go with it."

"I think Nick is at the heart of these murders," David said. "We can connect him to every one of the three victims. We can't connect the senator and Bevis to Tiffany or Amber."

"Like Nick is going to cop to anything," Cameron said.

"Unless…" Mac's voice trailed off.

"Unless what?" Archie asked.

"Nick loves to role play," Mac said. "So let's give him a role to play."

With his arms folded across his chest, Nick Fields was sitting back in his seat at the table. "So when are you going to spring me from this hole?"

After slapping the case file down onto the table, Cameron slipped off her jacket to reveal her tight shirt, which hugged her slender body, and slid into the chair across from him.

Nick looked across the table at her. Maybe it was because they were in the bright light of the interrogation room that he noticed more color on her face. The green specks in her eyes jumped out at him. The waves of her auburn hair brought out her cheekbones. The corners of his lips tugged upward at the sight of her.

"Nick," Cameron said, "you've got quite a reputation with the ladies." The corner of her lip curled.

"It's a talent." Nick grinned.

"Amber Houston…" She leaned forward. He could see down the front of her shirt. "That strip club was packed that night she went with her friends. What was it about her that made you pick her out of the crowd?" she asked in a breathless tone.

He gazed into her eyes. "She wanted me. She was crazy about me, and she let me know it. After the show when the club closed, all of the women would go home with their fantasies. Not Amber. She wanted me, and she stayed after to let me know that I could have her—anything I wanted, she'd let me have." He wet his lips. "All I had to do was ask, and it was mine to have."

"A lot of money disappeared out of her bank account before she went missing," Cameron said. "Did it go to you? Is that what you asked for?"

He pulled back. "It isn't what you think."

Cameron got up out of her chair to position herself closer to him. Moving into his space, she leaned against the table. Her slender curves were so close that he could feel her heat. "Tell me what I think, Nick."

"That I'm for sale," Nick said. "That I can be bought like a piece of meat. That's not what it's like."

She leaned in closer. "Tell me what it's like, Nick."

"If someone wants me…" he sighed. "If they want me on call—twenty-four-seven…it's like how doctors and police and other professionals are on call for when they are needed, and they expect to be paid for it. Also, for someone like me—a first-class companion—then there are expenses that go into my upkeep."

"And that is where Amber's money went to?" Cameron asked.

"But since then, my prices have gone up," Nick said.

"You're moving up," she said. "Your parents must be proud of you."

"They think I'm a rock star," Nick said. "They have no idea."

"How much did Tiffany have to pay for your expenses?"

Moving in closer to her. "Not every woman has to pay for my attention." Nick chuckled.

"What does a woman have to do to get such a premium man like you for free?"

His eyes wide, he wet his lips.

"Did Khloe have to pay for your…attention?"

"Oh, no," he said. "Khloe and I were friends. We went way back."

"How far back?" she asked. "Back to her staged disappearance?" She flashed him a grin that betrayed her appreciation for the publicity stunt that won Khloe a reality show deal.

His grin was wicked. "Khloe and I hooked up around the same time Amber and I were together. After Amber disappeared, I told Khloe that I knew her, and Khloe about wet her pants at all the publicity that she was getting on account of her being missing. She told me that she wished it was her—only not that she'd be dead—but alive. She said she knew how to use the fame that she would get when she came back alive and became a star. So…" He lowered his voice to a whisper. "We did it."

Cameron fought the hint of disgust that wanted to rush to her eyes. Nick was perfectly playing the role of a potential lover sharing his secrets.

"We did nothing wrong," he said. "She didn't call her mother to say she was kidnapped. We just set things up and let the police and media run with it. Khloe never expected her mother to go ape the way she did."

"What did you and Khloe do while she was missing?" Cameron held up her fingers to signal quotation marks in the air.

"That part of what Khloe said was true," Nick smiled. "We were shacked up in a motel having a grand old time." He touched her knee. "I gave her the time of her life."

"Did you give her the time of her life the day she died?" she asked.

The smile fell from his face.

"We know you were with her," she said.

"No you don't."

"What if I told you that your DNA sample is a match for the semen we found on her body?" For the first time, she saw fear come to his face. She bent over to whisper into his ear. "I want to help you, Nick. I can't if you don't tell me the truth."

"I was with her," he said. "But it's not like you think. We weren't lovers."

"Then what were you?"

"Friends with benefits."

Cameron nodded her head. They were friends who had sex without any ties or commitments.

"We got together. Partied. Had tremendous sex—it was always tremendous between us," he said. "And then I left. She was alive when I left."

"And then she just so happened to get murdered," Cameron said, "just like what happened to Amber and Tiffany." She screwed up her face in doubt. "I'm going to have a real hard time selling that to those two." With a roll of her eyes and a slight cock of her head, she indicated the other two investigators who were not in on the interview. Continuing with her role of good cop, she confided, "Mac Faraday, he's ready to lock you up and throw away the key. The police chief ... well ... he's young and trying to build up his reputation of being a tough guy." She shook her head. "If you want me to help you, Nick, you need to give me something."

He sat up. "After I left Khloe's place, I went to a party at the Wisp. That was where I met Katelyn."

"Who's Katelyn?"

"The hot babe that you guys scared off," Nick said. "We spent the rest of her vacation together, and I went back to Washington with her on Tuesday. I was with her from late Sunday afternoon through Tuesday. Khloe was alive and posting some stuff on the computer when I left."

"If you didn't kill Khloe," Cameron said, "Who would have wanted to kill her? If you want us to stop looking at you, then it would be helpful if you pointed us in another direction."

Nick stared up at her.

She gazed at him with wide eyes.

Silence stretched between them.

"He knows who did this," Mac whispered to David in the observation room.

"He certainly does." When his phone vibrated on his hip, David answered it without taking his eyes off Nick and Cameron. "Hello..." When he heard who it was, he turned away from the two-way mirror to concentrate on his conversation.

Willing Nick to tell them who killed the three women, and maybe even Dee Blakeley, Mac stepped up closer to the mirror.

"Khloe was going to make a public announcement in an interview on Thursday," Cameron said when Nick did not respond. "Do you know what that was about?"

"Yeah," Nick said in a low voice. "She told me all about it." His eyes grew wide. "It was big. It was going to put her name and face out there again. Guaranteed."

"What was it?" Cameron asked.

Mac could see his breath on the glass of the two-way mirror.

"I can't," he could hear Nick telling Cameron. His head was shaking. "It'd ruin everything."

"Thank you. That is very helpful." David pressed the button to disconnect the call. "That was the lab. Nick's DNA is a match for the semen on all three women. He had sex or raped each of them right before their murders."

"Which begs the question," Mac replied, "did he kill them, or is he connected to the killer?"

"We certainly have enough to hold him," David said.

The intercom buzzed, followed by Tonya's voice informing them that Nick's lawyer, an attorney from Washington, had arrived to take his client home.

"I'll call Ben." David whipped out his cell phone.

"Good," Mac said. "I'm dying to take a closer look at his eyebrows."

CHAPTER FOURTEEN

"Okay, so my client had sex with these three women," Russ Burton, a young attorney from a small firm in Washington, told the prosecutor and police chief sitting on the other side of the table in the interrogation room. "Did he ever deny that?"

Ben shook his head while David said, "Yet he never volunteered it, either. All those days that Amber Houston was missing, he never came forward. Same thing when Khloe Everest was missing."

"She was never missing," Nick said.

"That's right," David said with a glare. "You two engineered her disappearance for a publicity stunt."

"That was three years ago," Nick said. "Get over it."

"The fact is," Russ said, "my client may have had a sexual relationship with the victims, but he didn't kill them. He had no motive and you've got nothing to prove he committed these murders. So we're leaving."

Ben launched into the astronomical odds of Nick Fields being sexually involved with three women in different parts of the country and all three being murdered in the same way without him being involved, let alone not being the killer himself.

While the prosecutor was speaking, his words went into David's ears and turned into muted sounds while the police chief eyed the defense attorney across the table. Sitting next to the young man whose livelihood was living off of women, it was clear that the defense lawyer was at least half a foot taller. His shoulders and chest spread out beyond the ends of the back of the chair. The muscles in his forearms bulged out against the fabric of his suit coat.

David remembered being struck by the strength in his grip when they shook hands when he had first arrived. Pretty strong grip for a legal weenie.

Glancing quickly at Ben Fleming for comparison, David noted the athletically slender prosecutor, who could be found playing tennis or golf or even working out at the club at least three times a week. Ben enjoyed his sports.

The defense attorney wasn't into sports as much as he was into working out and building up his muscles—like a soldier or police officer whose work depended on him always being in top physical condition.

Noting Russ's closely cropped hair, David surmised that it was a military haircut. Maybe he had been enlisted before going to law school and never shook it. He was jarred out of his thoughts when Russ Burton stood up.

"We're going, Nick," he told his client.

"I'm afraid Nick isn't going anywhere." Ben sat back with a smirk. "We're charging him."

"And I'll get the charges dismissed like that." Russ snapped his fingers.

"I don't think so, considering that we have a confession."

"I confessed to nothing," Nick turned to his lawyer. "I didn't say nothing."

"Actually, we have you on tape admitting to it twice," David said.

Seeing their confused expressions, Ben said, "We're charging your client with obstruction of justice in Khloe Everest's phony disappearance. The statute of limitation is five years, so we're well within our limits, and your client admitted during our interrogation to helping Khloe stage it. One of those confessions was right here with you present. If found guilty, he could spend five years in prison."

"I'm sure we'll have no trouble finding that little dive hotel he and Khloe hid out at while we were wasting our manpower and resources looking for her." David took his handcuffs out of their case. "Turn around and put your hands behind your back."

"Not to mention his participation when she lied again about it on national television," Ben said. "That's the problem with lying. There's no telling when that lie is going to come back to bite you in the butt."

"They can't do this," Nick yelled.

"Oh, yes we can," Ben said. "And we will."

"Who do you think did it?" Chelsea asked Archie after hearing about the day's events during the short drive from Ben Fleming's office to Spencer Manor.

"It changes on the hour," Archie said with a sigh while pulling her SUV in through the stone pillars of Spencer Manor.

"I hope this case doesn't mean David can't help me move," she said.

In the backseat, Molly stood up and pressed her snout against the window. She was anxious to see her best friend, Gnarly.

"David will do everything he can to be available to help you." After turning off the car's engine, Archie grinned at the blush that came to Chelsea's cheeks while thinking about David. The mention of David's name made her ivory cheeks turn bright pink. "Even if he can't, I'm here."

"I guess this is something that you have to get used to when involved with a police chief or detective."

"Are we involved now?" Archie asked. "Something changed. I thought you were only friends because you don't need a man."

Chelsea leveled her gaze across the front seat to Archie. "You knew Cameron was a homicide detective and that they were working together. Why didn't you tell me?"

"Because I thought it would help you to come to terms with how you really feel about David."

Chelsea let out a deep breath. "Well, it worked, damn it."

"Loving someone is not a weakness." Archie unclicked her seatbelt and threw open the door. "Come on. Mac is driving back to Potomac, Maryland, to search Fields' house. David is working with Ben. How about a girls' night? We'll have chocolate mousse for dessert."

"Works for me." Chelsea opened the rear door to let Molly out. The shepherd took her spot at her mistress' side.

Archie came around the SUV and wrapped her arm around Chelsea's shoulders. "I am so glad you and David are working things out. It's like having a sister. I never had a sister."

"Neither have I."

The two women and the dog made their way up the steps and went through the front door.

As soon as they stepped inside, Archie sensed that something was off. Instead of running to greet her with his paws on her shoulders and a wet kiss on her face, Gnarly was sitting up on the living room sofa. Irving, Cameron's huge Maine

Coon cat, was sitting next to him. Both seemed to be sitting at attention. Their faces were emotionless.

Sensing that something was terribly wrong, Molly hid behind Chelsea instead of running to greet Gnarly.

"Something's not right here," Archie said in a low voice. "Gnarly, what did you do?"

Gnarly's head dropped. His ears fell back against the top of his head. Uttering a low whine, he dropped down onto the sofa.

Irving looked over at him and uttered a growl. As the cat's growl grew in volume, it seemed to take on the sound of a word: traitor.

Gnarly slinked off the sofa and crawled back behind a chair in the corner of the living room.

Chelsea searched the floor for a mess in addition to the one made by the burglar the night before. After all, they had both been inside all day. She could find nothing.

Suspicious, Archie hurried back into the kitchen. As soon as she entered, her scream filled the house. Its volume and tone was filled with fury like none that Chelsea had heard come from the mild-mannered editor.

When Chelsea rounded the corner to come into the kitchen, she was unable to express her disbelief in words. The refrigerator door rested open, and the food was spilled across the floor. Every cupboard door was open. Even the shelves up near the ceiling were empty of their food, which comingled with the food from the fridge on the floor. Out of Gnarly's reach, Irving had managed to somehow climb up to open the doors and make his way inside.

"I just cleaned all of this up this morning after that burglar trashed the place!" Archie wailed. "Augh! Gnarly! I'm going to kill you!"

"How did they do this?" Chelsea asked. "Maybe it wasn't them. Maybe another burglar broke in."

"No, it was them," Archie said. "They conspired and pulled off this heist together." She picked up the treat jar in which she kept Gnarly's treats. "Exhibit A. This was stashed in the cupboard. It was full yesterday. It is empty now."

As if on cue, they heard Gnarly throw up on the other side of the kitchen door.

"Ugh!" Archie whirled around. "Gnarly, I'm going to kill you—and that goes for your feline partner in crime, too."

"Listen, my client did not kill those women," Russ Burton told Ben and David after Nick was locked up in the holding cell in the basement of the police station.

"He's not under arrest for killing those women," Ben said.

"I heard you," Russ said. "He's under arrest for a publicity stunt he pulled three years ago. We both know what this is about. You're putting pressure on him to make him tell you what he knows."

"If he tells us what he knows, it may help us to be more sympathetic towards him in the obstruction of justice case," Ben said.

"If he didn't kill those women," David said, "then he knows who did. We want a name and the motive for doing it."

Russ stood up straight. He was a good couple of inches taller than David. His chest bulged against the front of his suit. "'Okay. I'll go talk to him in his cell and see what he says." He turned and went to the door leading down to the cells.

Bogie came out of his office. "Fields' alibi is a little less than airtight."

"How's that?" Ben asked.

"This Katelyn says she did hook up with Nick at the Wisp maybe around four o'clock. She's not sure. Definitely before five. However, according to Dora, Khloe could have been dead before then. She was killed less than an hour after having sex with Nick."

"Dora?" Ben asked.

"Doc," Bogie corrected himself.

"The last posting that Khloe made on her social media sites was at four o'clock," David said. "Her laptop was right there in the room. Nick could have killed her and done the hatchet job and then posted that on Khloe's Facebook page from her laptop right before leaving the house. The Everest home is only twenty minutes from the Wisp. So he would have been at the Wisp to hook up with Katelyn between four and five."

"Yeah," Bogie said, "but the dismemberment took time. With all those stab wounds, the killer would have been covered in blood. Doing it in less than an hour and being at a happy hour the next mountain over is cutting it close."

"I wish Doc could give us a closer timeframe for the murder," David said. "All we know is that Khloe was killed very shortly after she had sex with Nick." He shook his head. "I think he knows who did it, but I don't think he killed those women."

"Let's hope Burton can convince Nick to cooperate with us," Ben said.

"Maybe Mac and Cameron can find something in his house to persuade him that it would be in his best interest to do so," David said.

For the second time in twenty-four hours, Mac and Cameron were driving across the state of Maryland. This time, Cameron was driving her police cruiser with Mac in the passenger seat.

With a broad smile across his face, Mac disconnected his phone call from David. "They've got the search warrant."

"Yes," Cameron said. "We're getting very close. I can feel it."

"Nick's alibi checked out for Khloe's murder," he added, "but it's not necessarily airtight."

"Do you think he did it?"

"He definitely knows something," Mac mused. "I think he knows who did it, but he's protecting them. We need to go talk to Sheila McGrath, the widow who's keeping him."

"But first, we search Nick's house." She swung the cruiser around the end of the cul-de-sac and pulled into the driveway of the yellow house.

The neighbor and her children were outside building a snow fort. Seeing Cameron and Mac climbing out of the cruiser, Sandy waved across the yard at them. "My, you police are certainly busy here today."

"Now we're here to search the house," Cameron strolled across the snow-covered yard in the direction of the fort. She stopped when she saw a look of befuddlement fill Sandy's face.

"Again?"

On his way to the front door, Mac stopped when he heard her say that.

"We didn't search it before," Cameron said. "We only took Mr. Fields in for questioning. Now we have a warrant—"

"But the FBI was just here," Sandy said. "They were searching the house, too. They had FBI written across the back of their coats. They didn't tell me what they were looking for, but I think they found whatever it was because they all left about an hour ago."

"Cameron," Mac said, "get descriptions of these guys while I go look."

Inside, the house showed every sign of being searched. Drawers were pulled out and the contents dumped. Furniture was overturned and the cushions ripped open. Mac yanked out his phone to call David.

"Did you find anything?" David asked.

"Someone else was here first." Mac went into the kitchen. "They were posing as the FBI, and this place is thoroughly searched." A plastic bag with used duct tape rested on the counter. Remnants of cabinet varnish were attached to the sticky side of the tape. Mac bent over to peer at the underside of the top cabinet. "I think they found it. It must have been the tape."

"Nick had a copy of the tape and blackmailed the senator after Khloe was killed," David said.

"Now that they have the tape, he has no leverage to stay alive," Mac said. "They have to kill him to keep him from telling what he knows about the senator being a sexual predator."

Looking around for another place to search, Mac yanked open the freezer door and peered inside. It was filled with boxes of frozen dinners. A freezer bag was tucked in one of the shelves built into the door. It was filled with three items that resembled frozen fleshy tulips.

"Mac, are you still there?" David called to him.

"Give me a minute." Mac pulled out the bag and held it up. He peered through the frost and ice to distinguish what it was he was looking at. "David, do you know what a uterus looks like?"

In his corner office at the police station, David hung up the phone.

There were possibly three uteruses in Nick Fields' freezer. Does that make him our killer? His alibi isn't airtight. Maybe he's not the killer, but he's certainly involved. Maybe it's his hostile wife. In either case, Nick Fields is in trouble up to his pierced ears.

Mac knows what he's talking about. He's gone up against Senator Palazzi before. Yes, Palazzi would send his cleanup team to get rid of Nick, which was why he was safe as a baby in his holding cell.

Russ Burton's muscles flashed before his eyes. Not your average lawyer.

David's heartbeat kicked up until he could hear it in his ears. Urgency propelled him out of his chair behind his desk and out the door. "Where's Burton?" He yelled down to Tonya while galloping down the steps.

"Who?" she asked.

"Russ Burton. Fields' lawyer," David called back to her while on a dead run to the stairs leading down to the cells.

"He left forty-five minutes ago," Tonya answered, but the police chief was already out of earshot.

The stairs came out to the Spencer officer on duty to guard the prisoners in the cells. Otto the cat burglar had already been arraigned and transferred to Virginia to face charges on the burglary at the bank in Williamsburg. The only prisoner left to guard was Nick Fields.

"I want to see Fields." David moved over to the door between the guard and the cells.

"Sure, Chief." The officer unlocked the door and slid it aside for David to go on through. "What's wrong?"

Without answering, David entered the cellblock area. The small police station had only four cells. Nick Fields had been placed in the furthest cell on the right. "Fields, get up!" David called to him when he came within sight of the cell and saw the young man under his blanket on his cot. "I want to talk to you!"

Nick Fields did not move.

David's heartbeat was so loud that it seemed to pound against his eardrums. "Let me in there."

"Maybe it's a trick," the officer said. "He's pretending to be sick or—"

"Open it up!"

The officer unlocked the door, slid it open, and pulled out his gun just in case. David rushed in and over to the bed. He threw back the blanket. Nick Fields was on his stomach. With one movement, David grabbed his shoulder and yanked him over onto his back to reveal his dead eyes staring up at him.

So much for being safe as a baby in a holding cell.

CHAPTER FIFTEEN

Driving up the beltway to the exit for Sheila McGrath's home address, Cameron almost swerved into the next lane and collided with a van in her blind spot when David announced Nick Fields' death from the speaker on Mac's phone.

"How was he killed in his cell in your police station?" Mac asked.

"The only one who was in there with him was his so-called lawyer," David said.

"So-called?" Cameron repeated. "Then he's not a lawyer?"

"What's the cause of death?" Mac asked.

"Doc isn't here yet," David said. "But from what I can see, I think his neck was snapped. The killer must have placed him in the bed to give him time to get away before we noticed and realized this guy was really a hired gun sent to kill Nick for blackmailing the senator. Tonya went onto the Internet to look up Attorney Russell Burton with this law firm in Washington. The real Russell Burton is at least twenty years older than the guy who showed up here."

Mac and Cameron heard a movement in the background.

"Doc's here," David said. "I've got to go. Let's hope the state police forensics team finds something else inside that house to tell us what's going on. Tell me what you find out from Nick's sugar momma."

Before they could say good-bye, David disconnected the call.

"From what we know, she wasn't involved," Cameron said.

"If she has enough money to support Nick in the lifestyle to which he wished to become accustomed," Mac said, "who's to say she doesn't have enough juice to have him exterminated."

"True," Cameron said. "We're making a lot of assumptions in this case. I mean, do you have any evidence to prove what Khloe's big announcement was going to be?"

"She knew that Senator Palazzi was her birth father," Mac said. "We have a text she sent Bevis saying that she was his sister. How could she tell him that without proof?"

"DNA," Cameron said.

"But where did she get the first suspicion that she was—after her mother's death?" Mac asked. "On the tape, Khloe's mother said she had more than one copy. If anything happened to her, one would be made public. We know one copy went to her lawyer. She must have had the second copy somewhere in that house, and Khloe must have found it. Since she had been disowned, she decided to cash in her insurance policy with Daddy."

"Nick said he knew what she was going to announce," Cameron said. "Maybe Khloe gave the tape to him for safekeeping—"

Mac shook his head. "That house had been searched. I think Nick found out that she had been murdered and, before her body was discovered, went there to find the tape to use for his own gain."

184

"He certainly was an opportunist."

"We know that," Mac said. "Only an extreme opportunist would pretend to be gay for money and fame."

Seeing that Cameron was pulling into the parking lot next to a nursing home, Mac sat up in his seat. Cameron was equally curious.

"Did you put the right address in the GPS?" Mac asked her.

She was already double-checking the address. "This is it. Maybe Sheila works here."

They climbed out of the cruiser and made their way in through the main entrance. Mac tapped on the glass at the reception desk and presented his badge showing that he was a detective with the Spencer Police department. "Excuse me, we're looking for Sheila McGrath."

The receptionist stared at the badge and then at Mac. From him, her eyes fell on Cameron, who was also showing her police shield. "You're the police?"

"Yes," Mac replied. "Does Sheila McGrath work here?"

This question prompted the receptionist's eyes to grow even bigger. "I better get Mrs. Phillips, the administrator." She scurried out from behind the desk and trotted down the hallway.

"That was weird," Cameron said.

"Everything about this case is weird." A grin crossed his face. "I love it, don't you?"

"That's why I do what I do."

"Excuse me," a big-boned older woman who resembled a prison warden strode down the hall toward them. The receptionist was directly behind her. "I'm Mrs. Phillips, the nursing home administrator. I understand you're asking about Sheila McGrath." She folded her arms across her abundant bosom. "What is this about?"

Mac and Cameron showed their badges, which Mrs. Phillips took her time examining. When she saw that Cameron was with the Pennsylvania state police, her eyes narrowed. "What interest does the Pennsylvania police have in Mrs. McGrath?"

"We believe that she may have some information regarding the murders of three young women," Cameron said. "One in Pennsylvania, another recent murder in Spencer, Maryland, plus there was a murder twenty months ago in Los Angeles, California."

Mrs. Phillips' eyebrows furrowed. "You say a recent murder in…"

"Spencer, Maryland," Mac said. "It is very important that we speak to Mrs. McGrath. This doesn't mean that she's involved, but she may have—"

"I guarantee she's not involved," Mrs. Phillips said in a sharp tone.

"With all due respect," Cameron said, "how well do you know Mrs. McGrath? Do you really know what she does when she leaves here?"

The corners of Mrs. Phillips's mouth curled. For the first time during their conversation, she looked amused. "I think I'd better take you to Mrs. McGrath and let you ask her that yourself."

Without another word, she spun around on her heels and walked down the hallway at a pace so brisk that Mac and Cameron had to practically jog to keep up with her. They made two turns to go down corridors before the administrator pushed through a door to a resident's room and threw out her arm like a master of ceremony introducing the headline act. "Here is Sheila McGrath."

Mac and Cameron followed her into the room and stopped abruptly at the sight of a bed with the figure of a woman lying on it. An oxygen tube was up her nose, as well as a feeding tube and every other type of machine possible. The room was filled with the noises of beeps and hisses.

"Mrs. Sheila McGrath has been here for close to four years," Mrs. Phillips announced, "ever since she sustained massive brain injuries in the car accident that killed her husband. It would have been a blessing if she had died alongside him. She's been on life support ever since. So if you're thinking she killed three young women, you're sadly mistaken."

Mac and Cameron exchanged glances.

"Does Mrs. McGrath have any living relatives?" Mac asked. "Anyone who could be using her identity?"

"A woman with a bad attitude maybe," Cameron said, "and humongous breasts."

"Mrs. McGrath has no living relatives," Mrs. Phillips said.

"This is a private nursing home," Mac said. "It's expensive. Who's paying her bills?"

"Her estate." She turned to Cameron. "Her account is handled by her estate attorney, Teresa Winston. She's the senior partner at Winston and Associates in Rockville."

"A woman," Cameron hissed at Mac.

"Do you have her phone number?" When the administrator's expression betrayed disgust, Mac added, "It's apparent that someone has stolen Mrs. McGrath's identity and is possibly stealing from her estate. I think Ms. Winston would want to know about that as soon as possible."

With the same brisk pace, Mrs. Phillips took them back to her office and dug through the giant stack of files on her desk until she found the one she was looking for. Rather than give the number to Mac or Cameron, she dialed the number on her phone and asked for Teresa Winston. After a long pause during which she stared out the window and refused to make polite conversation, she greeted the lawyer. "We have a couple of detectives here asking about Sheila McGrath. They seem to think some killer has stolen her identity. Now I told them that you're the most reputable lawyer in the area, but they claim to have some evidence to say otherwise." She thrust the phone out to Mac. "Ms. Winston wants to talk to you."

With a deep sigh, Mac took the phone.

"This is Teresa Winston," the gruff voice that sounded more like a man than a woman said from the other end of the phone line. "Who is this?"

"Mac Faraday," he replied.

There was silence from the other end of the line. "Faraday? As in...are you the same Mac Faraday—"

"That would be me."

The impatience in Ms. Winston's tone disappeared. "What evidence would you have to suggest that Sheila McGrath's identity has been stolen?"

"Well," Mac drawled, "considering her current condition, I guess she would have no need for a luxury home in Potomac, Maryland, or to purchase a red jaguar and a black Ferrari, both registered to her. Both of those purchases have been made in the last eighteen months. We also have evidence of her taking numerous trips during the last three years."

"Don't forget the lip implants," Cameron said in a harsh whisper.

"This wasn't done by my firm," the lawyer said. "You know how rampant identity theft is. It had to have been stolen by the Chinese who somehow got access to her name and social security number, or maybe one of the employees at the nursing home—"

"Now wait here, Ms. Winston," Mrs. Phillips said.

Mac held up his hand to shush the administrator. "So you haven't seen any large sums of money suddenly disappear from her account, or weird bills come—?"

"Like for liposuction?" Cameron asked. "Why would a woman in a coma need liposuction?"

"I'm sure the attorney handling her estate would have brought any irregularities in her account to my attention," the lawyer said.

"Do you mean you're not personally handling Mrs. McGrath's finances?" Mac asked.

"I am a senior partner," she answered. "We're talking about a monthly routine of paying bills, handling investments— I'm more concerned with bigger cases than this. So I handed it off to one of my junior partners—a very capable young attorney. Bevis Palazzi. His father is Harry Palazzi, the senator. Why wouldn't I trust him?"

Cameron saw Mac staring straight ahead with a glazed look in his eyes when they climbed back into her cruiser. "I know that look," she said. "Josh gets the same look when he gets to a certain point in his cases."

Mac was still staring.

"It goes without saying," she went on, "that Teresa Winston is going to go into Bevis' office and demand to see Sheila McGrath's account. Now, she could do something about it and nail Bevis, or she could cover it up. What do you think she'll do?"

"In either case, Bevis will know we're on to him and cover it up before we can say 'embezzler,'" Mac said. "Who stole Sheila McGrath's identity to play house with Nick Fields?"

"I still think it's Teresa Winston," Cameron said. "We only have her word that she knew nothing about it. As the senior partner, she had access to everything, plus the power to make Bevis keep quiet about it. He probably even demanded a percentage for his silence."

"Tell me again what that neighbor said about Nick's wife," Mac said.

"Nastier than a junkyard dog," Cameron said. "Somehow Sandy offended her from the get go. She was jealous—like she was afraid of the lady stealing Nick from her."

"She hated her."

"According to Sandy, it was like for no reason." She asked him, "What are you thinking?"

Mac strapped on his seat belt. "Take me back there. I want to talk to her myself." He took his cell phone out of its case.

"She doesn't know her name." Cameron started the car engine.

"That's okay. She can still tell us who she is." Mac pressed the button to call Archie.

Chapter Sixteen

"You're right," Dr. Washington told David, "his neck was snapped." Kneeling next to Nick Fields' body stretched across the bed in the holding cell, she pointed to the bruising around the back of his neck. "Whoever did it knew exactly what he was doing. We have bruising on the jaw where the killer grabbed it in his hand and jerked his head all the way around until he snapped it like a twig. Happened so fast, Fields probably didn't know what hit him."

"They teach that in the military." Bogie peered at the wound from over her shoulder.

The officer who had been guarding the cells looked like he was going to be sick. "Chief, I am so sorry," he said for the dozenth time.

"It's not your fault, Brewster." David patted the officer on the shoulder.

"Hon, can you hand me my camera from my bag over there?"

David jerked around to watch Bogie reaching into the medical examiner's bag to take out her camera. He caught the smile Bogie gave her when her hand touched his when she took it. *Interesting. Way to go, big guy.*

"I didn't hear a sound," Brewster recalled. "Not a peep. You'd think—"

"Cause he was a pro." Unable to look at Nick's dead body—in his jail cell—anymore, David turned around. "I need air."

He was up the stairs and in the squad room before Bogie caught up with him. He had to grab him by the arm to get his attention. "You okay?"

"No." Fighting to keep from punching the wall, David paced in place. "This happened in our house, during our watch. Palazzi is behind this—you know that. Fields had gotten his hands on Khloe's copy of that recording and was blackmailing him—"

"How did Palazzi know we picked Fields up?" Bogie asked. "Bevis was here when you brought in Fields, but he was in the interrogation room. He never saw him, and no one said a peep to him."

"Somehow the senator found out." David shook his head. "Fields' phone call. When we picked up Fields he called his lawyer—"

"Who ended up being a killer," Bogie said.

"Fields' phone is with his personal effects," David said. "Let's check the call log to see exactly who he called."

The state forensics team was clearing out when Mac and Cameron arrived back at Nick Fields' house.

"Find anything else?" Mac stepped over to the van to ask the chief investigator.

"We did identify those frozen body parts as women's uteruses," he responded.

Mac rubbed his hands together to warm them up. The sun had set and the temperature was down below freezing. "DNA should match them up with our three victims, which will connect them to someone in this house."

"We did find something else that might help you," the officer said. "When we were lifting the Ferrari onto the tow truck to take down to the lab to search, we found a GPS tracker clipped inside the wheel well. Based on the amount of mud, we think it's been there a while."

"Someone was tracking Nick Fields," Mac said. "That was his car, or rather, the car he drove. Is there some way to trace the GPS?"

"We can trace the serial number to the store where it was bought and possibly match it up with a receipt if it was purchased with a credit card."

Doubting that anyone connected to covering up for the senator would be careless enough to use a credit card for the tracing device, Mac jogged up the walk to the house next door where Cameron was already explaining their return visit to Sandy and her husband.

"I tell you," Sandy said while shaking Mac's hand, "I've seen more police today than I have in my whole life." Impressed by her sudden importance, she left her kitchen to be cleaned up later and invited Cameron and Mac into their living room.

"I always did get a weird feeling about that couple." Her husband sat next to her on the loveseat. "That wife would launch into Sandy, but never when I was around to defend her. Classic sign of a bully, if you ask me."

"We're concerned about her extreme jealousy," Cameron said.

"Like that maybe she would come after me." Sandy clutched her husband's hand.

"Right now," Mac said, "we want to find her. Now you gave a description of her to Detective Gates here. I had an artist come up with a composite picture of her." He brought up the picture on his smart phone and handed it to Sandy. "Is this the woman that you saw living next door?"

Sandy only had to look at it for a second before she nodded her head. After showing it to her husband, he confirmed her identification. "Yes, that's her." She handed the phone back to Mac. "Do you know her name?"

Mac showed the picture to Cameron. "We do now."

Cameron waited until they were outside walking to her cruiser before she asked. "Who is that in that picture you showed her?"

"Bevis Palazzi wearing a wig." Mac climbed into the cruiser. "I asked Archie to do a trick with Photoshop."

Cameron fought to regain her voice before climbing into the driver's seat. "Are you serious? You mean he's—how did you know?"

"The first clue was his plucked eyebrows," Mac said. "David tried explaining that it's not unusual for men in important positions to have their eyebrows cleaned up—"

"Josh doesn't pluck his eyebrows."

"Bevis goes beyond cleaning up," Mac said. "He plucks his eyebrows so that they look like a woman's. Then, while Ben and David were questioning him, he kept going back to Archie provoking him. He couldn't let that go."

"Because he hates women," Cameron said.

"Probably learned from his father," Mac said. "Toss that in with a liberal dosage of jealousy—" He sat up straight in his seat. "I bet you I know when Khloe signed her death warrant."

"When?"

"One of my employees at the Spencer Inn used to be friends with Khloe," Mac said. "She stayed friends with

Khloe's mother. When Khloe came back to Spencer, she started going to the inn and running up charges on her dead mother's account. Lily called her on it, and Khloe was told that she needed to pay cash or put it on a credit card—not in her mother's name. Well, Khloe was with Nick at the time, and he whipped out a card with the name of Sheila—probably McGrath—on it. Not trusting them, the inn ran a check on the card and found that it was good—at which point the two went to town on it."

"And since Bevis was in charge of Sheila McGrath's estate," Cameron said, "those bills came to him—so he could see that Nick was fooling around with someone else—that someone else being a woman."

"I'm willing to bet that was when the GPS was attached to Nick's car, so that Bevis could keep tabs on him." Mac sat back in his seat. "That gives Bevis two motives to kill Khloe. To protect his father's reputation, on whose shirttails he plans to ride into political office, and jealousy, because Khloe was sleeping with his man. As much as he hates women, I think killing Khloe came easy for him."

Cameron stopped with her hands on the keys in the ignition and frowned.

Seeing that she wasn't turning on the cruiser for them to leave, Mac asked, "What's wrong?"

"We've connected Bevis to Nick, which connects him to Khloe and Tiffany Blanchard," she said. "But we can't prove any connection between Bevis and Amber Houston, my case."

"When you were questioning Nick, he said that he was seeing both Amber and Khloe at the same time," Mac said. "Bevis was a theater groupie, hanging out with Khloe and her theater friends. He had to have met Nick through her during that time period."

"Had to have met," she repeated. "A defense attorney can turn that into reasonable doubt in a jiffy, Mac. Bevis could have met Nick for the first time when he was visiting Khloe in Hollywood. We need to know when Bevis first meet Nick and became obsessed with him."

He was already listening to the ring on the other end of the line on his cell phone.

"Who are you calling?" she asked.

"I'm going to get a stronger connection for us," Mac told her before turning his attention to the voice that answered the phone. "Hello, Lily. It's Mac Faraday."

"Mr. Faraday, how are you?" There was a note of fear in Lily Carter's voice.

Mac recalled that the last time Khloe's ex-best-friend had seen him, he had Senator Palazzi by the front of his shirt. "Lily, I don't have a lot of time to talk about this. You do know that Senator Harry Palazzi had raped Khloe's mother. He was her father."

Silence came from the other end of the line before Lily replied in a low voice, "Yes. My mother had told me. She and Florence were best friends. Khloe never knew, at least while her mother was alive. Florence really freaked when Khloe and Bevis started hanging out together, not that Khloe slept with him or anything like that. But I guess that thought crossed her mind."

"I suspected you knew the truth about why Florence reacted the way she did when Khloe lied about being abducted," Mac said. "Now, Lily, this is important. Khloe's twenty-first birthday. According to something she had said on her show—"

"I never watched her stupid show." Judging by the annoyance in her tone, Lily was insulted by the suggestion that she would have followed Khloe's career on television.

"That's okay," Mac said. "On her show, Khloe said that she had met Nick Fields, that friend that she brought to the inn, when he was singing in a rock band at a club that she and her friends went to on her twenty-first birthday. Were you there that night?"

Again, there was a moment of silence from the other end of the line before Lily said, "Yes, I was there." Excitement came to her voice. "I didn't remember him because he didn't strike me as being that great, but Khloe was really into him and swore that she was going to sleep with him. I remember us making a bet. A hundred dollars on whether or not she could seduce him. I lost."

Mac grinned at Cameron while asking Lily, "Was Bevis Palazzi with you that night?"

"Yes, as a matter of fact he was," she answered with a laugh. "Khloe invited him because she knew he'd pick up the tab, which he did. He paid for everything."

"Did he take any special notice of Nick Fields?"

"Well," Lily said with a drawl, "since you mention it, Bevis kept talking about how talented the band was. He even predicted that the lead singer, with the right financial backing, could be as big as David Bowie." Her voice sped up as the memory came racing back. "I remember now. Bevis was going on and on about how much money you can make by promoting rock singers and by the end of the evening, he said he was going to back this lead singer. After that show, Bevis went back stage with Khloe to meet him. Was that the same guy that Khloe had brought to the inn? Did he kill her?"

Cameron's and Mac's eyes met.

Having confirmed a connection between Bevis and Nick Fields before Amber Houston's murder, a smile crept to Cameron's lips as she turned on the cruiser to go find their killer.

"Hey, Chief..." Tonya led Archie and Chelsea into the squad room. She stepped into the doorway to Bogie's office where David and the deputy chief were examining Nick's phone. "You've got visitors bearing big boxes of food for everyone. Should I send them away?"

The mention of food reminded David that he hadn't eaten lunch and that it was closing in on ten o'clock at night. Without answering, he stepped into the squad room where Chelsea and Archie were emptying their packages.

Gnarly jumped up onto the sofa to make himself at home while Molly sat next to her mistress. In spite of the smell of food, Molly showed no interest in getting anything. However, Gnarly held his head high and sniffed at everything. Both women had big boxes with take-out containers filled with dinners from the Spencer Inn.

"When Chef Iman heard that all of you were working late, he insisted on sending dinners from the Spencer Inn," Chelsea said, "on the house."

Archie was glimpsing inside the containers to see what each held. "We have steaks, pork chops, and chicken. Iman went through his mental inventory of what each of you usually order and tried to match the meals up." Seeing a chicken dinner, she turned to hand it to Tonya. "Chicken à la Spencer."

Chelsea handed David a box. "Rack of lamb with a loaded baked potato." She reached up to kiss him when he took it. "Don't forget your salad." She pointed to another box containing tossed salads. "And we have fresh rolls, too. They put them in hot out of the oven."

"I love this job." Tonya cut into her chicken dinner at her desk.

"Doc, I believe we have a salmon dinner with your name on it," Archie said.

"How did Iman know I was here?" the medical examiner asked.

"We told him that there was a dead body in the building," Archie replied.

Doc Washington pulled a chair over to Bogie's desk in his office to eat next to him. When he saw her move in, Bogie sat up straight and peered out the door to make sure no one noticed her in his office, which Archie and Tonya had.

The delicious food took their minds off the brutal murder in the cells directly beneath their feet. Even Brewster, the officer who was responsible for Nick Fields, was enjoying his pork chops with a brown sauce and rice pilaf.

"Well," Chelsea asked after they were all settled down, "do you know who your killer is?"

"Fields' lawyer," David said. "But he was working for someone. We need to find him and connect him to whoever hired him. He used the name of a real lawyer to get in here." He looked across the squad room to where Archie was breaking a roll into bite-sized pieces and feeding it to Gnarly. "Archie, can you access your face recognition software to get a name for this guy? I'm almost certain he's got a military background. He should be in the database."

"I can get to it from Bogie's desktop." After giving Gnarly the rest of the roll, she stood up from where she was sitting next to him on the sofa. "But I do need his picture."

Hearing that she was going to need his computer, Bogie picked up his plate and moved from his desk. "We scoured through our security pictures. He was pretty camera savvy, but we managed to get one of him getting out of his car in the parking lot. We also got the license plate number." Bogie and Doc moved out of his office to allow Archie to go to work at his desk.

"The car ended up being a rental," Tonya said. "And the name used was Russell Burton, the phony name he used when he showed up here."

"But first," David said to Archie, "I need you to hack into the cell phone records for Bevis Palazzi's account."

"That's illegal," Chelsea said. "You need a warrant to go hacking into people's phone records."

"Nick Fields is dead," David told her. "We don't need a warrant to look at his cell phone that was left in our possession. The call record shows us that he called Bevis Palazzi."

"I remember him getting a phone call," Archie recalled, "while he was in the interrogation room before Bogie went in. He was really mad when he got that call. He said not to say anything—"

"Standard lawyer line," David said. "Nick told us that he was calling his lawyer. That lawyer must have been Bevis."

"And Bevis is a lawyer," Bogie said. "So why didn't he stick around to defend Nick Fields?"

"Because he wanted him dead instead," David said. "He must have been covering his own butt. After all, he's a suspect in Khloe's murder."

"Are you thinking he called the hit man?" Archie asked. "What's his motive for wanting Nick dead?"

"Most likely to cover up their relationship," Mac said as he came in to overhear the end of their conversation. "Bevis and Nick Fields appear to have been pretty tight."

"Tighter than we ever suspected." Cameron came in behind him. "Nick's sugar momma is Bevis. Food!" Spotting the box of food, she dug through the containers to select a dinner. "I'm starved."

"Bevis?" David said. "Nick's sugar momma? Are you sure?"

"He's the lawyer handling Sheila McGrath's account," Cameron said. "Sheila has been in a coma for the last four years. It looks like Bevis stole her identity, took trips and bought cars and a house and set Nick up to play hubby to

Bevis in a dress, wig, and humungous fake boobs." She showed a roasted chicken dinner to Chelsea. "Can I have this?"

"Help yourself." Chelsea turned to her when the detective sat down at the desk across from her. "That's just totally bizarre."

"Bizarre, but true." Cameron cut into her baked potato. "The neighbor ID'd Bevis in a wig. So we think Bevis paid Nick well to play house with him, but then when he found Nick cheating, he'd pitch a bitch fit and kill the women in a fit of jealousy—then he'd steal their uteruses since he didn't have one of his own." Searching, she looked around. "Is there any sour cream left?"

"Three uteruses were found in the freezer. Bevis has killed at least three women." Mac handed Cameron a sour cream container from out of the box. "Lily Carter confirmed that Bevis was with them the same night that Khloe met Nick Fields."

"At which time he was dating Amber Houston," Cameron said while opening the container of sour cream. "Bevis killed her to get her out of the way to make room for him. However, it didn't work. Nick took off for Hollywood with Khloe instead."

Mac took up the story. "Khloe and Nick kept their sexual relationship a secret because Nick was pretending to be gay. For some reason, he thought he'd go further if he was a homosexual. Bevis must have bought Nick's lie and didn't realize Khloe and Nick's friendship had benefits that included sex until Nick and Khloe went on a spending spree at the Spencer Inn on Sheila McGrath's credit card. That's why Bevis didn't kill her until just recently."

"Sheila McGrath's finance records show a lot of trips out to the West Coast," Cameron said. "Must have been Bevis chasing after Nick, under the pretense of visiting his friend

Khloe. He killed every woman who got in his way—Amber Houston, Tiffany Blanchard, and Khloe Everest."

"Actually, he killed four women." Doc Washington wiped her mouth with her napkin. "If Bevis killed Khloe Everest, then I believe he also killed Dee Blakeley, which would make it four women."

The corner of Mac's lips kicked up. "You did your comparison?"

She nodded her head. "And to be sure, I sent the reports to a forensics expert friend of mine in New York. He confirmed it. While there are differences, like Dee Blakeley wasn't butchered the way the other women were, there are a number of similarities. All four women were first stabbed in the small of the back, and their spinal columns were severed, which paralyzed them. Then, the killer rolled them over onto their backs and sat on them. There were bruises on the hips that are consistent with great weight resting on them and him pressing his thighs against their sides and ribs to hold them in place. Then, the rest of the stab wounds were in the chest and stomach. The angles of the stab wounds are consistent with him sitting on them and thrusting straight up and down, not at an angle." She concluded, "That part of the M.O. is the same in all four cases."

"We need to pick up Bevis for these murders," Mac said to David.

"I agree," David said, "but the problem is that a United States Senator is claiming to be his alibi for Khloe's murder."

"Nick had an alibi for her murder, too," Cameron said.

"It's not as solid," David said.

"Or as impressive," Cameron noted with an arched eyebrow. "His alibi isn't a US senator."

"If Doc is correct in that whoever killed these three women also killed Dee Blakeley, then that eliminates Nick

Fields," Mac said. "He was only about twelve or so when Dee Blakeley was murdered."

"Plus, he was living in a small town in Pennsylvania," Bogie said.

"We have the uterus in the freezer that was in the house that Bevis had purchased with stolen money from a woman in a coma," Mac said. "Once DNA matches them to the three women—"

"Wasn't Nick living there, too?" Chelsea asked. "Sounds to me like Bevis has a case for an easy dismissal. He's going to be saying it was Nick that killed the last three victims to keep them quiet about him stepping out on Bevis, who was keeping him in a lavish lifestyle in exchange for sex, which is warped and perverted."

"Hey," Cameron said, "women have been playing house for money in exchange for sex for a long time."

"We're talking about a straight man having a homosexual relationship in exchange for money," Chelsea said.

"I didn't say it wasn't perverted," Cameron said. "I'm simply saying the concept is not new."

"Due to the inconsistencies of the M.O.s in those three murders with Dee Blakeley's, Bevis' lawyer will put reasonable doubt in the minds of the jurors," Chelsea said.

"With Nick dead," David said, "he can't dispute Bevis' defense, nor can he testify against him."

"Who's to say Bevis wasn't home with his daddy the senator at the time of Khloe's murder?" Mac asked with sarcasm.

"How much do you want to bet Bevis' boss will cover up the identity theft and embezzlement?" Cameron said. "Give him four years, and Bevis will be running for president. I can see it now. Bevis the Butthead for President."

"If the DNA from the uteruses connects with the three victims," Doc said, "then we should have enough to arrest Bevis."

"But not convict." Disgusted, Mac plopped down on the chair next to the desk David was sitting at. "Senator Palazzi's lawyer and cleanup team will somehow manage to steal them like he did the tape."

His appetite gone, David placed the lid over his plate. "I'm really ready for a break in this case."

"I've got one for you." Archie came into the squad room from where she had been working on Bogie's desktop computer. "We got a hit through the face recognition program. Lincoln Northrop. You're right, David. He was in the army—disciplinary discharge. The military tried to nail him for the murder of his CO but couldn't get enough evidence for a conviction. He ended up cutting a deal for a dishonorable discharge."

"How did you get all that?" Chelsea asked her.

"I have my sources." Archie shrugged her shoulders.

"Did you hack—?"

"I know where he is," Archie interrupted her to hand a slip of paper to Mac. "I found where the FBI has been looking for him. He's suspected in four murders—as a hired gun. A credit card with one of his aliases was used to check into a hotel off Route 70 in Washington, PA, this evening."

"PA! My jurisdiction!" Cameron slapped the lid shut on her dinner and stood up. "We're going to nail ourselves a hired gun, men! Let's roll!"

CHAPTER SEVENTEEN

Lincoln Northrop was checked in a roadside motel in Washington, Pennsylvania. With a few phone calls to her department in the Pennsylvania State Police, homicide detective Cameron Gates managed to have six state police troopers and three cruisers surrounding and watching the hotel by the time they arrived. Cameron had two Spencer police cruisers following her during the ninety-minute drive west and then north up to Pennsylvania. David and Mac were in one, with Bogie and Officer Brewster following in the deputy chief's cruiser.

Just on the off chance a canine was needed, David had loaded Gnarly into the back seat of the cruiser.

With the time approaching midnight, David had assumed the silence in his cruiser was due to exhaustion after an exceedingly long day. The only sound in the cruiser was Gnarly's snoring in the back seat. Afraid he would fall asleep at the wheel, David broke the silence. "You need to take Gnarly to a sleep clinic for his sleep apnea."

"Sometimes I feel like putting Archie's mask on him," Mac replied.

"Archie?"

"Forget I said that." Mac realized he had broken a confidence.

"She has sleep apnea?"

"A lot of people have it," Mac said.

"I never would have guessed."

"She looks like Hannibal Lector with her mask on," Mac said with a smile.

With a loud snort, Gnarly sat up and looked around. Seeming to remember where he was, he dropped back down and resumed snoring.

"It's a dog's life," David said.

Mac glanced over his shoulder back at Gnarly, who was lying on his back with his legs spread out in four directions and his head tilted back. "Gnarly needs to learn how to relax."

He turned back to look out the front windshield. The caravan of cruisers was turning onto the expressway that went around Morgantown, West Virginia. Even though the hotel Lincoln Northrop was hiding out at was only ninety miles away, they were going across three states to get him.

"We need to get him alive," Mac said.

"I always try to get them alive," David replied.

"Think about it," Mac continued. "Northrop is three removed from those murdered. Northrop was probably hired by Cooper, who works for Brooks, who's Senator Palazzi's lawyer. Alive, he can turn on Cooper. Knowing Cooper, he'd turn on Brooks in a heartbeat, which would force him to turn on the senator. If we can't get Northrop alive—"

"Northrop is a hired gun," David said. "He won't give up without a fight, I can tell you that right now."

"We need to try."

"I always try," David said. "That I can control. I can't always control what happens at the other end."

They followed Cameron's cruiser off an exit from Route 70 and into the heart of downtown Washington, a small town that had seen the worst of hard economic times. They pulled in off a side street before a two story-motel that contained approximately twelve rooms, six on each floor. Two Pennsylvania State Police cruisers were tucked in the alley beside a convenience store next to the motel. A car junkyard was on the other side of a chain link fence behind the store and motel. Six state troopers got out of their cars to meet Cameron when she climbed out of her cruiser.

David pulled in to park across from her cruiser on the other side of the alley.

"He's in the third room from the right on the second floor," one of the troopers told them. "He took a woman up there about a half an hour ago. She's a known prostitute. He must have picked her up in the bar across the street." Seeing the gold police shield on David's chest, he asked him, "Do you have a warrant to pick him up?"

"Right here." David patted his chest.

"Then let's do this." Cameron was already putting on her bulletproof vest. Bogie and Officer Brewster had the back of the deputy chief's cruiser open and were putting on their equipment. Mac opened up the back door of David's cruiser to let the German shepherd out.

"Gnarly, come," David called out to him after opening up the rear compartment of his cruiser.

When Gnarly came to him, David took an oddly shaped vest out of the back and knelt down next to the German shepherd.

"Is that a dog vest?" Mac asked.

"A bulletproof dog vest," David said. "After the last few times, I decided it was worth the investment."

"He's not an official K-9." To Mac's surprise, Gnarly stood still while David strapped the vest on across his back and secured it around his midsection. The vest was black with "Spencer Police" stenciled across the side straps in gold bold block letters. The vest even had a section that covered his chest and back across his hips.

"He still needs to be protected," David replied. "Archie said he can't come with us anymore unless he wears this."

"Do you have a badge in that box, too?"

With a wide grin, David took a police badge, still wrapped in plastic, out of the box and unwrapped it. The badge number was K-9-1 "Consider him your partner." He clipped the badge onto the vest.

Mac and Gnarly exchanged glances. "First partner I ever had who drank out of the toilet."

"Admit it, the three of us work well together." David thrust a ballistic vest toward Mac. "Suit up."

"Aren't you going to put it on me with all the love and tenderness that you just gave Gnarly?" Mac asked.

David shook his fist in Mac's face. "Here's your love and tenderness." With a chuckle, he took off his jacket to put his own vest on.

Mac took off his winter jacket and slipped his arm into the vest. At his feet, Gnarly sat with his chest thrust out. Before him, he could see Gnarly taking on a whole different attitude—from kleptomaniac German shepherd to a serious K-9 going on duty. He had seen it happen before. Gnarly seemed to sense serious situations and knew when to stop goofing off. The vest amplified it. Staring up at Mac, Gnarly was waiting for his partner to take the lead.

"Be careful out there," Mac told him. "This guy is a professional killer."

His eyes trained up at Mac's, Gnarly licked his chops.

Mac picked up an assault rifle and checked the cartridge.

"Let's get him, partner." With a pat of his hand on his thigh, Gnarly fell in beside him to join David over at Cameron's cruiser, where the officers from the Pennsylvania State Police and the Spencer Police were meeting. Two Washington County Sheriff Deputies had joined them to be kept in the loop.

David let Cameron take the lead since Northrop was in her territory and she was familiar with the layout. "Since he's got a woman with him, he won't be looking out for us," she said. "I suggest we move as fast as possible. He'll be at a disadvantage if we catch him with his pants down."

They split up to take the two sets of stairs leading up to the second floor. With Gnarly, Mac hung back behind Bogie. Directly behind Detective Cameron Gates, David went up the opposite set of stairs. Eight armed officers approached the door from both sides. Since the room was on the second floor with no balcony and a frosted bathroom window that looked out on the auto junkyard behind the motel, they concentrated on capturing him through the front door.

After insuring everyone was ready to move, Cameron banged on the door. "Lincoln Northrop, this is Pennsylvania State Police with Police Chief David O'Callaghan from the Spencer police department. We have a warrant to take you back to Spencer, Maryland, for questioning in the murder of Nicholas Fields. Open up."

A woman uttered a high-pitched scream from inside.

"Northrop, open up now!" Cameron yelled. "You have until the count of three, and then we're coming in after you. One ... Two—"

Before she could count off three, a gunshot blast blew a hole through the door.

"That door's coming out of your budget," Cameron told David.

As a single unit, Cameron, David and the officers barged inside to find a screaming naked woman hopping up and down on the bed.

"Where is he?" Cameron demanded to know.

Too hysterical to form words, she pointed to the bathroom. Bogie kicked in the door and they charged inside. Mac and Gnarly ran into the room to meet David and Cameron running out of the bathroom.

"He went out the bathroom window," Cameron said while running past. "He jumped into a dumpster that's under the window. He's making a run for it. How good is Gnarly at tracking?"

Spotting a shirt on the floor, Mac picked it up and showed it to Gnarly. "Let's go find him."

Gnarly was still getting the scent when Cameron took a call on her radio and reported. "He's in the junkyard."

Keeping the shirt for his scent, Mac took Gnarly out of the motel room and ran around to the back.

In his radio earbud, Mac could hear David giving orders to the officers while they reported sightings of the hired gun. Without the benefit of the radio, having only his nose to depend on, Gnarly broke into a run as soon as they stepped through the gate. "Gnarly's got a scent," Mac reported into his radio while following Gnarly's barking as best he could. In the middle of the night, and with only the benefit of his LED light, he was unable to keep track of where Gnarly had taken off to. The black and tan German shepherd had instantly disappeared into the darkness among the piles of crushed cars piled up like Leggo pieces and others compressed into cubes, with still others waiting to be demolished.

Not wanting to give away his position to the professional killer, Mac tried to call out to Gnarly in a low voice while listening for the dog and to the voices on the radio.

"Anybody see him?" David asked after a long moment of silence on the radio.

The answers were negative.

"Mac, how about Gnarly?" David asked in a low tone. "Does he still have a scent?"

Not hearing or seeing Gnarly anywhere, Mac replied, "I think he lost it. He'd be barking if he still had it."

"He's got—" David broke off with a cry of pain followed by a curse.

"David!" Mac cried out. His call was mixed with others from Cameron and the other officers searching.

"Where is he?" Bogie yelled is a hoarse voice.

Off the radio, Mac could hear a fight around a stack of flattened trucks. He ran around the column to find David and Lincoln Northrop wrestling on the ground. David was fighting to pin the man, who was naked from the waist up, while keeping him from grabbing his baton or other equipment on his belt.

"Hold it right there!" Mac shouted while aiming his rifle at them. "Police! You're under arrest!"

When David jerked around to see who had come to his aid, Northrop took advantage of his dropped guard to kick David's legs out from under him. As quickly as David went down, Northrop drew a knife from a sheaf he had on his ankle. In the swift movement of a trained killer, he grabbed the police chief, who was struggling to keep away from the knife, pulled him to his feet, grabbed hold of him around his shoulders, and pressed the point of the knife to David's throat.

"I don't think so!" Northrop said.

"There's no way out." Mac kept his rifle aimed at him.

"Bad news for your chief," Northrop said in a low voice. "If I don't get out of here, neither will he."

Mac could sense rather than see Bogie, Cameron, and the rest of the officers arrive. Some broke off to take positions surrounding their captive. While taking stock of the situation, Mac spotted David's rifle lying on the ground a few feet away. Northrop must have knocked it out of his hands when he jumped him.

Seeing them closing in, the killer yanked back David's head to press the blade more tightly against his throat, right against his jugular. All he had to do was slice it open and David would be dead in a matter of minutes.

"Tell them to back off," Northrop ordered David.

"I can't do that," David said through clenched teeth.

"Do it!" He pressed the blade against his neck. "I swear! I'll kill you now!"

When Mac saw David flinch, he yelled, "Wait!"

"Shoot him, Mac!" David ordered.

"Shut up!" Northrop shouted into his ear.

"No deal!" David said. "Mac, kill him!"

In the dark corner around the column of cars off to his side, Mac could see Bogie, hiding behind a truck, taking aim with his rifle.

"I'm not fooling around," Northrop said. "If I don't walk out of here, neither will he."

Bogie caught Mac's eye.

"I've got the shot," Mac heard Bogie say.

Mac could see that David had heard him through his earbud.

"Drop the knife, Northrop," Mac said, "or this won't end well."

Northrop chuckled, "You order everyone to drop their guns and let me walk out of here, or he's going to be bleeding all over his white shirt."

David said, "Kill him. Kill him now."

"No!" Mac yelled.

"I told you to shut up!" Northrop jerked David back several feet.

"Damn!" With a shake of his head and a frown, Bogie fought to regain his shot.

"You got until the count of three for all of you to back off!" Northrop shouted while glancing around at the officers who had taken position around them. "I'm going to start cutting. One…"

He pressed the knife against David's throat again. David closed his eyes while fighting to pull Northrop's arm down from where he had the blade pressed against his throat.

Mac saw a movement up at the top of the pile of cars. He was at least twelve feet up.

How did he get up there?

He crouched down low in Northrop's blind spot.

"Two!" Northrop yelled.

Gnarly sprang.

His front paws landed on both of Northrop's shoulders. A hundred pounds of fur and teeth slammed onto his shoulders and back while he dug his teeth into the back of the killer's head.

David yanked the knife down and away to free himself while Northrop dropped to the ground. After rolling away from the man intent on killing him, he grabbed his rifle and, in one smooth action, sprang back up onto his knees and fired at Lincoln Northrop, who was determined to not go out alone. He had his arm up in mid-air to strike at the dog who had taken him down.

David shot off two rounds through Northrop's back and chest. From a few feet away, they blew holes right through him.

Mac ran up to roll Lincoln Northrop over. There was no hope of him living. "Damn!" Mac cursed at the loss of the connection back to Senator Palazzi.

David was still climbing up to his feet.

"Are you okay?" Mac heard Cameron ask David.

"Yeah." David's answer held a note of disgust in it. Mac assumed he was appalled about getting ambushed by Lincoln Northrop and taken hostage.

While Cameron went to check on Gnarly, who was being praised by the various officers for his deed, David moved on to Mac. Instead of a hug, he greeted Mac with a punch to the shoulder. "Why did you contradict my order for Bogie to take the shot?"

"I was going to take the shot, David," Bogie said. "I had it, but then I lost it when Northrop pulled you back."

"Because Mac started negotiating after I gave the order for you to shoot," David said before turning his glare back to Mac.

"Because Northrop was using you for a shield," Mac said. "If Bogie had shot him, he would have taken you out, too. Gnarly had a better chance of saving you without the risk of you getting shot."

"I had a head shot, Mac," Bogie said in a gentler tone. "I could have gotten Northrop without hurting David. He would have gotten covered with his brains, but the chief would have been fine."

"You don't know that," Mac said.

"There's always a risk," Bogie said, "but David made the call, and I would have taken the shot if I hadn't lost it."

"Because you stepped in where you didn't belong, Mac," David said.

"Hey, I may have made a mistake," Mac said. "I didn't know Bogie had a head shot—"

"It isn't your job to know!" David was yelling. "You wanted Northrop alive to get Palazzi, and you were willing to risk my life to make it happen."

"That's not true," Mac said. "I would never have put you in danger to get a collar. You know that."

"I'm the chief of police," David said, "You're not." He poked him in the chest to make his point. "You have a tendency to forget that, Mac. I'm in charge, and when I give an order, I expect it to be carried out without question. You got that?"

Not wanting to continue the argument that then had the attention of everyone around them, including Bogie and Cameron, Mac gritted his teeth. As much as he wanted to argue, he didn't like doing it in public. He felt like a child being chewed out by his teacher in front of the whole class. David's glare demanded a response from him.

"Got it," he bit out.

"Good."

CHAPTER EIGHTEEN

At four o'clock in the morning, there was no traffic on the freeway heading south from Washington, Pennsylvania, to Morgantown, West Virginia.

Halfway home already, Cameron Gates had declared that she was going back to Chester, West Virginia, to spend the morning with her husband and get some sleep. It wasn't until they were on the road that Mac remembered that she had left Irving, the skunk cat suffering from separation anxiety, at Spencer Manor.

Seeing that David was still livid, Bogie had invited Mac to ride home in his cruiser. Claiming to be man enough to take it, Mac declined the offer. Besides, Gnarly was already in the back seat in David's cruiser.

During the drive back to Deep Creek Lake, the tension in David's cruiser was so thick that you could have cut it with a knife. Mac suffered the ride in tension-filled silence, broken only by the continuous sound of Gnarly's licking, until they came upon Morgantown.

Too angry to speak, both men refused to voice the growing agitation and instead listened to Gnarly lick and lick and lick. Neither one wanted to break the silence for fear of appearing to be the weaker one. So, they both suffered with every lick that came from the back seat.

Finally, Mac couldn't take it any longer. "Gnarly, will you stop that infernal licking?" He whirled around in the seat. "Stop it!"

With a whine, Gnarly dropped back into the seat and began panting.

Mac turned around to face the front.

David turned the cruiser to exit the freeway and turn onto Route 68 to head east.

Gnarly resumed licking.

"What's wrong with you?" Mac turned around to see that Gnarly, still in his bulletproof vest, was licking away at a spot on his side. "Is that vest uncomfortable?" He asked David, "Why didn't you take the vest off him? It's probably scratching him."

"He's your partner," David replied.

Mac reached back to grasp one of the Velcro straps on the vest to release him. When his hand touched a moist vest, he assumed that it was drool from Gnarly's licking. Unable to get a hand on the vest, Mac reached up to switch on the interior light to see Gnarly better.

When the back lit up to reveal a blood-covered vest and a bloody snout, Mac let out a stifled gasp. As much as he tried to contain himself, his horror was evident.

"What's wrong?" His eyes on the road, David could only guess at what Mac was gasping about.

"Gnarly's bleeding."

"What did you say?"

"Gnarly's bleeding." Mac tore at the blood soaked vest.

Now that he had his master's attention, Gnarly laid down with a whimper. His panting was mixed with an undertone of high-pitched whining.

"Are you sure?" David was still unconvinced. "He probably got blood spatter on him from when I shot Northrop."

Seeing a hole in the vest from which the blood was seeping, Mac whirled back around in his seat to face David. "There's a hole in his vest. Gnarly was stabbed, David—in the chest. He's bleeding."

"Why are we only finding this out now?" David asked.

"I don't give a damn!" Mac's anxiety was increasing. "We need to get him to a vet—now!"

David slipped on the lights and siren. "Hang on. We're minutes away from an emergency room." He pressed his foot on the accelerator.

When Bogie and Officer Brewster discovered that Gnarly had been stabbed, they fell in line behind David in the race into Morgantown. Mac had no idea where David was taking them. He didn't care. He assumed it was a veterinary hospital that had a pet emergency room.

When David pulled the cruiser into the West Virginia University hospital emergency room and right up to the ambulance entrance, Mac argued, "David, you're wasting time we don't have. In case you haven't noticed, Gnarly isn't human."

"They'll take him," David said in a firm tone that dared Mac to object. "Follow my orders and we'll be fine." With one hand he unsnapped his seatbelt while shouldering open his door. "Get Gnarly out of the cruiser and onto a gurney and cover him completely with a sheet."

Bogie followed David through the automatic doors. Spotting a gurney, the deputy chief commandeered it to wheel over to the cruiser for Mac, with Officer Brewster's help, to deposit Gnarly on. Once the dog was on the gurney, Mac urged Gnarly to keep still whileBogie and Brewster draped the sheet that had been on the gurney over him, including his head and ears.

"We have an officer who's been stabbed," David told the nurse who came running out to greet him. "He's bleeding from the chest."

"Is he conscious?" she asked.

"Yes, but he's in a lot of pain and losing a lot of blood." David glanced over his shoulder to where Mac, Bogie, and Brewster were wheeling Gnarly in through the door. When he saw Gnarly's tail hanging out from under the sheet, David stepped in front of the nurse to block her view. "I don't think you should look. He's really ugly."

She didn't appear to notice the furry appendage. "Emergency room two." Without pausing, they wheeled the gurney in the direction of the emergency room. "You go talk to admissions to get him admitted," she instructed the police chief.

"You know they're going to kick our butts out of here," Mac told Bogie in a low voice once they were in the room.

"Keep your faith," Bogie said. "Help me move him over onto the examination table. On the count of three."

Mac and Brewster took one end of the mattress while Bogie took the other. When Gnarly, still panting, attempted to sit up, Mac and Bogie eased him down. "Lie down, Gnarly," Mac ordered.

"I understand we have a police officer with a stab wound," a nurse came rushing in with a doctor behind her.

Mac felt a pang in his chest when he saw that the doctor looked not much older than his grown son who was a third-year student at George Washington University. He would have preferred someone old and gray with a ton of experience under his belt, placed directly below his tubby belly. This doctor looked like he was barely old enough to be shaving, let alone treating patients who were bleeding all over the gurney.

"Yes." Bogie stood up to his full height and stuck out his chest. His build was intimidating before, but as he took on the demeanor of a man to be reckoned with, he dared the doctor and nurse to defy him. "Officer Gnarly here took a knife wound to the chest while saving our chief of police's life from a murderer."

Behind him, Gnarly lifted his head and looked over at the doctor and nurse. His ears fell back and he uttered a pain-filled whine. Panting to alleviate the pain, he dropped back down onto the examination table.

"That's a dog," the nurse said.

"He's also a police officer," Bogie said. "He needs help now."

"We can't treat a dog," the nurse said. "The health department'll shut us down quicker than you can say fleas and ticks."

While she objected, the doctor stepped forward, pulled back the sheet, and put the stethoscope into his ears. "We need to get a blood pressure reading on him," he ordered while checking Gnarly's heartbeat. "His heartbeat is acceler-ated. Get me some gauze and an IV. We're going to need to sedate him. Tell the anesthesiologist to use our mildest medi-cation. Different species and breeds react differently to human drugs." He looked up to tell Mac, "It looks like it could be close to the heart. Good thing he was wearing this vest. It's tight enough that it slowed down the bleeding—"

"We can't treat a dog," the nurse interjected loud enough to be heard over him.

"Maybe you can't, but I can," the doctor told her over his shoulder. "Get me a nurse willing to assist in treating this officer, and make it quick. He's losing blood and needs help now!"

When she stared at the doctor with wide eyes, Bogie said, "You heard the man. Move it!" The boom of his voice was enough to propel her backwards into the swinging doors. She spun around and ran out of the examination room and down the hallway.

Seconds later, four nurses arrived with equipment and supplies. Unsurprisingly, they were all pet owners who tended to the fallen German shepherd with the same devotion as they would have with a human patient. One young nurse sat at Gnarly's head, cooing at him with her lips so close to the dog's snout that she was a hair's breadth from kissing him, while he drifted off to sleep under anesthesia. Only after Gnarly was asleep and they were ready to stop the bleeding did the doctor allow them to remove the vest to examine the wound. Eventually, Mac, Bogie, and Brewster were ushered out of the examination room and to the waiting room while the doctor operated on him.

David was already sitting with two cups of coffee. One, he was drinking. The second, he handed to Mac. "He's going to be fine."

"Did you get him checked in?" Mac asked with a sigh.

"Yes," the police chief said. "Oh, if anybody asks, you got stabbed in the chest tonight."

The corners of Mac's mouth kicked up. "Thank you."

"Don't mention it."

Mac took a sip of his coffee. After a moment of silence, he said, "You were right."

"I'm always right," David replied before asking, "About what?"

"While Northrop was holding that knife at your throat, I was thinking about how we needed him alive to make a deal for Palazzi. I was thinking that there had to be some way to have it both ways—for you to come out okay, and for us to take Northrop alive and make a deal."

Staring straight ahead, David sat up in his seat. "I know you see how young I am and you assume that I haven't been around long enough to understand the type of things that you're going through—like this vendetta you have against Palazzi. You blame yourself for Blakeley's murder, but it's not your fault."

"It is my fault," Mac's voice hissed. "Her parents looked me right in the eye and told me that it was my fault their daughter was dead. They didn't want her to testify. They convinced her not to testify, and I talked her into it. I promised her that she'd be safe." He hung his head. "I thought I could keep her safe, and I was wrong. Maybe I'm trying to vindicate myself for being wrong."

"You want her death to be for something," David said.

Mac sipped his coffee in silence.

"Do you think that hasn't happened to me?" David asked.

Mac didn't answer.

David stared into the coffee that was left in his cup. "Do you know why the chair of the town council, Bill Clark, hates my guts?"

"Because he's an arrogant jackass," Mac said.

"As true as that is, it's not the whole story," David said.

"What is the story?"

David sat forward in his seat and rested his elbows on his knees. "When I was active duty—it was after my first tour in Afghanistan—I'd just come back home, and ATF came to me. They had uncovered a group that dealt in illegal arms and transported them from overseas using troops that were coming home. The weapons were going to major drug dealers." He paused to take a sip of his coffee. "It was a big operation. A lot of weapons. A lot of money. A lot of really nasty people involved. Bill Clark's little sister was right smack in the middle of it."

Mac stared at him. "I never knew Clark had a sister."

David broke his gaze. "Lisa and I went to school together. We graduated the same year. She was a friend of Chelsea's. That's why they sent me in." He added, "Chelsea knows nothing about any of this, by the way."

"How was Lisa involved?"

"Lisa worked in logistics and scheduled the flights. She was a key operator and living with the guy who was running the whole operation. He was in charge of base security. She'd schedule the transportation of the arms. He would arrange security so that his people would inspect the shipment and the smuggled goods would get into the country without the good guys knowing."

"Slick operation," Mac said.

"It'd been going on for years right under everyone's noses until one of Lisa's supervisors noticed something fishy and started asking too many questions and ended up dead. During the murder investigation, they uncovered the operation and got circumstantial evidence that Lisa's boyfriend had killed the supervisor. Problem was, they had no concrete proof. They knew that Lisa had enough information to put them all away and bring down the whole operation."

Mac saw where he was going. "And since you two were old friends…"

"I was sent in undercover to turn her." David said, "The old high school friend from back home who just so happened to be transferred to the same base cover. My story was that I was in a financial fix due to a gambling problem that I had picked up and needed some quick cash. She vouched for me. They cut me in."

His cup empty, David stood up. "Want a refill?"

After draining his cup, Mac handed it to David, who went over to the coffee maker to pour their fresh cups. "Am I right in assuming it didn't turn out well?"

"When I got close, I saw what was happening behind the scenes," David explained. "Sid, Lisa's boyfriend, was the ringleader. He was abusive to the point that she was nothing like she had been back in school. She used to be alive. Funny. Clever. He'd beaten her down so far physically and emotionally that he'd broken her. It took a lot of work for me to earn her trust. I promised her that if she helped me to nail him, I'd protect her and he'd never hurt her again." His face contorted in emotion. "I promised her."

Mac's mind raced back to when he had made the same promise to Dee Blakeley. It was a promise that he ended up not able to keep. Choked with the emotion of his own broken promise, he asked softly, "What happened?"

David stood over Mac when he handed the cup to him. "We both wore wires," he whispered. "I was with her, but Sid sent me with some guys to go check a shipment." He sat down next to him. "I was wearing an earbud to hear orders from the surveillance van. I could also hear what was going on at her end, too. Sid was a jealous bastard. He'd noticed that she had been spending a lot of time with me. He suspected that we'd been sleeping together."

"Were you?" Mac asked.

His silence answered Mac's question.

"It was a set up," David said. "The guys Sid sent me with were supposed to beat me up, but not kill me. They told me Sid wanted to do that. They were just supposed to prep me for him. I took out one of them, and my backup took out the other two. By the time the smoke cleared, I heard her in my earbud." He swallowed. "While beating the crap out of her, Sid had found her wire."

"Oh, geez," Mac breathed.

"The whole time I was running across the base to get to her, I could hear her screaming and begging—begging for me to save her while he was stomping the daylights out of her."

224

He stopped to swallow. "Her last words were 'David, you promised me—you promised.' He shot her between the eyes a split second before I got there—"

"I'm sorry, David."

"So don't tell me that I don't know what you're going through." He took a sip of his coffee. "My point is…" He paused to clear his throat. "Mac, I respect the hell out of you. When I look at you, I see Dad."

Out of the corner of his eye, Mac looked at him.

"Maybe it's because of that that I give you a lot more free rein than I would any of my other officers." David swallowed. "But I am the chief of police. My people have to trust me enough to follow my orders. You may have the experience and instinct to solve these types of cases, but I'm still the guy in charge. When I give an order, you have to follow it. If I let you get away with disobeying my orders, then what's the rest of my department going to think about my authority? Do you understand?"

"Understood." Mac waited for David to drain his second cup of coffee before he asked, "What did you do to Sid after he killed Lisa?"

"I blew his brains out."

The doctor and nurses at West Virginia University Hospital didn't want to press their luck with keeping the hospital administration from finding out that they were treating a non-human patient. Luckily, the stab wound went through Gnarly's shoulder. While it punctured the chest cavity, it did not strike any major organs or arteries. As soon as they finished with Gnarly and made sure he was out of danger, they wheeled him, covered completely by a sheet, out to the cruiser and loaded him, IV and all, in the back with instructions to drive him home gently. He was still heavily sedated.

While each of the nurses fussed over Gnarly, giving him kisses and stroking the drowsy shepherd, Mac shook the doctor's hand. "I know you took a huge chance treating Gnarly."

"I'm a doctor," he replied. "When I swore to preserve life, I didn't put any boundaries on species."

Mac slipped his business card into his palm. "If there's ever anything I can do to repay the favor, don't hesitate to call me."

After glancing at it, but not registering Mac's name or importance, the doctor pocketed the card. "Thank you very much, but you don't owe me anything. I'm glad to help." He patted Mac on the shoulder. "I need to join the rest of the team in the examination room. We need to sterilize it before any human patients come in." He waved a farewell to David, who was waiting in the driver's seat of the cruiser. "Drive safely and take it easy. Don't bounce him around. We don't want to tear his stitches."

Archie, Chelsea, and Molly came out onto the porch to greet them when they pulled the cruiser through the stone pillars marking the entrance to Spencer Manor. As soon as the door opened, Irving came running out to see if his mistress was there. Seeing that she wasn't, he whirled around and went inside to have a proper snit in the chair next to the fireplace.

David took one end of the blanket that Gnarly was on while Mac took the other. Gingerly, they carried him inside and placed him on a dog bed that Archie had set up in front of the fireplace, which had a roaring fire in it. As soon as he was on the floor, Archie knelt down on the floor next to him to pet and caress him. Still out of it from the heavy drugs, all Gnarly could offer was a weak cry.

Mac carefully adjusted the IVs and covered Gnarly with a blanket to keep him warm.

Gazing imploringly at him, Molly curled up next to him and rested her head on his hip.

"Northrop is dead?" Chelsea asked.

"Yep," David said.

"That means he can't turn on Senator Harry Palazzi and his son, Bevis," she said.

"I know that," David said with a sigh.

"Did you have to—?" she started to ask.

"He tried to kill me," David replied. "He stabbed Gnarly. He left me no choice."

Chelsea's eyes grew big. "I'm sorry, I didn't know ... it was you?"

"Yes," David said. "I shot him. I killed him. He wasn't the first man I've killed, and I'd do it again."

Unable to find something to say, she stared at him.

Sensing that this discovery had changed her image of him, David turned away. "I'm tired. I'm going to bed." Without giving her a chance to stop him, David went through the dining room to the deck doors, and went out to go to his cottage.

CHAPTER NINETEEN

Spencer Manor—Next Morning

Chelsea let herself into David's cottage. She half expected David to still be in bed since he had only gotten home two hours before. Archie had offered to drive her and Molly into work at Ben Fleming's office if he was still in bed, so she let herself into the cottage to check. The sound of the shower running told her that he was awake and would be taking her into work.

Molly slipped in behind her and went over to a basket of dog toys that David had on hand for his canine guests. After nosing through them, she selected a dog bone. While waiting for her owner, she stretched out on the floor next to the basket to enjoy a good chew.

David's coat was slung over the back of a chair at the kitchen table. His utility belt was draped over top of that. When she set her laptop case on the table, Chelsea noticed everything that David carried in his utility belt: baton, flashlight, cell phone, handcuffs, pouch to carry extra gun cartridges, and, of course, his gun.

All that stuff. Must be heavier than my purse.

She picked up the belt and weighed it with her hand. It was heavy—just as she had thought. As a wicked thought crossed her mind, she glanced up into the loft. The shower was still going.

Should I? ... Yeah! He'll never know.

Her heart beat faster while she shrugged out of her coat and slipped the belt around her waist to let it rest on her hips. Her frame was so tiny that there were no holes in the belt in which to buckle it, so she was forced to hold it in place with her hands. Still, the weight made her wonder at how police officers were able to go around all day wearing something that heavy—let alone run after a fleeing criminal.

When she set the belt back onto the chair, her hand landed on the gun in the holster. The Beretta, black in its leather holster, resembled a child's toy beckoning to her.

A child's toy that can kill someone—like the man David killed last night. It looks heavy. Something that can take away a man's life should be heavy—it deserves to be heavy.

Sucking in a deep breath, she unclasped the case and slipped the gun out of its holster. Reminding herself that this weapon had the power to take away a life, she tightened her grip on it and pointed it across the room. Closing one eye, she held it up to look down the sights.

"What are you doing?"

Chelsea jumped. In doing so, she raised the gun while looking up into the loft at where the call had come from.

Seeing the gun pointed in his direction, David, dressed in his bathrobe, dropped to the floor. "Chelsea! Have you lost your mind?"

Realizing what a stupid thing she was doing, Chelsea fought to keep hold of the weapon, while at the same time trying to put it down as quickly as possible. "I'm sorry, I…I wasn't thinking."

"Obviously." David rose up to peer over the railing. "Did you put it down?"

Holding up both of her hands to show him that she was unarmed, she nodded her head. "I put it back."

David hurried down the winding staircase from the loft. "You know better than to play with a gun. What got into you?"

"It was sitting there…" Even as she said it, Chelsea realized how childish her excuse sounded. "I was thinking about you killing that man last night and I wondered what it was like. I wanted to put myself in your place—understand what had to be going through your mind—see what it was like."

"By shooting me?" David felt his heart racing inside his chest. Clutching his chest, he realized that he was still moist from his shower and wearing only his bathrobe.

"I'm sorry," she said. "I was wrong. It was childish and stupid of me."

"Are you waiting for me to argue that point?" After checking the safety, the round in the chamber, and the magazine, David slipped the gun back into its holster.

"I just want to understand what you go through when you have to kill someone," she said. "The way I was raised, you don't kill people—"

"I was raised that way, too," David said. "But there are people who think nothing of that, and it's my job to protect the rest of us from them. When I signed on for that job, I knew full well that sometimes I would end up in situation where I would have to take a life. It goes with the job."

Her eyes fell to the gun in the holster. "Did you use that gun?"

"No," David said, "I used an assault rifle. I don't have that for you to play with because the Pennsylvania State police took it into evidence."

"I don't fault you for what you did." She rested her hand on his. "I'm trying to understand—"

"I feel horrible," David said. "I always feel horrible after killing someone. I run it through my mind over and over again to see if there was something I missed, something else I could have done to have had a different outcome—but it always comes down to the same thing—I had to do it. There was no other way."

"If you didn't feel horrible, then that would make you as bad as the bad guys," she said.

"Exactly." Seeing her eyeing the gun in the holster, David asked, "Would you like to hold it?"

She backed up a step. "I don't know. What if I shoot you by accident?"

"Now you think about that." Chuckling, David took the gun out of its holster. He removed the magazine and took the bullet out of the chamber. "This is where most accidents happen," he said. "They take out the magazine, but forget about the one in the chamber." He turned on the safety, just in case, and held out the gun with its grip to her.

Frightened, she gently took the grip into her hand. "It feels a lot lighter," she noted.

"No bullets," he said. "Point it to the floor."

With both hands on the grip, she aimed the gun to the floor. "How, in the types of situations that I imagine you and Mac get into where everything is happening at once, you can take this and aim and actually hit anything, I don't know."

"That's why there's a lot of training," David said, "to get us used to it to the point that it becomes second nature. You're right. We never know what's going to happen until we get into the middle of it. Then, we have a split second to make a decision and act on it. " Seeing her trying to look down the sights, he grasped her hand holding the gun. "Let me show you how to hold it and aim."

Stepping behind her, he held her against his bare chest and placed both hands on hers and the gun. "Relax." He jiggled her arms to help her loosen her grip.

Easy for you to say. Chelsea was aware of the heat from his body pressed against her back. His flesh felt hot. The rapid beating of her heart made it difficult for her to relax her grip.

Resting his cheek against her head, he helped her to aim at an imaginary target on the lower wall. "Look through the notch and down the barrel to the tip at the end. You line that up with the target, and then you fire," David said. "This is a condensed version of target practice, but you get the idea."

Feeling her back against his body, he tried to ease the quickening of his breath. Her scent was filling his head. He lowered his hands down to her waist. The back of her hips pressed against his body.

"David?" She was still peering through the sights on the gun. "Did you hear my question?"

"What?" He was startled out of his fantasy of ripping off his robe, lifting her up into his arms, and taking her upstairs to the loft.

"What about the kick I always hear about?"

"What kick?" he replied in a dreamy voice.

She turned around to ask him, "Isn't there supposed to be a kick when you fire a gun?"

"Oh, the kick," he said. "From the gun. Yes, there is a kick." Trying to take his mind off his fantasy, he rambled on. "You have to fire a gun a few times to get used to it and know what to expect. That's why they say when you get a gun, even if it is only for emergencies, you need to take it out to practice, so that you know how it will fire." With the back of his hand, he wiped the sweat from his forehead and busied himself by taking the gun from her hand and reloading it. "A lot of novices, knowing that a gun will have a kick, will press down to fight against the kick while firing the gun. That's how you end up with a crotch shot."

"Crotch shot?" She cocked her head at him.

"That's what I call it." He slipped the gun back into the holster.

"Is that what it sounds like?" she asked him.

"It's exactly what it sounds like. Since the shooter is pulling down on the gun to fight the kickback before he or she fires, the shot goes low. You're aiming for the perp's chest, but instead you get him in the crotch."

"Have you ever seen that?"

"It's not pretty," David replied.

"You look flushed," she said.

"That's because the shower was hot." David tightened up his robe. "I only got a couple of hours sleep and needed to wake up."

A slow grin came to her lips when she caught sight of a bulge from his arousal inside his bathrobe. "I guess I woke you up." She stepped into his arms and wrapped them around him.

"You certainly have." He pulled her in tight.

"I'm sorry I went off on you last night." She pressed her lips against his jaw.

"When you apologize like that, how can I not forgive you?"

She raised up on her toes to reach beneath his robe and wrap her arms around his shoulders. He covered her mouth with his. He took in a deep breath to fill his head with her scent.

The chiming of the anniversary clock on the mantle jolted her back to her senses. With effort, she pulled out of his embrace. "I have to go to work," she whispered.

He cupped her face in his hands. "I have to take you to work."

She pried her gaze from his eyes and lowered them to his body, visible through the opening of his robe.

"I don't think Ben will mind if you're a little late." He gently kissed her.

"It's a new job," she argued while reaching up to steal another kiss.

"He knows you can't drive." He took her back into a tight embrace.

"I don't want Ben to think I'm privileged just because I'm dating the police chief."

David gazed down into her eyes that were the lightest blue he had ever seen. He could stare into them forever. A naughty grin crossed his face. "Is that what we're doing? Dating? We've actually moved out of the friend category to lovers?"

She uttered a groan while burying her face into his neck. "I hate it when you win."

Irving the skunk cat was in a snit. He hadn't seen Cameron, his mistress, for two days, and that stoolie dog who as good as squealed on them for tearing up the kitchen was getting all the attention. That Gnarly was sentenced to wear the Cone of Shame while recuperating from his daring rescue of the police chief was of little consolation.

At least Molly knew enough to respect the skunk cat's authority by staying away from him. Her mistress cared enough to take her everywhere with her. Irving recalled when he used to go to work with his mistress, until she married that man.

Life was so grand until she met him. Perched on top of the back of the love seat, Irving stared out the front window in an effort to will Cameron to come back to him. It finally worked.

Cameron's police cruiser came through the stone pillars and around the circle driveway.

Irving jumped down from the back of the loveseat and raced to the front door. When Archie pulled herself away from where she and Gnarly were staring at each other to answer the door, Irving rejoiced only long enough to notice that Cameron Gates was not alone. She had brought company with her.

Spotting Joshua Thornton, Irving whirled around, hitched his butt up in the human's general direction, and raced up the stairs to hide under a bed. Joshua had quickly learned that Irving's butt hitch was a feline version of giving him the finger.

"Well, there's one who's not happy to see you," Cameron told Joshua before stepping inside.

When the tall, slender man, approximately the same age as Mac, followed her inside, Archie wrapped her arms around him and gave him a kiss on the cheek. "I understand congratulations are in order."

Pulling back, she admired his blue eyes, framed with laugh lines, and the wavy silver hair that he wore down to the collar of his leather jacket. The prosecuting attorney for Hancock County in West Virginia, Joshua Thornton was not your average legal weenie, as police officers and those on the front lines liked to characterize lawyers. During his long career as an officer in the navy, the JAG lawyer had investigated crimes ranging from espionage to serial murders—and had convicted the perpetrators. He had as much investigative experience as any detective before moving his family back to his small hometown after his first wife's sudden death.

Archie was in awe of how quickly the single father's romance had taken off. Only twelve months before, Joshua had met the homicide detective who worked across the state line from his jurisdiction. "I knew when you two were here last that it was going to be a short time before you got married. I was right."

"Great to see you again, Archie." Joshua kissed her on the cheek.

"I only wish you had a wedding and invited us so that we could have met your children," Archie said while leading him and Cameron over to the fireplace where Joshua knelt across from his wife to examine Gnarly's injury in the line of duty.

"Well," Joshua explained, "with five kids, four of whom are grown and out of the nest, it was just too hard to find a date for all of them to have been there for a wedding. I didn't want to wait that long."

Archie caught Cameron shooting Joshua a look. While she didn't doubt that he was telling the truth about not wanting to wait, there was something in Cameron's greenish-brown eyes that told her that it was not the whole truth. *Maybe not all of Joshua's children approved of their new stepmother?*

Joshua shifted the conversation with one question. "Is Mac home?"

"I hope you aren't bringing me another case," Mac asked on his way down the stairs. A few hours of sleep and a shower were enough to refresh him.

Joshua met him at the bottom of the stairs to clasp his hand. "I was hoping you'd let me in on your case."

"Don't you have enough crime in West-by-God-Virginia that you have to come to Spencer to dip your toe into our murders?" Mac asked.

"I hate crooked politicians," Joshua said.

"Is that because you're one?" Mac shot back with a grin.

"I'm not a politician."

"Yes, you are," Cameron and Mac said in unison.

"You were elected prosecuting attorney," Cameron said.

"I want to help you get Palazzi," Joshua told Mac.

"Are you by any chance in the same party he is?" Mac asked. "Does this desire to bring him down have anything to do with party lines?"

"This isn't about politics," Joshua said. "It's about law and order. Now do you want my help, or don't you?"

"How do you propose to help me?"

"You think the senator had Nick Fields killed because he was blackmailing Palazzi with a copy of the tape where he confesses to raping Florence Everest," Joshua said.

"Either that," Mac said, "or Bevis had Fields killed because Fields knew Bevis was a serial killer who murdered women Fields had slept with." He turned to Cameron. "Those uteruses in the freezer did come from our murder victims."

"I knew it," she said.

"Unfortunately," Joshua said, "since Nick Fields was living in that house, Bevis Palazzi can, and will, point his finger at Fields. After all, his sperm was found on each of the victims."

"Exactly," Mac said. "How do you propose we get him?"

"If this was my case, I'd put pressure on the father."

"But Bevis is the weak link," Archie said. "He's the most unstable. He'll break before Palazzi."

"And Harry Palazzi is a narcissist," Mac said. "He'd let his own mother burn to save himself."

"That's what I'm thinking," Joshua said. "Harry Palazzi is the one with the power to protect Bevis. All we have to do is remove that safety net, and he'll as much as hand us Bevis. After all, who was it Fields called when you arrested him?"

"Bevis," Archie said.

"And from that one phone call, the hit man showed up to kill Fields," Joshua said. "Therefore, that hit had to have originated from Bevis."

"Bevis called his father after he got Fields' call," Archie said. "That's what we found from his call records. The senator set up the hit."

"Possibly from Bevis' orders, or maybe not," Cameron said from where she was still stroking Gnarly on his bed. "We don't know what Bevis said in that phone call."

"Unfortunately, there's a lot we don't know," Mac said. "We do know a lot, but then we don't have enough evidence to make any arrests and make them stick."

"But we do know enough to nail the senator," Joshua said. "We know that every time someone becomes a threat to Senator Harry Palazzi, they end up dead."

"Very true," Mac said.

"We know how he works," Joshua said. "He has enough of a history that we can count on that, and send someone up against him. Then, when Palazzi sends someone to take care of the problem, you'll be ready."

"Who do you propose to go up against him?" Mac asked.

"Me."

Ben Fleming came out with a look of concern on his face when he heard David and Chelsea enter the office.

"Sorry I'm late," Chelsea apologized before Ben could greet them. "David had trouble getting out of bed." Realizing the innuendo as the words came out of her mouth, she hurried over to the coffeemaker to conceal the bright blush that covered her face.

"That's perfectly okay," Ben said, "I heard all about what happened last night. How's Mac?"

"He's fine," David said.

Perplexed by his nonchalant tone, Ben said, "Even after getting stabbed in the chest and spending the night in the ER?"

"Oh, that wasn't Mac," Chelsea said. "It was Gnarly who got stabbed while saving David's life." She returned from the coffeemaker with two mugs, one of which she offered to David.

"But the news said—"

"Which goes to prove you can never depend on the news getting the facts straight," David said.

"Well," Ben said, "while you were in bed trying to catch up on some sleep, our case has been developing at warp speed."

"What happened?" Chelsea asked him.

"Bevis Palazzi is in the wind," he said. "I just got a call from Samuel Brooks, his lawyer. Teresa Winston, Bevis' senior partner, was found dead this morning in her office. Her assistant said she had told her that she was going to confront him about the identity theft and embezzlement from Sheila McGrath's accounts last night after everyone had left. Winston had been stabbed multiple times with a letter opener and the garbage from her trashcan was dumped over her dead body. There's a warrant out for Bevis' arrest. It's hitting the news now."

"What about a warrant for him killing Khloe Everest?" David asked. "Do we have enough now to nail him for that?"

Ben nodded his head. "I just called forensics. They're notifying you now. DNA matches the uteruses found in Bevis' house to our three murder victims, including Khloe."

"But there is nothing to tie him or his father to Dee Blakeley's murder," David said.

"Evidence tying Bevis to some of the victims is better than nothing," the prosecutor said.

"Is there anything I can do?" Chelsea sat down at her desk and grabbed her keyboard. She was ready for action.

"Get started on the warrant for Bevis Palazzi's arrest."

"Bevis is going to point the finger at Nick Fields," David said.

"We have enough to arrest him and get him off the streets," Ben said. "Meanwhile, you and Mac work at getting enough for us to place him in the Everest home with the knife in his hands so a jury will convict him. Maybe with Willingham's copy of the tape and a threat of public exposure, the senator will recant his alibi for his son. We need to get Bevis off the streets."

"He's a maniac," David agreed. "We have no way of predicting who this psychopath is going to go after next."

"We do know one thing," Chelsea said.

"What?"

"He hates women," she said.

"That should narrow down his potential victims by fifty percent," David said.

Chapter Twenty

Senator Harry Palazzi was stretched out on his masseuse's table waiting for his personal masseuse, a Vietnamese girl with a thick accent who he never understood, to dig her strong hands and claw-like fingers into his fatty shoulders. With his eyes closed, he anticipated the thrill of her working her fingers down his naked body. He could hear the light footsteps come into the room.

Abruptly, the light instrumental mood music ceased, and his own booming voice came through the speakers:

Slap!

"Oh, I forgot how you like it rough," a male voice said. "If you want it like the last time—"

"Last time was not rough! Last time was an attack. I said no—"

"Of course you said no. They all say no, but they don't mean no."

"You pinned my hands down and you raped me!"

"You call it rape, I call it playing rough."

Senator Palazzi practically fell off the table in rolling over to see the man peering at him with his eyes narrowed to blue slits. The unwanted visitor's silver hair was combed back off his forehead and fell in a wave at his neck. The senator's towel fell away to reveal his bulging stomach that covered up most of his private parts. "Who the hell are you?"

"I don't believe we've met." Joshua stuck out his hand. "Joshua Thornton. We had a mutual friend. Florence Everest decorated my home when I lived in Washington some years back. After my wife died, we renewed our relationship." He grinned at the senator while he lowered his voice to a whisper. "Only our relationship was consensual. Unfortunately, your daughter never did approve, and eventually we had to go our separate ways. But recently, I received a package from Florence." He chuckled. "You just heard what that package contained. She also left me a detailed letter telling all about your 'relationship' with her. How you raped her when she came to your home to give an estimate for decorating it…"

"Bruce!"

A huge, bald-headed security guard came rushing into the room.

"Show this bastard who he's messing with!"

When Bruce came at him, Joshua delivered a kick to his groin so hard that it dropped him to his knees. Before Bruce could come back up, Joshua picked up the recorder and whacked him against the side of his head to knock him down and out.

"Now, where was I?" With both hands, Joshua smoothed his silver hair back against the side of his head.

The senator was gazing at the smashed recorder.

"Oh," Joshua said, "we don't have to worry about that tape. You can keep it as a gift."

Seemingly speechless, the senator looked back up at him.

"Do I look stupid to you?" Joshua grinned. "Like I would have only one copy and bring it here to face you. There are more copies of that tape, plus the master. It will cost you a million dollars, cash, small bills, to get all of them. You have until tomorrow morning before they are automatically shipped out to various media outlets and will be uploaded to the Internet everywhere." He picked up the tape and thrust it into his chest and held it there. His sheer will made Palazzi look at him. "I'll call you."

Joshua leaned in toward him. "Oh, and you had better pray that I don't have any accidents or run into any maniacs with butcher knives, because as soon as that happens, my partner will be uploading that recording. It will go viral. I wonder what your women voters will do when they discover that you're a serial rapist."

After shoving him back down onto the table, Joshua sauntered out of the room. When he encountered the senator's masseuse, he said, "Sorry about the mess. I'm sure the senator will clean it up."

Bogie was snapping away to capture pictures of Kevin Cooper, private investigator.

Senator Palazzi's personal cleanup man was meeting with two of his men in his office. In the passenger seat, Cameron was listening in on the meeting with a bug that she had planted during her earlier visit to the brownstone.

"Right on schedule," she told Bogie. "They're on a conference call with Palazzi and Brooks. The order is to dive into Joshua's background for dirt to use against him—"

"I hope he's clean," Bogie said.

Cameron gasped. "They're getting another assignment— to take care of Mac."

In the cruiser's back seat, Irving let out a growl.

"Quit complaining," Cameron told the cat. "You're just going to have to learn to get along with Joshua."

"Are you surprised?" Bogie asked her.

"About him being jealous of Josh? No."

"I mean about targeting Mac."

"Nope," she said. "I just hope they don't get ahead of us."

CHAPTER TWENTY-ONE

Darkness enveloped Spencer, Maryland.

Stings are, by their very nature, stressful. Trying to anticipate every move and every angle and expecting the unexpected makes for a stressful situation.

In a vain effort to keep Palazzi's men from finding a connection with Mac Faraday so that the senator would not sense a trap, Joshua Thornton had checked into a roadside hotel in McHenry.

Mac and David staked out Joshua's room from the connecting room next door. Bogie and every man available, dressed in plain clothes, were scattered around the hotel and lounge.

Mac felt like a voyeur listening to Joshua and Cameron in the next room, which was wired for video and audio. Even though they were aware of the audience, and Joshua was not one to offer public displays of affection, the chemistry between the newly wedded couple was evident.

"You know you don't have to do this." Cameron lay down next to him on the bed and wrapped her arms around him.

"I wouldn't be here if I didn't want to do this," he replied while hugging her close. "Besides, if I wasn't here, then you would be here without me and I'd be home with a teenager with raging hormones and a mopey dog missing your neurotic cat."

"Ah." She started to sit up. "So you're doing this for purely selfish reasons?"

"Of course." Joshua pulled her back down and held her tight so that she couldn't escape. "I'm a lawyer. I wouldn't be doing this unless I got something out of it. I'm expecting teeth chattering sex from you after all this is done."

She sat up and looked down at him. "Okay. Do you want payment in advance?"

"No," Mac hissed in the adjoining room as if they could hear him. "Pay up later on your own time."

"Prude," David muttered to Mac.

Bogie's voice came across the earbuds. "You are about to have company. Three men just parked over next to the employee entrance and came in through the kitchen. They do not look like dishwashers. They are all carrying."

"Three?" David asked.

"One of them is Kevin Cooper," Bogie said.

"He'll recognize Cameron from the interview at his office." Grabbing his gun out of his holster, Mac leapt from his seat and ran for the door connecting the two rooms. He threw open the door to catch Joshua and Cameron in the midst of a kiss.

Instinctively, Joshua pushed Cameron away and went for his gun on the bed stand while she went for hers in her holster.

"They're on their way and Cooper is with them." Mac waved for the detective to hurry. "Cam, you have to come with me."

"They're on their way up to the room," Bogie reported. "Everyone get ready."

"You need to get out of there, Cameron," Mac said.

She ran for the door, but stopped halfway across the room before turning back to grab Joshua's face in both of her hands and kissing him passionately. "I love you," she whispered when she pulled back before running through the open doorway.

Mac closed the door as the pounding started on the door to Joshua's room.

Joshua took his time checking the gun he had in one ankle holster and the knife he had put in a sheaf on the other ankle. For show, he had tucked a gun into the back waistband of his pants.

When he opened the door, he was greeted with a fist to the face that knocked him backwards. He was still tumbling backwards when he got a fist to the gut that doubled him over. Two men then grabbed him by the arms and shoved him back onto the bed where they continued punching him to the stomach and chest after disarming him of the gun tucked in his belt.

In the next room, hearing Joshua taking a beating, Cameron ran for the door, only to have Mac block it. "I can't let them—"

"Had enough?" One of the thugs asked Joshua.

"No," Joshua called out with a forced laugh. "I can take it."

Monitoring the audio and video feed, David, Mac, and Cameron sensed the comment was meant for them.

"He knew this going in," Mac told her in a low voice.

"Well, Joshua Thornton, I presume." Kevin Cooper sauntered in. "You made a big mistake trying to cash in on your relationship with Flo Everest. Instead of the senator paying, it's going to be you." He asked the men who were searching the room, "Is his partner here?"

Spotting her purse on the table, Cooper grabbed it. "Where is she?" He started to open up the purse.

Realizing Cameron's police shield was inside her handbag, Joshua snatched it out of his hand. "Out getting us a bottle to celebrate." He tossed the purse across the bed and into a corner, where it was out of their reach. "She'll be back soon." With the back of his hand, he wiped the blood from a cut on his cheek.

"I hope she's good looking." Cooper uttered a lewd chuckle. The other men joined in. "After driving all the way out here from Washington, we're in the mood for a party."

"Oh," Joshua said, "and you're going to have one, too, when she sees the looks of you guys."

They all laughed until Kevin Cooper saw shakes of his men's heads indicating that they had not found what they had come to search for. "Where are the tapes?"

"What tapes?" Joshua asked with a wicked laugh.

Cooper backhanded him across the face. Before Joshua could regroup, Cooper grabbed his jaw in his hand and squeezed. With a gunman on either side pressing their guns into his ribs, Joshua had no escape when Cooper bent over him and glared into his face. "Wrong answer. You told Palazzi that you had a master and a number of copies. I want them all, and I want them now." He pressed his fingers, squeezing Joshua's jaw so that the inside of his cheeks pressed against his teeth until his jaw and mouth hurt.

Cooper shoved him back onto the bed. "Now, let's try this again. Where are the tapes?"

"I should expect such stupidity from an elected official," Joshua laughed. "I told Palazzi that if anything happened to me that those tapes would be made public. So what does he do? He sends you to rough me up."

"Not just rough you up," Cooper whirled around to face him. He shot a cold glare at him. "You're the one who isn't very smart, Thornton. Haven't you figured it out yet? We're going to kill you and your lady partner when she gets here—after having some fun with her, of course. If you're lucky, we'll let you stay alive to watch." He grabbed Joshua by the shirt. "Now where are the tapes?"

"If Palazzi's ruthless enough to send you to kill me for blackmailing him, what do you think he's going to do to you when those tapes end up on every news station and Internet site all over the world after you kill me without getting them?" Joshua asked. "Do you think he'd hesitate about killing you for being so sloppy? In other words, if you kill me, you'll be writing your own death warrant."

"I don't think so," Cooper said. "Palazzi has enough friends in dark places that he'll never get voted out of office."

"Unless the voters get so physically ill of having a sexual predator representing them that they'll walk, run, and crawl to get rid of him."

"So what?" Kevin Cooper broke into such a deep cocky laugh that Joshua wondered if he had lost his mind. Seeing that Joshua didn't get the joke, he shrugged his shoulders. "I guess I can tell you. After all, you're going to be dead. It isn't like you're going to tell anyone. Haven't you ever heard of voter fraud? Palazzi has greased all the right palms in all the right places. As long as the senator pays his bills, the computers inside the voting machines will always say he wins. He's in for life." He scoffed. "And he's not the only politician in Washington who's found a way to take the worry out of elections. So what the voters think really doesn't matter."

"Unless Palazzi ended up in jail," Joshua said. "Like for having you kill Khloe for him."

"Hey," Cooper said. "'I did not kill Khloe."

"You're Senator Palazzi's cleanup man, right?" Joshua asked.

"Enough talk," Cooper said. "You're asking too many questions." He ordered his men, "Kill him."

When one of the men grabbed him by the arm, Joshua countered with a kick to his knee that caused the thug to drop to his knees. When the other man grabbed him and pinned his arms behind his back, Joshua turned to Cooper. "Even if Palazzi has the voting machines stacked in his favor, people are going to be asking questions and looking into how he can keep getting voted into office when the overwhelming public opinion is against him because he's a rapist. So it's in his best interest that those tapes aren't made public. You're never going to find them without me, and I'm not going to give them up unless I get answers."

"What do you need answers for when you're going to be dead in a few minutes?" Cooper asked.

"Wouldn't you want to know who killed you?" Joshua answered. "Who gave you the order to kill me? Palazzi? Does he give you his orders directly?"

The gunman he had knocked down hobbled back up onto the bed.

"Senator Palazzi didn't get where he is by being stupid." Kevin Cooper laughed.

"His son." Joshua shifted to ease the discomfort of the two guns stuck in his ribs.

"You're a lawyer, right?" Cooper said. "Haven't you had clients who have special needs?"

"Samuel Brooks," Joshua said. "He takes the orders from Palazzi, who passes them on to you and then hides behind lawyer-client privilege."

"That's how it works."

"So the order to kill me and my partner came from Samuel Brooks," Joshua said.

"After we collect all of the copies you have of the recording," the private investigator said.

"Do you know what's on that recording? Palazzi admitting to Florence Everest the he raped her and got her pregnant."

"Fat lot I care," Cooper said with a shrug.

"As long as you get paid."

"As long as Samuel Brooks pays me my retainer every month to take care of his big money clients and keep the skeletons in their closets behind closed doors, I do what I have to do."

"How many clients does Brooks have you doing cleanup for? How many politicians have gotten themselves into office via this voter fraud scheme?"

Cooper and his men answered with wicked laughs.

"Come on," Joshua said. "You're going to kill me and my partner isn't here yet. It isn't like I can spread this around."

"Okay," Cooper said. "You want to know?"

"I have a right to know."

"Palazzi is Brooks' big client," Cooper said. "I mean, this man has two serious problems. He can't keep his fly shut, and he hates women. Bad combo. It's like a couple of times a year we need to go convince some bitch to take the payoff that Brooks offers her to not go blabbing to the police and the media."

"Where does Bevis fit into all this?" Joshua asked.

"You ever hear the nut doesn't fall very far from the tree?" Cooper said. "Bevis hates women, too—only it's worse than his daddy. No chance of the senator ever becoming a grand-daddy with that one. He's a royal whack job. He blames women for everything. If he's got a big account coming in and it falls through—doesn't matter that it's the male client who pulled it—Bevis will blame the client's wife, or if he's not married, his girlfriend, or the client's female assistant." He paused. "It's always the woman's fault for everything."

"What cleanup have you had to do for Bevis?" Joshua asked.

Without answering, Cooper stared at him.

Joshua could almost see the wheels turning in the PI's mind while he was thinking.

"What's taking your partner so long?" Cooper asked.

Holding his breath, Joshua wondered if he had pushed too far with the questions. On both sides of him, the muzzles of the guns pressed against his ribs.

"Sounds like the senator has a sweet setup," Joshua said. "His lawyer handles the payoffs. You guys provide the muscle to the victims who have too much integrity to accept money."

"Too much integrity and not enough brains," Cooper said.

"Or, they could just plain be stupid," Joshua said.

"We've had some of them, too."

"Like Nick Fields," Joshua said. "He had no integrity or brains. That's why you had to send Lincoln Northrop to kill him at the Spencer Police Department."

Cooper's cocky grin fell as Joshua's stretched across his face. "It's a set up!" Grabbing his gun from his holster, the private investigator ran for the door, only to have it fly open. He came face to face with Bogie and the muzzle of an assault rifle. Seeing that he was outgunned, he spun on his heels and ran for the connecting door. When he threw it open, he came face to face with Cameron's and David's guns. Throwing up his hands, he backed up into the room while Cameron grabbed the gun from his hand.

Before both gunmen could fire their weapons, Joshua reached up behind them and slammed their heads together. In the seconds that they reacted to the sudden head butt, Joshua somersaulted backwards over the bed. When the two assailants dove across the bed to pursue him, they froze when Joshua came back up with a gun in each hand and aimed at them. It was only then that they realized that Joshua had managed to disarm both of them simultaneously after butting their heads.

A look of disbelief filled their faces as Joshua aimed their own guns at both of them. "Told you we were going to have a party," he told them before they were cuffed and taken down to Spencer police department.

"You're wasting your time. Palazzi will have us out by morning," Kevin Cooper said when Bogie shoved him down into a chair at the table in the hotel room.

"I don't think so," David said. "We have enough on you to nail you for conspiracy to commit murder in this case, and once we get a warrant for your phone records, we'll connect you to Lincoln Northrop and prove that the order to kill Nick Fields came from you."

"Not to mention all the big name clients who Brooks has had you doing cleanup for," Joshua added.

"I want a deal," Cooper said.

"Oh," Mac said. "I can imagine that. You're going to say it was Brooks, and Brooks is going to hide behind lawyer-client privilege. Someone is going to jail, and we'll settle for you."

"There's no hiding with what I have to offer," Cooper said. "I have recordings—video and audio. Sometimes, Palazzi wanted his messages delivered in a special way, and he wanted to give his orders in person." He chuckled. "I have him on tape telling where all the bodies are hidden…" His grin was like that of a cat who had eaten a very plump canary. "… including his wife's."

They all exchanged glances before Mac said, "You went to work for Senator Palazzi a dozen years ago. His wife disappeared over twenty years ago."

"That's right," Cooper said. "She disappeared with her best friend. Palazzi had me move their bodies ten years ago when they decided to build a subdivision on top of an old farm in Virginia where he had buried their bodies. He killed them because he raped the friend and she told his wife. She believed her friend and was going to leave him and tell the media about him being a rapist. So he killed them both and framed some guy he had arrested who had just gotten out of jail."

Cooper chuckled. "I got it all in both audio and video, in Palazzi's own words. Samuel Brooks was there in the meeting, too. Plus, I can lead you to their bodies. Is that good enough to get me immunity and protection?"

Every officer and detective in the hotel room gazed at each other in silence, too stunned to form words to respond to the private detective's news. The only noise in the room was Kevin Cooper's arrogant laughter.

Mac's words were very low. "Do you mean to tell us that you not only knew, but got evidence a decade ago, that Senator Harry Palazzi killed his wife and her friend, and framed an innocent man, and you did nothing?" His voice rose in anger. "All these years, over twenty years, an innocent man has been rotting in jail for something he didn't do while you—a former police officer—did nothing to make it right!"

"If he had, then he wouldn't have been making all the sweet money he has been making helping Brooks and his powerful political friends who have gotten sweet jobs for life," Joshua said with sarcasm.

"Yeah," Cooper said. "I want my lawyer, and I want a deal. Once I get the deal in writing, you'll have Brooks and Palazzi."

"Do you have any idea what a reputation you would have gotten if you had turned over this evidence a decade ago?" Mac replied. "You would have put Senator Palazzi away, solved a double homicide, prevented the rapes that Palazzi has committed since then, and freed an innocent man."

"Do you have any idea how much Brooks and his friends pay me to keep them in power?"

Mac raged. "You were a cop!"

"Hey," Cooper shrugged, "shit happens. Where's my deal?"

Afraid of what he would do if he got too close to the private investigator, Mac turned away.

Cameron stepped into his space. "I've got an idea that will make us all feel better." She took the gun that she had taken from the private investigator from out of her waistband. "We'll shoot him."

The officers and detectives in the room were uncertain if they should believe her or not. They looked to David for his reaction. He was equally unsure.

Joshua's smile stretched across his face.

Confident, Cooper laughed. "Yeah. Right."

Cameron went on. "We know what's going to happen. We'll take Cooper to the police station. He'll call Brooks or another lawyer. Since he knows where all the evidence that we want is, he will refuse to talk until he gets a deal, which he'll get because that's the only way we'll get to Palazzi and Brooks and all of their bottom-sucking friends in Washington. Cooper here is going to get immunity. He will skate and be taken into witness protection where he'll get a new life without any payback for the slimy existence that he has lived. Meanwhile, all of the women who Palazzi has raped, something he got away with thanks to Cooper's protection, will continue to suffer for the rest of their lives."

She waved Cooper's gun. "Well, this is our chance, men—our only chance—before the slimy lawyers get their hands on him—"

"Hey!" Joshua interjected.

"No offense meant."

"None taken," Joshua replied with a grin.

"As I was saying," Cameron continued, "This is our only chance to give Cooper here the payback that he deserves.

Here's what we're going to do. I'll shoot Cooper dead. Then, we'll say that when we burst in, Cooper pulled his gun and took a shot at me and I had to kill him in self-defense. If we all say that's what happened, no one will ever know, and there will be one less slime ball wasting oxygen."

"We can't forget to shoot his gun," Joshua said.

"Of course we'll do that," Cameron said. "Do I look stupid? I've done this before."

Seeing the sly grin on Joshua's face, Mac said, "Sounds good to me."

"Now we can't contradict each other," Cameron said, "but we can't all tell the same story in the same way. If we all use the same words then they'll know that we got our stories straight."

"Now wait a minute," Cooper objected.

"Shut up, "Cameron ordered.

"I want to shoot him," Mac said.

"Can I hit him before you shoot him?" Bogie cracked his knuckles. "I want to break his nose."

David said, "You know, it would be more believable if we had an actual gun fight before we killed him. I think we should shoot out his kneecaps and wound him really good before we actually deliver a kill shot."

"How about if we make it a big gun fight," Joshua suggested. "We'll all get to shoot him."

"But I get the kill shot," Mac insisted.

"Then we're going to need a bigger gun to explain how he was such a big threat that we all had to shoot him," Cameron said.

"I have a throwaway assault rifle in my cruiser," David said. "I'll go get it while you stage the scene."

"Who wants to shoot out his kneecaps?" Bogie asked.

"You can't do this!" Cooper struggled while the deputy chief pulled him up to his feet.

"Oh, yes we can," Cameron said while leaning over to tell him in a low voice. "We have the badges. We can do anything we want."

"Be a man, Cooper." Mac cocked his gun. "Shit happens."

Chapter Twenty-Two

Knowing the justice department would quickly accept Kevin Cooper's offer for a deal in exchange for the evidence he had been collecting for a dozen years, David waited until the private detective had broken into hysterical pleas for mercy before ending their charade of planning to kill him. Even if Cooper didn't change as a result of thinking he was going to be killed, at least the detectives got their frustration off their chests.

Hours later, armed with arrest warrants, David, Mac, and his officers swooped in on the senator's mountain home to take him in for questioning about his wife's disappearance and murder. Senator Harry Palazzi had a seasonal home on Spencer Mountain that provided a view of the whole lake and surrounding mountains.

The house was dark when the cruisers swarmed in from all directions. Mac was hoping that they would wake up the senator. He deserved to be woken up. When no one answered the door, they broke it down and the police poured in with their assault rifles, ready for a fight.

Wanting to see Senator Harry Palazzi's face when they snapped the cuffs on him, Mac was jogging up the steps behind the police when he heard the lead agent come to the door to tell them, "You need to see this."

Mac followed David inside. The first thing they noticed when the lights came on was the blood spatters on the walls and doorframes leading into the living room.

Lying in the middle of a blood-soaked rug was the senator, dressed in what had to be a smoking jacket. His body had been mutilated.

"Revenge for one of his attacks?" David asked.

"This one's still alive!" one of the officers called out from another room.

Expecting to find Bevis, Mac rushed into the den where they found Samuel Brooks lying in the middle of the floor. Like his client, he had been stabbed several times in the chest and stomach.

That he's still alive could only be a miracle. Mac knelt down next to the man struggling for every breath. "Brooks," he asked, "who did this?"

"Be-Bevis," the lawyer gasped out while clutching Mac's jacket with his blood soaked hand. "He's crazy."

"Why?" Mac ignored the EMTs coming in with their first aid equipment. Fearing that Brooks would die before he could give them the whole story, he refused to move.

"Crazy...he found out...Harry had to...ordered Fields killed. Bevis flipped out...said he...he was husband." Brooks let out a pained gasp. "He thought...money he was paying...he believed it. He thought Fields was his hus...band. Fantasy...thought real."

The grip on Mac's jacket loosened. As he stared up into Mac's face, Samuel Brooks's eyes filled with fear. His mouth dropped open. In death, he released Mac and his hand dropped down to his side.

"Excuse me, Mr. Faraday," one of the EMTs ordered him to move so that they could tend to the lawyer.

Mac found David with Cameron and Joshua outside. Afraid of missing Senator Palazzi's arrest, Joshua had refused medical treatment for the cuts and bruises he had suffered in the fight at the hotel.

"Bevis?" Cameron asked.

"He's lost it," Mac said. "Brooks said he killed his father because he thought he killed his husband—he believed Fields was his husband."

"And killed his father?" Joshua said. "Avenging his husband's murder. Now he's killed a man. Remember Cooper said he blamed women for everything."

"Maybe there was no woman here to blame," Cameron said.

"No woman here," Mac said. "He had to strike out upon learning the news. This is a crime of passion. Now that he's had time to think, what's he going to do?" When none of them answered, he concluded, "Find a woman to blame."

As much as she loved Mac and their friends, Archie Monday loved those occasions when she was home alone at Spencer Manor.

Well, on this particular day, she wasn't really alone.

Irving had just as much attitude as Gnarly. Unlike Gnarly, who was an independent sort, Irving didn't like being alone. So he had spent the day following Archie while she went from room to room in the huge manor home doing laundry, cooking lunch, stretching out across the sofa while editing a book, and then cooking dinner to eat with Chelsea after Ben had driven her home.

After they had dinner, Chelsea took Molly out for a long walk, which she did every evening. It had become a habit for David to take Gnarly and go walking with them, but on that night, David was out closing the case, and Gnarly was still recovering on a bed Archie had made for him up in the master suite.

After Chelsea had left for her walk with Molly, Archie resumed busying herself. All the while, she was under the penetrating emerald green gaze of the Maine Coon that looked like a giant skunk.

No wonder Joshua Thornton refused to let Cameron leave him alone with Irving in Chester, West Virginia. It's creepy the way he stares. Does he ever blink?

She finished folding the last load of laundry, which consisted of her Victoria Secret silky lingerie, and took it upstairs with Irving leading the way. In the bedroom, she smiled while placing the intimate clothing away in the walk-in closet and dressing room. Each piece brought back memories of special moments she had shared with Mac.

Life is good. I have been blessed to have him in my life.

When she came out of the closet, she realized Irving was missing. Gnarly was still sacked out in his bed.

Don't tell me Irving has finally decided to let me out of his sight.

Picking up her clothes basket, she stopped to listen for any sound of the stealthy feline. The house was too quiet.

Maybe it's because I'm used to hearing a hundred pounds of fur, paws, and teeth getting into everything. Maybe Irving decided to make a lone raid on the kitchen.

Leaving the basket behind, Archie started for the door only to be stopped with a sense of dread. Ben and David's warning about Bevis had sounded serious.

He wouldn't be crazy enough to come after me—after that little argument…but his rage was out of proportion—and he is crazy.

She grasped the gun that she had tucked in the pocket of her sweater. *As long as I have the gun close at hand, Bevis won't show up. If I don't have it, he surely will.*

At the top of the stairs, Archie peered over the bannister down to the foyer and sitting room. "Irving? Are you down there?"

His leaving her side was certainly strange. Irving suffered from separation anxiety, which was why Cameron took him everywhere. When left alone, he would tear up the house. He had only recently adjusted to spending his time with Donny, Joshua's teenaged son. Not so much with Joshua, though.

Her hand on the gun in her pocket, Archie descended the stairs one at a time while searching for the cat. As big as he was, he certainly would have been hard for her to miss. But then, cats can be quite clever and devious—as evidenced by the kitchen raid.

He must have needed a litter box break.

With a shrug of her shoulders, Archie went into the kitchen. *Time for a snack. How about a delicious chocolate mousse?*

She went through the kitchen door and went to the fridge. Yanking it open, she reached in to take out the crystal dessert cup. She felt drool form in her mouth at the sight of the rich creamy chocolaty dessert. Closing the refrigerator door, she went to the silverware drawer and pulled it open to reach in for a spoon. A reflection of movement in the silver tray propped up against the splashboard under the cupboard caught her eye.

Irving, what are you up to? She turned around to face the skunk cat, only to see Bevis, his eyes wide and red with rage coming at her with a butcher knife poised to thrust into her back.

Her hands full of chocolate mousse and spoon, Archie had no way of grabbing her gun. Her only defense was to duck out of the way of the knife and drop the mousse. She dodged out of the way and ran across the room.

The crystal dessert bowl hit the floor with a shatter and mousse went everywhere.

Bevis lunged forward and the knife plunged into the oak drawer.

In her escape across the room, Archie reached for her gun and turned around. As she was taking the gun out of her pocket and turning, her feet hit the chocolate mouse and she slid across the floor. The gun flew out of her hand.

Catching herself against the kitchen counter on the other side of the room, she stood up and turned around to face her attacker. For the first time, she got a good look at him.

What's he wearing?

Bevis' fat, hairless legs were fully exposed up to where the hem of his blue dress covered his butt. If he hadn't been intent on killing her, Archie would have laughed out loud.

Her delay gave Bevis time to wrestle the knife free from where it was embedded in the wood. He spun around for her to see his heavily made-up face, complete with false eyelashes. The eyelashes were overshadowed by his huge bosom.

"You've got to be kidding?" she blurted out.

"Go ahead! Laugh, bitch!" He raised the knife up over his head. "It's because of you he's dead! My husband! The love of my life! You're going to pay!"

Shocked into action, Archie searched for where the gun had fallen.

The assault was launched from the top of the fridge where Irving had been taking a nice nap on the warm appliance. When he landed on top of Bevis' head, the wig went soaring like a flying carpet.

Archie dove for the gun, only to hit another blob of chocolate mousse that sent her feet out from under her. She landed on her stomach. When her hand hit the gun's grip, she sent the firearm spinning across the room.

Bevis was still trying to determine what had happened to his wig when Irving bounced off the kitchen counter and landed on top of his head to imbed ten sharp needles into his' skull. The cat's high-pitched cry filled Bevis' ears. Forgetting about the knife, his hands flew to his head in an effort to free the enraged feline that was ripping through his scalp to his skull.

Seeing that the knife was closer, Archie got up onto her knees and crawled toward the weapon. All the while, she was aware of the fat man in the blue dress whirling around in the kitchen while grappling with the black and white cat who was holding on for all it was worth. When his feet hit the choco-late mousse, Bevis slipped and landed on the kitchen table. Chairs fell over, which caused him to tumble to the floor. His dress flew up to reveal his bare bottom. His eyes filled with blood, he groped about to climb up onto his knees.

Still, Irving refused to stop in his attack.

Cursing, Bevis grabbed the cat, ripped him from his head, and hurled him away.

Irving bounced off the table and on to the floor.

Spotting the knife block, Bevis replaced his weapon. Seeing his blood-covered hand, he felt his face and learned that it was coated with his own blood.

Directly below him, Archie, still on her hands and knees, grabbed the fallen knife.

"You bitch!" Bevis screamed in rage, "Look at what you did to me! I'm going to make you pay!"

Archie rolled over onto her butt and thrust out the knife to him. "Bring it on!" She was at a disadvantage with him standing over her, but she couldn't risk taking her eyes off him to climb up to her feet.

Refusing to back down, the cat jumped up onto the table and hissed at him as if to say, "That makes two of us."

"You have no idea who you're messing with! I'll show you who's boss!" Bevis raised the knife and lunged forward.

He was so enraged that he didn't hear the gunshot that tore through his lower back at a downward angle, ripping out his testicles and penis. Bevis' bloody body parts splattered over Archie. The bullet ricocheted off the granite floor between her legs and hit the wall.

With one hand, she wiped the blood from her eyes while holding up the knife to defend herself.

Stunned, Bevis looked down at his mutilated lower body. With a roar, he raised his knife and stumbled forward, but he only made it one step before a second bullet tore through his midsection.

This bullet flew over Archie's head to ricochet off the refrigerator. It shattered the cookie jar on the kitchen counter. Ginger snaps went flying everywhere. Irving leapt from the table onto the kitchen counter.

Archie ducked to avoid the second shower of blood and body tissue. Luckily, she was able to scurry away before Bevis collapsed onto the floor. Any chance of survival was thwarted when he landed on top of his knife.

Expecting to find Mac waiting for her, Archie stood up to find Chelsea standing in the kitchen doorway, Archie's gun in her hand. Her naturally pale face was white. Her hands were shaking. Tears seeped into her eyes.

Molly had scurried under the breakfast table with her tail between her legs.

"Chelsea?" Slowly, Archie moved toward her. She spoke softly. "It's okay, Chelsea." She held out her hand to her. "Give me the gun."

"Is he dead?" she whispered. "Archie, did I kill him?"

"I believe so." Gently, Archie took the gun from her hand.

"I had to do it," Chelsea repeated what David had told her. "I didn't want to, but there was no other way. He left me no choice."

"That's right." She took her trembling friend into her arms. "He left you no choice."

Ready to fire again, Archie approached the still body to ensure that the threat was over. His head looked like it had been through a blender.

Definitely a closed casket funeral for you, Bevis Palazzi.

Once again, the manor was filled with silence…except for the sound of Irving helping himself to the ginger snaps on the kitchen counter. Archie went over to pet the cat, who welcomed her touch on his head. "You're not such a bad cat after all."

The buzz of her cell phone startled her so much that Archie jumped with her gun ready to take on the next attack. She saw by the ID that it was Mac. "Hello, hon…"

"Archie, the state police are coming out to the manor." Mac's voice was filled with worry. "Is everything okay there? Bevis—"

"I know," she interrupted him.

"Are you and Chelsea okay?"

"Oh, Mac, there's blood and chocolate mousse everywhere." She looked at Bevis Palazzi's body bleeding out across the kitchen floor. His blood was mixing with the chocolate mousse to make a grotesque-looking ooze. "I'm going to have to clean up the kitchen again."

Frantically pawing at a ginger snap hiding out of his reach, Irving knocked the only canister to have survived the previous attacks on the kitchen to the floor. The glass canister shattered into a hundred pieces. Chelsea jumped at the sudden noise. Molly scrambled to get close to her mistress. The flour housed inside formed what resembled a mushroom cloud across the floor to cover Bevis and the chocolate mousse.

Startled by the crash, Archie jumped and grabbed her forehead.

"What was that?" Mac asked.

"Irving decided to get a start on dusting for fingerprints."

EPILOGUE

Twelve Hours Later

At forty-four years of age, Charles Dawson had spent most of his adult life in the prison with no visitors. Deserted by his family upon his conviction of a double homicide after years of being a screw up, he had had no contact with the outside. For that reason, he found it peculiar when the guard fetched him from his cell saying that he had a visitor. He found it doubly puzzling since it wasn't visitors' day.

His curiosity was piqued when he was escorted into the conference room to find a gray-haired man in what appeared to be a very expensive suit sitting behind the table with a note-book, laptop, and folder. Upon his entrance, the man rose from his seat and stuck out his hand. "Charles Dawson, my name is Edward Willingham, senior partner at Willingham and Associates."

Charles held up his hands to show that his handcuffs made it difficult for him to shake hands.

"Take off those cuffs," Ed ordered the guard.

The guard objected. "Our policy is for prisoners—"

"As of three minutes ago, this man ceased being a prisoner," Ed said. "Call your warden, who may not be able to take your call because he's rushing around to get the paperwork completed so that this man can leave by five o'clock today." He smiled at the man standing before him in the prison uniform. "I was on the phone with the governor when he signed the pardon."

Charles Dawson was too shocked to notice when the guard took off his cuffs. When he found his voice, he asked in a gravely tone, "What...?"

"Let me begin by telling you that Senator Harry Palazzi, the man who killed the two women he framed you for murdering, is dead." Ed went around the table to sit down behind his laptop. He opened up the folder.

"Good," Charles said. "If he wasn't, I'd end up back here." Slowly, he sat down across from him. Numb from disbelief, he didn't quite feel the chair. Realizing he could find no reason why this man was there to free him, he asked, "Who are you again? Why are you here?"

"I'm a lawyer."

"The last lawyer I met rolled over and died and let me get railroaded in here," Charles said. "I told him that Senator Palazzi killed those women. Hell, he told me so to my face, and when I told my lawyer he said that even if it had been true, that no one would believe an honorable man like Senator Harry Palazzi would do such a thing."

Ed referred to the folder in front of him. "That was Francis Miller, a public defender appointed by the court to defend you?"

"Yes," Charles said.

"Are you aware that after your conviction he became a junior partner at Samuel Brooks and Associates? He is now a senior partner," Ed said. "We're naming him in your law suit, along with everyone else who has played a role in this injustice."

"Why?" Charles sputtered out.

"Most likely money," Ed said. "Power. A nice office—"

"I mean why!" Charles shouted. "Why me? Why are you here now when I have been saying for years that I didn't kill those women? No one believed me. I lost everything. I don't have a family. Now I'm free, but I have no place to go! That man and his powerful friends who proclaimed him an honorable statesman stripped me of everything. What good does it do letting me out now? Like you're going to give me back the last twenty years? My youth? I have nothing! What good is it going to do for you to sue them for me? Like—" he laughed, "and how much of whatever we get are you going to take for yourself, Mr. Fancy Lawyer!"

Ed looked at the man sitting across from him in orange overalls with tears filling his eyes. They were tears of shock, anger, betrayal, relief and fear.

"Nothing," Ed said in a soft voice. "I'm taking nothing of how ever many millions the jury will award you—and I know that once they see the evidence we have, they will award it all to you."

"What about your fee? Certainly you aren't doing this for nothing." Charles gestured at his suit. "Someone has to pay for that suit."

"My fee is paid by the Forsythe Foundation," Ed said. "Named after Mickey Forsythe, a fictional character created by Robin Spencer—

"I heard of her."

"Everyone has," Ed said. "Our purpose is to right injustices and provide aid, financial or otherwise, to right wrongs like this one. Your case is a perfect example. Now, the man who had the evidence of Senator Harry Palazzi killing his wife and her friend has had this evidence for many years, but chose to do nothing with it for his own selfish reasons. Last night, he turned it over to the authorities in exchange for immunity from criminal prosecution."

"So he can't be arrested for letting me rot in jail," Charles sneered.

"He got immunity from criminal prosecution," Ed said with a smile, "but not civil. He's going to be named in our lawsuit. He's got a nice big house in the Outer Banks. Have you ever thought of living on the beach?"

"Sounds lovely." The tears in his eyes turned to ones of joy. In spite of his best effort, they spilled from his eyes.

Ed returned the smile. "Where would you like to go when you leave here?"

"I have no place to go," Charles said. "I told you. I have no one. Even my family believed those lies those bastards told about me—about what I did to those women."

"Well, the truth is coming out." Ed gestured to the guard. "I took the liberty of making a few phone calls and brought someone here to walk out with you."

The guard opened the door to allow a young man and woman, holding a small boy in her arms, to come in.

Charles stood up.

"Let me introduce you to your son," Ed said, "your daughter-in-law, and your grandson. I thought maybe having a family would help you get your life back on track."

Holding his son, Charles Dawson was unable to hear the lawyer over his sobs of joy.

A week later, the news of the day was about the late Senator Harry Palazzi, murderer and rapist.

First, there was the discovery of his murdered wife's body, along with that of her friend in a grave under a work shed in the Maryland Mountains. Then, it was released that a witness had recorded evidence of the late senator detailing how he had killed them when they had confronted him about raping his wife's best friend.

In Charles Dawson's behalf, Edward Willingham filed a two hundred million dollar lawsuit against the Palazzi estate, Samuel Brooks' estate, Kevin Cooper, Dawson's defense attorney, and others for railroading an innocent man into jail. His chances of winning looked very good.

The senator's political party was still reeling to come up with a suitable spin for the revelation of who had really murdered Senator Harry Palazzi's wife and her best friend when Florence Everest's rape tape was leaked to the media. When Mac asked his lawyer about how the tape got leaked, Ed Willingham had said, "Why Mac, to make public any information given to me by a client would be a violation of client-lawyer privilege."

"But Florence Everest is dead, Ed."

"Good thing for me then, huh?" the lawyer said. "Dead people can't sue."

After the tapes had been made public, human nature had taken its course. It seemed as if every day a woman or two would come forward to say that she, too, had been raped by the senator. Apparently, Harry Palazzi, confident that his people would cover for him, had attacked at will.

Any good that Senator Harry Palazzi may have done in office was overshadowed by the statements of the women, well over a dozen, whom he had brutalized and then intimidated into silence. In spite of efforts by the late senator's media friends to ignore his attacks on women and the violent way he had died at the hands of his own homicidal son, the sheer volume of rape victims and the brutality of his own actions on the recording made it impossible to spin the facts.

Within seven days, the count of women who had come forward was up to fifteen women, with the earliest rape going back to when Palazzi had been a sheriff deputy.

Senator Harry Palazzi was going down in the history books as a rapist and murderer.

The late senator's political party was scrambling to find a suitable candidate to take his place in the senate who could make voters forget about the monster who had formerly held his seat. There were rumors that calls were being made to Catherine Davenport Fleming, Ben's wife, to accept the appointment to finish his term and run for his office in the next election.

When asked, Catherine flashed her stunning smile and demurred, "A wise woman once pointed out to me that it took only one person to get prayer yanked out of our schools. Why can't one person put our country back on the right path to greatness? I have to wonder if I have the strength and determination to be that one person our country needs."

The senator's son, Bevis Palazzi was going down in the crime books as a sexual pervert, an embezzler, and serial killer.

Further investigation of Bevis' activities proved that he had stolen his comatose client's money to get cheek implants, a nose job, liposuctions, and lip implants. He had also used her money to take Nick Fields on lavish trips in an effort to court him. Khloe Everest's theater friends confirmed that the aspiring politician was a homosexual, kept in the closet by his father. According to statements from witnesses who knew the two men, Nick was not a homosexual, but he did like money and would do anything for it—even play husband to Bevis' role of wife.

As part of his agreement for immunity and protection, Kevin Cooper filled in the blanks. "I caught Bevis Palazzi leaving the scene after he killed Dee Blakeley. He claimed it was an accident."

The private investigator was sitting across from the Garrett County prosecutor in a state police jail interrogation room where he was staying before leaving with the US Marshal to go into protection.

The thick case files stacked up in front of him, Ben Fleming laughed. "He accidentally stabbed her over twenty times."

Cooper chose to ignore the remark. "According to what Senator Palazzi told me, Bevis went over to her apartment to plead with her to withdraw her charges. If they had been taken seriously by the jury, they would have destroyed his father's reputation. Then, Bevis had no hope of going very far in his own political career. All that she had to say was that it was all a misunderstanding. He even offered her a bribe. But she wouldn't listen, and she ordered him to leave. She walked away from him, and he lost it. He grabbed the knife, and the next thing he knew, she was dead. Luckily for him, I caught him and took him home. I was agreeable. I knew a good thing when I saw it."

"Say that to the families of the three other women Bevis killed because you didn't arrest him for his first murder," Ben replied.

"It's Nick's fault that those other women are dead," Cooper said. "Bevis paid him very well to be with him. He offered to support him so that he didn't have to work as a male stripper. If Nick had taken the money the first time Bevis offered it to him, then he never would have killed Amber Houston. Bevis offered an allowance plus a sports car if he didn't follow Khloe to Hollywood, but no, Nick wanted to be a star. If he had stayed, then Tiffany Blanchard would still be alive."

"Was it Bevis who outed Nick as being straight and ruined his career in order to get him back here?" Ben asked.

"I'm sure it was," Cooper said. "When Nick came back, his Hollywood career was over. That was when Bevis offered him a house, a Ferrari, and a big allowance. All he had to do was be faithful to Bevis, even if he was just faking. It wasn't like Bevis was asking for that much. If Nick had kept his zipper shut, then Bevis wouldn't have gone berserk and killed Khloe."

"And cut out their uteruses and put them in his freezer as trophies," Ben said. "Face it, Bevis was a serial killer with an insane jealousy and hatred toward women. He learned that hatred from his father. You knew all about it, and you did nothing to put an end to it. That makes you an accessory after, if not before, the fact."

"Call it what you want," Kevin Cooper sat back in his seat and smiled. "I've got immunity. Hey, if it weren't for me, the justice department would never have found out about the voter fraud, which has launched a huge investigation. In a few months, about a dozen senators and congressmen in both parties are going to wet their pants when the feds come knocking on their doors. And the justice department will be thanking me."

"What a great American," Ben's tone dripped with sarcasm.

Chuckling, Kevin stretched out his arms and laced his fingers behind his head. "Hey, with all the stuff that Brooks' clients have been mixed up in, I knew that it was only a matter of time before the authorities would eventually catch up with one of them. That's why I kept copies and recorded everything. I've made myself much too valuable to send to jail. While those guys are going to jail, even if it is a country club jail, the US Marshal is setting me up with whole new life. This time next week, I'll be fishing and working on my suntan."

"That's right." Ben closed the file and stood up. "I heard the marshals have got a nice place and job picked out for you."

Sitting forward, Kevin rested his elbows on the table top. "I know a good thing when I see it."

"That you do."

Ben didn't bother shaking hands with the private investigator, whose license was then revoked since his identity had been erased. The prosecutor waited until he had left the jail and was in his car before he allowed himself to smile.

It does pay to have influential friends in high places. One of Ben Fleming's friends happened to work for the United States Marshal's office, in the department of placement for protected witnesses. Ben had asked her to select a very special place and occupation for Kevin Cooper. He didn't care to know where or what Kevin would end up doing. He only asked that it be a place and job that would befit such a man.

Thirty days from the day of Ben's final interview with Kevin Cooper, Charles Dawson was sunning himself on the private beach of his house in the Outer Banks, which was a small part of the settlement that Kevin Cooper's attorney had recommended their client make to keep his assorted dirty dealings from being made public in court. The Mercedes convertible in his garage was part of another settlement from a recently disbarred defense lawyer. Then, there was the several millions of dollars that had been gifted to him from a mysterious benefactor. His lawyer, Ed Willingham predicted that millions more would come in after the civil trial against the Palazzi and Brooks estates.

It looked as if he would not have to work a day for the rest of his life. Maybe there is justice after all.

Charles' grandson was burying him in the sand while he tended to his fishing pole. He hadn't caught any fish yet, but that was okay. He was happy enough to have the sun in his face and the wind coming in off the ocean to toss his hair.

"Grandpa, I think you got a fish! Your pole!"

"I'll get it tomorrow," Charles said while drifting off to sleep.

Meanwhile, Kevin Cooper was freezing his butt off on a fishing boat in Alaska.

"Hey, butthead, quick goofing off and get to work!" the boat captain yelled at him when he caught him throwing up the so-called food that he had for breakfast.

Even if Cooper wanted to run off to start a new life on his own, separate from the Witness Protection Program, it turned out that he couldn't. Some hacker had drained every penny from the millions of dollars that he had stashed away in two offshore accounts. He had nothing, and he couldn't even report the theft. To whom do you report the theft of your bribe and otherwise ill-gotten money?

Cooper slipped on the icy deck to land face first in the holding bin for recently caught fish, which gave his crewmates a good laugh.

"Shut up, you bunch of morons! Can't you see I don't belong here! This was some sort of mistake! I'm supposed to be in Hawaii!"

"Quit yer bitchin," one of them replied with a shrug. "Shit happens."

Detective Cameron Gates and Joshua Thornton returned to their quiet life in Chester, West Virginia. The state homicide detective would have been happier if she had captured Bevis Palazzi, but she took consolation in knowing that Irving had a paw in thwarting his latest murder attempt.

Sick of hearing about Senator Harry Palazzi and his perverted son who invaded their home in a blue dress and humongous fake boobs, Chelsea ordered the news off-limits during her move into her condo on the lake. Mac and Archie joined in helping her and David.

Like small children, Molly and Gnarly enjoyed the empty boxes and packing that scattered the two floors of the condo. They took turns chasing each other from room to room.

Mac was carrying in boxes of dishes into the kitchen when David abruptly laughed.

"Care to share what's so funny?" Mac asked him.

"Really?" David turned to him. "Plucked eyebrows? Was that really the first clue that told you Bevis was the killer? His plucked eyebrows?"

"And you tried to shrug it off saying that a lot of men pluck their eyebrows."

Cutting open the box of dishes, David shook his head. "Not pluck. Wax, and only enough to clean them up."

"Did you get a look at Bevis' eyebrows?"

"The last time I saw him, he looked like his head had been shoved into a blender that had been turned on." David opened an overhead cabinet and put a stack of dinner plates inside.

"Before Irving got his paws on him." Mac took out a stack of salad plates and handed them to David. "Can I ask you a question?"

"Nothing has ever stopped you before." David cut open the second box. That one contained glasses.

"How is Chelsea dong?" Mac asked him in a low voice. "She was really shaken up, and now she refuses to talk about it."

David looked around to see if she and Archie were in hearing distance before answering, "She's having nightmares."

"I was afraid of that." Mac shook his head. "Good thing Ben is being fair about it and not giving her a hard time."

"She's going to need some counseling," David said. "But she'll come through it okay. She's strong. She'll be fine."

"Of course she will. She's got you."

"That's exactly right."

They bumped fists.

"Time for dinner!" Chelsea came down the stairs. "I'm starved. I hope you guys are hungry."

"Starving," Mac said.

"I have a six-pack of beer in the fridge for you and David," Chelsea said. "Archie, I have a bottle of white wine for you. I also have a Chianti for dinner for you three. I've got my own bottled water, and for dinner, I have…" She threw open the oven to reveal a lasagna. "I made it at the manor last night and put it in the oven to cook while you guys were out getting supplies."

They all "ooh'd" and "ahh'd."

Delighted at the impression she gave as an ace hostess, Chelsea beamed when she announced, "And for dessert, I made a fruit torte from scratch." She turned to the kitchen counter, only to find the torte not there.

"Maybe it's under the packing." David picked up loose packing paper and tossed it to the floor in search of the dessert.

Archie opened the refrigerator to look inside. "Maybe someone put it in the fridge."

After searching the small kitchen everywhere the dessert could be, Mac asked, "Where are the dogs?"

The four of them froze. They looked at each other, and Chelsea said, "Molly would never…"

Mac went into the sunroom off the sitting room, where he saw two tails sticking out of either end of the sofa. David took one end of the sofa, while Mac took the other. On the count of three, they lifted the sofa and pulled it out from the wall.

How the two dogs had managed to take the dessert from the kitchen counter, carry it out to the sunroom, hide it behind the sofa and devour it in their own private party, no one would ever know.

"Molly!" Chelsea gasped. "How could you?"

The white German shepherd's ears lay back flat against her head. She crawled on her belly against the wall to hide behind Gnarly, who was licking the creamy filling from his snout.

"So much for Molly being a good influence on Gnarly," David said. "It looks like the other way around to me."

Fighting the smile that came to his face, Mac said, "Gnarly, I'm going to kill you."

The End

About the Author

Lauren Carr

Lauren Carr is the international best-selling author of the Mac Faraday, Lovers in Crime, and Thorny Rose Mystery series.

She lives with her husband, son, and three dogs on a mountain in Harpers Ferry, WV.

Visit Lauren Carr's website at www.mysterylady.net to learn more about Lauren and her upcoming mysteries.

CHECK OUT
LAUREN CARR'S MYSTERIES!

Order! Order!

All of Lauren Carr's books are stand alone. However for those readers wanting to start at the beginning, here is the list of Lauren Carr's mysteries. The number next to the book title is the actual order in which the book was released.

Joshua Thornton Mysteries:

Fans of the *Lovers in Crime Mysteries* may wish to read these two books which feature Joshua Thornton years before meeting Detective Cameron Gates. Also in these mysteries, readers will meet Joshua Thornton's five children before they had flown the nest.

1) A Small Case of Murder
2) A Reunion to Die For

Mac Faraday Mysteries

3) It's Murder, My Son
4) Old Loves Die Hard
5) Shades of Murder
    (introduces the Lovers in Crime: Joshua Thornton
    & Cameron Gates)
7) Blast from the Past
8) The Murders at Astaire Castle
9) The Lady Who Cried Murder
    (The Lovers in Crime make a guest appearance
    in this Mac Faraday Mystery)

10) Twelve to Murder
12) A Wedding and a Killing
13) Three Days to Forever
15) Open Season for Murder
!6) Cancelled Vows
17) Candidate for Murder
   (featuring Thorny Rose Mystery detectives
   Murphy Thornton & Jessica Faraday)

Lovers in Crime Mysteries

6) Dead on Ice
11) Real Murder
18) Killer in the Band

Thorny Rose Mysteries

14) Kill and Run
   (featuring the Lovers in Crime in
   Lauren Carr's latest series)
19) A Fine Year for Murder (January 1, 2017)

A Lauren Carr Novel

20) Twofer Murder (featuring the entire cast of the Mac
Faraday, Lovers in Crime, and Thorny Rose Mysteries) -
Summer 2017!

TWOFER MURDER

A Lauren Carr Novel

It all starts when David O'Callaghan invites his half-brother Mac Faraday to go fishing. Having never been fishing, Mac declines the invitation to a week of boredom between long periods of quiet boredom--until Archie reminds him that he would then be free to attend a huge mystery writers conference in Pittsburgh in order to accept a posthumous lifetime achievement award for Robin Spencer.

The thought of spending a week with murder mystery writers, literary agents, and publishers makes fishing suddenly look very good. Mac's daughter Jessica Faraday, who has a masters in forensics psychology and has actually studied Robin Spencer's murder mysteries, agrees to accept the award.

Like a snowball rolling down a mountain, the two trips turn into his and hers outings—and his and hers murder mysteries!

David and Mac from the Mac Faraday mysteries, Murphy Thornton and Tristan Faraday from the Thorny Rose mysteries, and Joshua Thornton and J.J. Thornton from the Lovers in Crime end up tasked with solving a murder mystery that is tearing a small town apart in rural West Virginia,

In Pittsburgh, Jessica, Archie, Dallas Walker, and Sarah Thornton join forces with Homicide Detective Cameron Gates to solve the murder of an up and coming murder mystery writer whose past turns out to be her biggest mystery.

Mark your calendars, mystery fans! Summer 2017, you are in for a treat with *Twofer Murder*—2 mysteries for the price of 1!

Coming Summer 2017!

www.ingramcontent.com/pod-product-compliance
Lightning Source LLC
Chambersburg PA
CBHW011458170626
46814CB00008B/2946